FOUR STORIES

MARCUS MCGEE

PEGASUS BOOKS

ISBN 978-0-9673123-0-9

LCCN 99-90734

Comments about *Four Stories* and requests for additional copies may be addressed to Pegasus Books c/o Ms. McGhee, P.O. Box 235, Neptune, New Jersey, 07754, or you can send them via e-mail to marcus.media@yahoo.com

For My Parents,
Richard and Sora,

who through their example
and wisdom
have sustained and
inspired me.

FOUR STORIES

Cover design: acrylic on canvas by Marcus McGee

THE FELINICIDE

I never really liked cats. In fact, there were times when I thought I hated them. The fourth of seven children, there wasn't much I remembered about my uneventful and generic/hand-me-down childhood, but those few things I could recall were revisited with amazing accuracy and detail. There I was, a three year-old at an integrated nursery school in Little Rock, Arkansas in 1963.

The fact that this facility was among the first to integrate had no relevance to me. What had mattered was that, for a first time, my baby brother was allowed to play in the sandbox with me. Then it happened.

Curious by nature, I discovered an odd-shaped mass of sand, picked it up, and squeezed it in my hand where it metamorphosed into a warm, gooey, smelly orange-colored paste that oozed between my fingers. My hand opened to mixed reviews: some kids groaned while others ran away holding their noses, but what I remember most was the kids who neither groaned nor ran away. These cruel kids just stood there and laughed at my misfortune and naïveté.

After a teacher explained to me that cats sometimes went to the bathroom in sandboxes, I distinctly remember thinking cats were devious and mean-spirited to play tricks like that on kids. Well anyway, I grew up and figured the cat guilty of that heinous crime was no doubt dead.

After college I got married, had two kids, and settled into what I hoped would be an uneventful and generic/hand-me-down life. My wife was of a medium complexion, but she was an exotically attractive woman who had lovely hair, though she dyed and cut or extended it so frequently that I never knew what color or length it actually was.

She was intelligent, but what I liked most about her was the fact that she produced strong, healthy kids. She was a good breeder.

My pretty fourteen-year-old daughter was a straight-A student, and my eight year-old son was both handsome and precocious. We had bought a large two-story home in a suburb of the suburbs and had a good life. My daughter and I wanted a dog, but my wife wouldn't let us have one. She and my son wanted a monkey, but my mother reminded us that monkeys were sex perverts, so finally we settled on a bird, a beautiful nine hundred and seventy-nine dollar cockatoo, who we named Edgar—until she laid an egg, at which time she became Erato.

Now Erato was a friendly, perceptive, lovable bird with cream-colored feathers and a beautiful reddish-orange streak in her crest. She was very large for a cockatoo and moved about on gray, scaly, four-toed, zygodactylous feet with a gracefulness that drew adoration and praise, endearing her to my small family and friends.

While we bought countless cassette tapes with little modulated voices in an attempt to train her to talk, it was quite by accident that she learned her first and only word. My son's teacher requested that each child in the class should memorize a poem, something "light, humorous, or inspirational."

I suggested Poe, my favorite, and not long after, right in the middle of a television news story on a cannibalistic serial killer, she said it, clearly, almost maniacally. Ever after, I had slight suspicions about that bird. It said ominously, "Nevermore."

Yet even as I boasted to friends and bragged about my profoundly literate bird, I became something of a bird lover and not long after joined the Audubon Society. I invested one hundred seventy-six dollars on an aggregate pre-fabbed birdbath, a large covered feeding station, and various seed and nut mixtures, which enticed as many as thirty-one species into my large backyard.

It was just feathers at first. I'd find a few in the grass by the hedges, take a few steps, and find a few more. "Molting," I thought, but then I began finding the long flight feathers in uncommon plenitude. By the time I found the bloody little black wing, I knew I had a slight problem on my hands.

Inside the house I'd draw the curtains, crouch on my knees, and peer into the backyard from the raised bottom right-hand corner of the drapes with my son's set of toy binoculars, but nothing out of the ordinary occurred: birds came, they bathed, they ate, they dropped the green and white blobs all over, and they flew away.

One morning I came out and found a little Stellar's jay, dead for no apparent reason. That same evening I found two young crows and a baby starling. I checked with the neighbors to see if the kids next-door were shooting BB guns into my backyard again, but the little imps were at their *real* father's house and had been there for two weeks.

"You're wasting your money and time by doing that," my resentful wife intoned as I dumped three five-gallon buckets of seemingly good gourmet birdseed into the garbage bin. "You could be taking me out to *dinner* with the money you're wasting on that. It's probably just a cat."

I hated it when she told me what I *could* be doing with my money.

"It's bad seed!" I snapped back. "The birds *aren't* being eaten! Any idiot knows that animals kill only for food, only to eat. It is humans alone who kill without a good reason or purpose!"

I was just about sure I had heard it somewhere. It *sounded* good anyway. Well, I spent ninety-eight dollars on new seed and everything was fine... until I found a mangled, ravaged thrush the next day, little bloody dots on its breast.

"So tell me, Honey," my smug wife said when she came home with that *told ja so* tone in her voice, "Find any dead birds today?"

"No!" I retorted.

I knew she'd ask so I had stashed the thrush's body away in a safe, hidden place.

"It was bad seed. I told ja so."

I faked sniffles as I called in sick for work the next morning so I could watch the bird feeder from my corner of the window. For three hours I sat there, waiting to see a bird eat the seed and suddenly keel over, but nothing happened.

Then, after lunch, as I sipped a light beer, I heard a squawk and saw birds flying out from the feeder in every direction. I stood in a panic, ripping open the curtains, to see a gigantic, horrific, savage, cruel black cat beneath the feeder's ledge, its powerful mouth clamped on the wing of a brownish warbler who chirped loud and ran about in semi-circles on skinny black legs as it struggled to get away.

Sadistically, the beast pinned the poor bird down with a bloody paw and pinched its tiny neck between sharp incisors. The wings flapped desperately, tensed, the poor bird warbled a last time and fell limp. I stood there in fear and amazement as this seemingly dead bird, once released, hopped to its feet and flew a few yards only to be pounced on by the brute, nipped, and released again.

This was sadism! This was torture! So I, barefoot with beer in hand, rushed out screaming feline obscenities and barely missed hitting the scurrying cat with the can as its black tail disappeared over the fence. I tried to resuscitate the little bird, but its many wounds proved mortal.

"Find any dead birds today, Honey?"

She held up a tuft of feathers found in the feeding area.

"No!" I snapped, snatching the feathers. "Any idiot knows its molting season!"

She circled the feeder and bath; she kneeled and peered under the hedges, scanning the ground for blood and bodies. I was too clever for her; I had hidden the warbler hours before she came home. Disappointed by her search, she conceded.

"I'm a big enough person to admit it, Honey. I was wrong about the cat. You were right. It musta been bad seed."

Now I felt smug.

"Yeah, bad seed. Told ja so."

When I found three sparrows the next afternoon, I realized I had to do something about that killer cat, so I rigged a box trap in the yard. It was simple: a stick, a large wooden slatted produce box obtained it the local supermarket and a little string. The stick held the box up; attached to it was the string; attached to the string was an imitation bird full of catnip. I also purchased yarn, expensive gourmet cat food and a toy mouse for the trap in case the criminal cat didn't like my bird.

I can't take full credit for the genius of the scheme, though. I had a collaborator who was a cat-hating psychopathic twenty year-old working in the pet store at the mall. Over coffee we worked out the details. I opted not to use the mustard gas, but everything else about the plan was perfect, except one thing: if my wife saw the trap, she'd know I had a cat problem.

After hours of labored thought, I found a solution. I called my boss and said that, due to circumstances beyond my control, I'd be in late every day for about a week. That way I could pretend I was leaving for work, park around a corner and wait for my wife to take off for her job, circle back around, and set the trap. Then I had to come up with an excuse for leaving work early so I could beat my wife home, disassemble and hide the trap. I was sure I would have my cat within a week.

I found a young robin the next day and after that a bluebird, but, unfortunately, the trap had not been sprung. A week and nine birds later I was a tortured mess.

As it turned out, the cat was much smarter than my brilliant pet store friend was: it ate the gourmet food every day, but it was clever enough to avoid the bird on a string. The bested cat-hater suggested I lace the food with cyanide, and I would have done it if the problem hadn't resolved itself so suddenly.

I got a call from my wife one afternoon. Apparently, she had gone home for lunch.

"Erato's out." she admitted, caution in her voice.

Working on a writing project, I showed little interest.

"Well," I sighed, "put her back in."

She laughed.

"No Honey," she said, "it's not exactly like that."

She cleared her throat in irresolution.

"Ya see, Erato was out of her *cage* when I saw this funny looking box thing in the backyard..."

She had my undivided attention as she continued.

"Well, when I went out to see what it was, Erato flew out right behind me."

"But you caught her!" I interrupted, "You put her back in the house!"

"No!" She blurted, "That crazy bird flew up into the trees! And now I can't even see her. I didn't know she could fly!"

By this time, I was standing on my computer chair.

"Doggone you! She's a bird! Of *course* she can fly! Sometimes you just don't think. Don't I always tell you that you have to be more careful!"

Suddenly it hit me: the vision of that wicked black cat with Erato pinned down, all ready to deliver the death bite.

"You better find her! Look out there! Do you *see* her?"

On came the emotion and the tears.

"No."

Nevertheless, I was unaffected by her histrionics.

"What the heck are *you* cryin for? *I'm* the one who spent a thousand dollars on that bird! And you, like an airhead, let her out there with that killer cat!"

OOPS! I hadn't meant to say it, but her crying suddenly stopped.

"Waitaminute! What cat?"

I was cursed to stutter whenever I spoke untruth.

"Ne, ne, ne, nevermind."

Unfortunately, she knew the curse.

"You're lying. What *cat* are you talking about?"

It was out of the bag. It actually felt good to get it off my chest.

"The one that's been killing all the birds out there! The one that's going to kill Erato!"

Her tone changed to one of defensive anger.

"I didn't know anything about a cat or I woulda been more careful. You never said *anything* about a cat! You said it was bad *seed*!"

She was onto me.

"Waitaminute— You've been *lying* all along, haven't you?"

I didn't like the direction the conversation had taken.

"That's, that's not important! We've gotta get Erato before that cat does. Keep looking for her. I'm on my way!"

By the time I got home, the kids were out of school, and we all took part in the search. After ten minutes, my fourth grade son's shriek brought me racing to the shrubbery where I found a small bloodstained patch.

A few feet away I found a long white feather that had obviously been chewed on. After a closer examination I recognized it as Erato's: the feather's clean, freshly-cut edge and the fact that she could still fly reminded me that we had had her wings clipped two days earlier by my twenty year-old friend.

There were a few more feathers and additional bloodstains, but we couldn't find a trace of the little nine hundred seventy-nine dollar body. My wife would resume the earlier discussion.

"You never did *tell* me. What's that crazy box doing on the lawn?"

I looked over toward my trap and, for a first time, I realized it had been sprung. Rushing over, I kneeled and peered between the slats to find two sinister, horrible eyes staring coldly at me. Then the fiendish creature hissed and barred wicked, dripping fangs. My wife knelt beside me.

"What is it?"

"It's the *killer*! I've caught my killer cat!"

Still a little baffled about timing, I scanned the yard.

"Waitaminute! How long has this box been down like this?"

Her expression was blank.

"I don't know. I don't *know*! I didn't pay attention to whether it was up or down."

I was sufficiently satisfied.

"It doesn't matter. This is my killer. He killed Erato, and now I'm gonna kill him!"

I found a dried mud-encrusted three foot long two-by-four near the fence, and just as I flicked the giant snails off it and was ready to smash the box, cat and all, my wife clasped my arm and spoke to me between clenched teeth and a sneered expression.

"Just *what* do you think you're doin?"

"Let me go! I'm gonna kill that savage cat! He *ate* Erato!"

Her nostrils flared in anger as her voice grew louder.

"*Look* at you! *You're* the only savage I or anyone else around here can see. Your kids are watching you!"

I glanced around without turning my head and noticed their shocked, terror-stricken expressions. There I stood, hair frazzled, grunting, groaning, hyperventilating with a stick in my hand. I felt like a Neanderthal with a club, but my wife reveled in such an advantage over me. She had that smug look again.

"Go ahead, you big tough man. Beat the poor little animal to a bloody pulp in front of your kids. Hafta wonder what that'll *do* to em."

Frustrated, I dropped the bat, turned, took a deep breath, and tried to put my cringing kids at ease.

"I'm not gonna kill this, this *monster* right now, guys—not like this. But ya gotta understand what's goin on here. See, this animal killed and ate Erato. She was part of our family. Don't you think we *have* to kill it for that? At least for Erato?"

I wasn't sure exactly why my daughter was crying, but ha! Here I had emotion. It was something I could work with.

"Yeah, poor Erato. We'll never... We'll never hear her squawk again. Yep... or burst another sunflower seed or kernel of corn. All we'll have is an empty cage, guys, an *expensive*, barren cage to remind us of our beautiful bird and the terrible thing this cat did."

On that note, my daughter busted out in a gut-wrenching, uncontrolled sob while my son's lip trembled as evidence of his own agony over the killing. I had succeeded, and now I would justify my position.

"We *have* to kill that cat, don't we, guys?"

Leave it to my wife to ruin my moment of glory. Wagging her head, she sighed in disgust and mumbled the words (intentionally loud enough for the kids to hear):

"I don't *believe* you!" and "Have you no scruples?"

Then she opened the box, took the darn cat out, cradled it in her arms, and started doing *baby talk* to it. Now this was confusing the kids, so I reinforced my point.

"Don't forget, it *killed* our Erato. It's a killer!"

She held it at arms' length, staring into its face.

"That's a good name. Killer. Killer Joe. Thank you, Honey."

I wanted to snatch that cat from her, but I didn't like the way it *looked* at me. I could tell it wanted to claw me but was just waiting for the opportunity.

"That cat has got to die! We have to kill it!"

I had been married for too long. My wife could sense my nervousness about the cat. Smiling, she held it out toward me.

"You wanna kill it? Take it."

I guess I recoiled a little and a little too quickly because she laughed out loud.

"Kids, I think your Daddy's *afraid* of the cat."

"I am not! I'm not afraid of him. I'm not afraid of *anything!*"

She extended him again.

"Then take him."

Here my image in front of the kids was at stake, but that cat, it had this kind of mean *look* in its eyes.

"There's a difference between fear and stupidity," I said, thinking I could reason with the kids. "See, I'm not afraid of that cat, but I can tell he wants to claw me. Now I'd be a very *stupid* guy if I let myself get clawed just to prove I'm not afraid."

She turned and placed the cat in my son's arms.

"See, you're not afraid of it, are you? But your *Daddy* is."

While the boy stroked the cat's head in a place between the ears, I turned to my wife.

"It doesn't want to *claw* him. It wants to claw *me*."

She was doing it again, making me struggle to justify my position. Gently, she took the cat from my son and gave it to my daughter.

"She's not afraid either."

"He doesn't want to claw her. He wants *me*!"

Sighing again, she gave me one of those looks that made me feel like I was being silly.

"Yeah, right."

Then came the doggone *chicken* sounds. She made chicken sounds. There was nothing I hated more than when supposedly rational people sank to the point of clucking and making animal noises. Embarrassed for me, my daughter looked over compassionately and spoke.

"Daddy, I don't think Killer Joe wants to *claw* you. Here, just hold him."

As the chicken sounds continued, I looked over at my son who seemed ashamed to have a father who was afraid of a cat.

"Give him here!"

Now I had the fiend in my hands, and I just wanted to get it out of them as soon as possible! Oh, I still planned on killing him, but I wasn't sure how.

In the meantime, I'd have to lock him up. I thought. *I had no cages, I had no secure boxes. Where could I possibly put him?* His body suddenly tensed and he hissed viciously at me. That's when I figured I'd just get *rid* of him! I figured I'd just get the little demon off my hands before he attacked, so I thought of a place. I could lock him in my office upstairs!

Panicking, I rushed into the house, hustled up the fifteen steps toward the little office, and I kicked open the door, but, just before I could put the cat down, just when I thought the danger was almost past, just as I knew it would happen right from the beginning, Killer Joe looked me dead in the eyes, barred his hideous fangs in a wicked cat-like smile, exposed his four gleaming straight-razors, and he *clawed* me, not just one time, but thrice: once on the arm, and once on each... back pocket as I fled the room.

While my daughter consoled me and nursed the wound on my arm at the kitchen table, my wife and son proved themselves traitors by siding with and even comforting the little black monster upstairs. They couldn't stay up there forever, though. I knew they'd eventually have to come down and answer for their treachery, but I wasn't exactly in a forgiving mood. Little Benedict Arnold led the way.

"Bad news, Dad."

"What?"

"The cat pooped on your computer."

"He *what*?"

Guinevere took over.

"It was *just* the keyboard. It won't cost you that much to replace it."

She extended her palm, though not in friendship.

"I'm gonna need some money."

I was aghast.

"What for?"

"Oh, ya know, cat litter, litterbox, food, toys, shots, ya know—*cat* things."

Ignoring the pain under my pockets, I bolted up in anger. This had gone too far!

"Are you out of your *mind*? I'm gonna *kill* that little murderer! I'm not buyin him anything!"

She laughed.

"Oh yeah? And exactly *how* do you plan on killing him?"

"Well, I don't know yet!"

Bad answer. But for the moment, I had no idea how I could kill him.

"I'll think of something."

"Well, while you're thinking, Torquemada, the *little beast* has gotta eat."

"That cat eats thousand dollar birds in case you don't remember. Let him starve. It would serve him right."

"Oh, and he's also gotta poop and pee. Now *you* tell me—do you want it all over your office?"

I had to think a while because she did have a point.

"How much?"

"A hundred and twenty dollars."

I choked on the words.

"A hundred twenty dollars! Are you crazy!"

"Pets are expensive nowadays. Come on. Give it up."

Reluctantly, I forked over the money, complaining the whole time that Killer Joe wasn't my pet.

I had never realized how much I took my office for granted. I could go in there and escape the world. I wrote in there, I daydreamed in there, I hid from my wife in there, but it no longer belonged to me. That cold-blooded criminal was living up there.

It may have been my imagination, but I got the distinct feeling my wife was starting to prefer his company to mine. On the first night, she spent five hours up there, and then, when she finally came to bed at three a.m., she woke me up and all she could do was talk about him. Three A.M.! She acted like she had known him for years, like they were old friends.

"Ya know, Honey, I really don't *think* it was Killer Joe who got Erato. Had to be another cat."

My wife was usually pretty smart, but now she was being ridiculous.

"Uh-huh, and what did you do? *Interview* him? Is that why you were up there for so long?"

Now I felt clever.

"Let me guess. He *told* you that, right?"

She put on her best poker face.

"In a sense, he did. There's no blood on his fur, not a shred of a feather in his mouth, he doesn't appear the least bit interested in the canary I brought home from the pet store and finally, there's his feces sample..."

"His *feces* sample?"

"I *told* you. He pooped all over the office and upon examination, I have determined his is *not* the feces of a bird eater. You wanna take a look yourself?"

I was standing in the middle of the bed in an instant.

"Don't tell me you brought cat sh, sh— cat *crap* into our bed!"

She laughed aloud, putting the plate on the nightstand.

"Don't be silly. This is a snack—Japanese food. The feces sample is in the refrigerator downstairs. You can have a look in the morning."

She woke me up at six a.m. with a question that came out of the black. I remember feeling put on the spot because she had angled the night lamp so that it shined directly in my eyes.

"Did you actually *see* Killer Joe or another cat kill that bird?"

"Of *course* I did! Oh come on, I already told you that."

"Did you get a good look at him? Tell me, how close up did you see him?"

I had no idea where she was going with this ridiculous line of questioning, but in that blinding light of interrogation, all I could do was answer to the best of my recollection.

"I saw him from ten—no no, from about five feet away."

"What did the cat in question look like?"

And she woke me up at six in the morning for this!

"He looked like Killer Joe! The cat was that Killer Joe you've got up there in that, that *Country Club for Kitties* upstairs!"

She wasn't finished.

"One more thing. Can you *describe* the cat you saw?"

I knew she was getting at something, but I didn't know what it was.

"It was a gigantic black cat with real mean eyes. I tell ya it was Killer Joe!"

Through the glare of the light I caught the glimpse of a tape recorder.

"Turn that thing off."

She ignored my request and continued.

"Well, what did you see? Did he have any markings, or was he completely black?"

I had had enough.

"Completely black! Look! I'm sleepy and I'm tired of answering your idiotic questions! Turn off that damn light and don't wake me up again!"

Pleased with herself, she sighed, she turned off the recorder and the lamp, and then she rolled over.

"Just thought you might like to know this, Honey, but Killer Joe *isn't* completely black. His paws and the tip of his tail are white and he has a large white patch on his chest that I'm sure you wouldn't have missed. Goodnight."

❖❖❖❖❖❖❖❖❖❖

I sat angry at the breakfast table staring insouciantly into my cereal-flavored chocolate milk. My daughter tapped my arm.

"Daddy, I hear Killer Joe isn't the cat who killed Erato and all those other birds. Mom says she's got proof. She said you confessed on tape. I hear it's some other cat."

My eyes flicked up toward the room where my wife was no doubt catering to if not conspiring with the criminal.

"Well, your mother doesn't know what she's *talking* about! I was there! The cat I saw torturing that bird was Killer Joe!"

By this time, little Brutus looked up from his Spookie-Os to take a stab at me.

"No Daddy. The cat *you* saw was all black. Killer Joe has white paws, a white bowtie on his chest, and white on his tail. You got the wrong cat. You caught an innocent cat."

My wife! What was she doing? Playing the recording and arguing a case before the children? Completely fed up with my son's disloyalty, I snatched two handfuls of his pajama shirt and pulled his young delicate face close to mine so that I spoke to him through a James Cagney-like sneer.

"Look, I say the cat I got upstairs is a killer! You callin me a *liar*?"

Not frightened by my baleful, menacing glare, he answered the question indirectly.

"Mom says the facts speak for themselves."

I pushed him away so I could address both kids. By this time, I could tell that neither understood that their *mother's* reasoning was absurd, that *I* was the rational one. My voice cracked as I exploded in anger.

"Forget the damn facts, guys! *Listen* to me! Killer Joe is guilty! He killed Erato and he deserves to die!"

Suddenly, a blood-curdling scream from above tore down the stairs and filled the room. While it was my wife's voice, I had never heard her shriek so horribly, so painfully, and then it hit me: a friend of mine at work told me she had heard of cats killing people and that in most cases, the cat had clamped with its claws on the victim's face and caused an agonizing suffocation.

I could see it: My foolish overly trusting wife suffering and Killer Joe gleefully toying with and torturing her the way he did the warbler. With her dying breath she would say, "I shoulda listened to my good husband. He's such a smart guy!" and "he was right about that cat!"

I flew to the bottom of the stairs, but I remembered Joe had something *against* me. If he was really killing my wife, he'd come for me next.

"Kids! You better get up there! That cat is *killing* your mother!"

Yet, even before they reached the top of the stairs, they literally ran into her. She seemed so sad, nearly in tears.

"The canary's dead."

I quickly seized this opportunity to further my interests.

"I *knew* it! Joe got im. I told you he was a killer!"

"No!" she interrupted, "Joe didn't kill him. I did." Her eyes swelled with tears. "I couldn't find the retarded bird when I went into the office. I looked for him, but I didn't see him. For a minute I wondered about Joe, but I should have known better. When I finally sat down on the couch, I heard a muffled squeak and there he was. I had squashed him."

I feigned compassion and empathy as she was crying.

"Sweetheart, don't feel *bad*. You didn't kill the bird. He was probably already dead when you sat down."

She knew at once what I was trying to do.

"No, he was very much alive! You want everybody to think Joe got him, but that's simply not the case. I admit I had my doubts, but they were completely unfounded. The bird was alive. I *felt* it."

"With what? Your butt? You're gonna tell me you can feel whether a bird's dead or alive in a split second with your hypersensitive *butt*?"

On this rare occasion, the kids found *me* a little amusing, and once again, my wife was a bad sport. She first stared the smiles from their faces and then continued.

"He was alive. He squeaked!"

"Of course! That's cuz you squished out his dying breath!"

She opened her hand.

"Does *this* bird look like the victim of a vicious attack?"

The bird seemed unmolested, and the kids apparently agreed with her, but I wasn't finished.

"Of course it doesn't *seem* like Killer Joe did it, but that's his MO! He makes it seem like it might be something else when he really did the killing! That's why I dumped out three bins of seed! Remember? I thought it was bad birdseed?"

No one seemed to remember. They just looked at me like I was losing it.

"I'll prove it to you!"

I hurried outside and, ignoring the smell, went immediately to my cache of dead birds, piled them in the wheelbarrow and carted them into the house. My wife and kids quickly recoiled and complained profusely for the stench of the rotting corpses.

"I know it smells bad, guys, but you've gotta see this! Look—"

I held up two victims in one hand and sifted through the maggot-infested carnage with the other.

"Look at this! Two larks—dead for no apparent reason, and here's a starling... and a crow. I could go on. There are twenty-five here in all and all of them, same MO as the canary. That cat is neat. He leaves no marks."

What I had failed to mention was that, in spite of the fact that Joe had been locked up for the past forty-eight hours, I had found the larks under the shrubbery near the fence just that morning and a sparrow the night before.

I rationalized though, that the birds may have been killed days before. Besides, additional information would confuse further an already frustrated, convoluted proceeding.

As I looked from my wife's appalled face to the revolted sickened expressions of the children, I felt a sense of accomplishment and success about this spontaneous stratagem involving the wheelbarrow full of dead bodies. This was sensationalism! This definitely had impact. I had my wife and kids right where I wanted them.

"This robin," I sighed in eulogy, "was just a baby, a beautiful baby. That cat killed a little baby."

The tables had turned. I had their hearts in my hand.

"Now think of *Erato*!" I said, driving the nails in Killer Joe's casket, "Poor Erato, her corpse would be rotting in this heap of foul bodies, but he tore her limb from wing, and he *ate* her!"

My daughter could always be counted on to behave theatrically, and she performed like a star. Throwing her head back, she let out a pathetic wail that cut me to the core of my being.

The effect on my son and wife must have been similar because both began to cry as well. I had never seen her so *human* before, so vulnerable. This aspect of my wife had been unknown to me until that very moment. In fact, I began to realize just then there was much about her I didn't know or understand. She sobbed as she spoke.

"Please Honey, take all that *away* from here! Please! Just take it out!"

Yet, even as I packed the soil on the mass grave with the back of a shovel, I felt like kicking myself for not describing in intimate detail to the family how Erato came to be unceremoniously dumped and splattered on my computer keyboard. I regretted the missed opportunity. I had been so surprised by my wife's emotional reaction that I forgot to make my point: Killer Joe had to die!

She had sent the kids upstairs and was seated on the couch when I re-entered the house. It was just her and me.

"Sit down, Honey."

Her smile was forced and her manner edgy. I sat.

"Honey, I just want to stop fighting about this cat. The whole thing seems a little ridiculous, don't you think?"

Her little laugh was just as phony as the smile. She was up to something.

"No." I said, "I think it's pretty serious."

The smile and affected manner disappeared.

"Fine. Then we can play it your way."

She stood and walked toward the patio sliding glass door, her back to me.

"What happened to the body?"

I had no idea what she was asking.

"What do you mean?"

"I mean what happened to Erato's body? Why wasn't *it* in your sick little collection? If Killer Joe has an MO as you say, why would he kill all those other birds for sport and eat only one: Erato? It just doesn't make sense."

"Well," I stammered, "maybe he likes the *taste* of cockatoos. I understand they're a, they're a delicacy in some parts of the world."

"Where?" She demanded. She knew I had made it up. She sighed aloud and she let me off the hook with a smile.

"Let's just *suppose* Joe killed and ate Erato. It didn't happen, but we'll suppose it. Ya know, it is in the *nature* of some creatures to kill, some are born into that nature. They can't help what they do. That being the case, killing poor Joe up there will do nothing to change the nature of other killers." She paused. "I mean, what good will it do if he dies?"

Was this a concession? Here she was making excuses for the killer cat. Very self-satisfied, I answered.

"It'll make me *feel* better, that's what it'll do."

She sneered and changed her tactics.

"And don't *you* feel a little responsible for all those dead birds you so proudly displayed?"

"What're you talking about? *I* didn't kill them!"

"But you created the *environment* in which the killing occurred. All those birds would still be flitting about if it hadn't been for you."

She had caught me off-guard with this undeserved accusation, this character attack, and as I stuttered to regroup, she pressed further.

"It was *you* who bought that blood-stained birdbath. It was you who got the feeder, but tell me something? Did you for once think that maybe you put them in a bad location? A location that would entice not only birds, but *cats* too!"

I glanced outside at my feeder and bath sitting precariously close to the hedge but was distracted by the sound of the kids coming down the stairs. Her crazy ranting had gotten their attention, and then she resorted to the cheap, underhanded tactic of playing to them.

"Did you for once think about putting the feeder in a less precarious location instead of in front of a hedge where cats could hide?"

How could I possibly respond to such a loaded, leading question? But she answered for me.

"No you did not! You were a doting, silly, quixotically-romantic, penny-ante, beginner of a birdwatcher who didn't know the first *thing* about what you thought you were doing. Your inexperience and just plain ignorance on your part killed all those poor birds! You can blame Joe all you want, but their blood and stench is on *your* hands!"

I looked over at the kids and watched as my son nodded in agreement with his mother. Such petty name-calling and silly emotionalism, but I could play just as dirty.

"Well, a friend of mine told me that uh, a friend of hers had a brother whose wife's cousin was *killed* by a cat like Killer Joe! They trusted him, but then he went all wild all of a sudden and attacked the lady. Clamped right on her face! They said she died a horrible, painful death."

The kids weren't buying into my scare tactic, but while grasping for another straw, I instantly realized I was under no obligation to convince them or my wife of anything. For all my wife's attacks, I had forgotten for a moment what I was: I was *the man*! I had the power. I was the law. *I could simply pull rank.*

"Okay. All right! Now I think I have been a fairly liberal and patient man because I have listened to everything you guys have had to say, but this debate is over! I've already decided. I'm going to kill that little fiend upstairs, and I'm gonna do it in exactly one week from today, and, and that's *final*!"

Nonetheless, my wife, who had no respect for finality, could not be dispensed with so easily.

"And just *how* do you propose to kill him, Vlad Tepes? You gonna impale im?"

"No. Of course not. Don't, don't be stupid."

My stuttering was actually a way of stalling so I could come up with a good intelligent answer.

"Well, I, I've thought about it very carefully, and I, and I even went to God in prayer, and what I, what I think is, yeah what I think I've decided to do is use the brick-bag method. Yeah, that's what I'm gonna do."

As I scanned the room, it seemed they were buying the act, so I continued with a new confidence.

"Yeah, I decided to use that particular method because I've heard it's painless."

I learned just then that *the macho routine,* used sparingly and at the right moment, was powerfully effective. They hung on my every word.

"You, you get an old potato sack, see? And then you put in two bricks, not big ones, you know, medium-sized. Then you put in the cat, see, and you tie it up. Then you swing it in a circular motion a couple of times around your head, and your throw the bag into a lake or any other large body of water. The bricks gently knock the cat out so he doesn't feel a thing when... when, when it, you know, kind of drowns."

Somehow I lost my sense of command and a general mutiny ensued so that I was forced to forsake the brick-bag method and consider "more humane" alternatives.

My son requested that we give the cat to a nice family, but I vehemently denied his plea. He then intimated that perhaps Killer Joe had a family or owner and that we should run an ad in the newspaper so the cat could be returned unharmed. Again, I denied his request.

My daughter suggested we declaw the cat and keep him, but my wife insisted that declawing would make him "less a cat" and would "put him at a disadvantage in his natural environment." She added that, since I may have made him a killer, I should take responsibility for his health and welfare for the rest of his natural feline life.

"Erato! You're forgetting all about Erato!" I argued then. "She was family! But you don't care about her. And you don't even care about Killer Joe for that matter! You're just arguing a side of an issue!"

She was in my face.

"And what about you! What was the meaning of you dragging that rotten, maggot-infested, *disgusting* pile of dead bodies in here? If that's your idea of love, Lothario, then I think you have a serious problem. At least I'm trying to save a life! All you want to be is right!"

I was losing ground. The *macho* thing had worked before, so I went to it again.

"Save your arguments! All of you! Just *save* your arguments. I'm the man in this house, and I've made my decision: Killer Joe dies in seven days!"

Well, getting through the first day was as difficult as anything I had ever done. My wife and son would not even look at me, let alone talk to me. Dinner for me was a tepid, colorless, tasteless, no calorie liquid served with a straw by my resentful daughter.

Sneers, sidelong glances, and scowls shot constantly at me, by me, through me, but I was all the more determined to carry out my order. I could not allow popular opinion to deter me from doing what I believed was right.

Nonetheless, I was still at a loss for an "acceptable" killing method. So, at a meeting for coffee with my psychotic pet store friend we discussed my many options. Somehow, he was very bent on *death-by-taser.*

After much consideration, though, I decided against anything accomplished by personal or electrical means and I called my brother/sandbox partner for his opinion. He uttered four syllables: S-P-C-A.

It was perfect! Why hadn't I thought of it before? There was a certain irony in it: here was an advocacy group that killed tens of thousands of cats annually while claiming they acted only in the best interests of animals. It was poetic. My wife even made yearly donations to the non-profit organization. I called the SPCA the next morning and was invited for an inspection of the facility.

Unfortunately, every truly great idea is infected with its unique problem. Wonderful, the SPCA could carry out this "humane" killing for me, but Killer Joe *hated* me. How was I going to get the animal to the execution site?

Where mere mortals lost faith, true genius took it all in stride. I paid my brave daughter eighty-five dollars to carry the cat for me and an extra fifteen for sitting in a way so that the beast's eyes could never fall on me while I was driving.

The girl at the SPCA front desk initially seemed so pleasant, but then, on seeing the demon in my daughter's arms, she started making those silly baby sounds my wife had made earlier. That doting, infantile smile quickly left her face when I, resolutely, stated my purpose. She then looked at me like I had asked her to assault her own mother.

"I'm sorry Sir, but we have a very strict criteria here with respect to these types of requests."

She stroked and caressed the black villain as she continued.

"The animal must be sick, old, or vicious in order for us to immediately euthanize it."

Now the little killer was purring and playing up to her, but I wasn't going to let him get away with it.

"Then he fits your criteria! He brutally killed and tortured twenty-five birds not to mention a fifteen hundred dollar cockatoo!"

She shook her head in disagreement and sighed.

"Bird killers can be handled with a little work, Sir, and they can be kept indoors."

By this time, I wondered if my wife had discovered my plan and secretly called ahead. I was becoming unglued.

"You don't understand, young lady! I don't want you to *handle* that vicious little fiend! I want you to kill it for me. And I want to watch!"

She looked toward my embarrassed daughter, as if she feared for the child's welfare, and answered rudely.

"I'm sorry, but since I don't deem this animal vicious, we will not automatically destroy it."

I tore my shirtsleeve open and exposed my raw arm.

"Just *look* at that! Claw marks! And I've got others I could show you. Don't tell me *that's* not vicious!"

"I'm sorry, Sir. I'd be perfectly happy, though, to *keep* your cat with the hope of finding this gorgeous animal a stable, decent home, but I'll try my best not to destroy him. This is the SPCA, not Animal Control."

I ordered my daughter to take Killer Joe from the boorish woman and left the facility. My daughter, who had been almost silent on the issue the entire time, never taking a side, finally decided to talk to me as we drove home.

"I'm a little disappointed with the SPCA too, Dad. But what do we do now?"

Was she finally showing a loyalty? To me?

"I'm not sure, Daddy's Girl, but I'll think of something."

I had to see more clearly where she stood.

"Tell me something: Are you on your *mother's* side about all this? Or mine? How do you feel?"

To my surprise, tears were streaming down her face when she looked back over at me.

"I'm on the *family's* side, Daddy! Look at what this cat is doing to our family! You won't bend, and Mom won't bend either. It's tearing our family apart! I don't care about this cat and I don't care about Erato either—not more than our family! They're *animals*, Daddy! But we're supposed to be a family!"

She paused and recomposed herself.

"I just want to get it all over with so things can go back to the way they were."

I was moved by her display of emotion.

"I want the *same* things, Baby."

"Then give in to Mom, Daddy. Let her have her way!"

Here I stopped being moved and we drove the rest of the way home in silence.

My wife was *very* friendly to me that night before we fell asleep, and she was even friendlier the next morning. As we languished in bed, she purred and whispered into my ear.

"Take the day off work today, Honey. I have a special agenda planned for you."

She then proceeded to tell me how much she loved me, how much she loved the fact I cared so much about a bird, and how, if only in my heart, she thought I could be a good, fair, and decent person. Finally, she proposed that I should spend a complete day with Killer Joe to see what he was really like. Well, after a night and morning like those I had had, how could I resist?

Anyway, knowing I'd be a little nervous about being in a room with the killer, she had bought protective clothing and gear to ease my touch of apprehension. I sat in the little cage as I watched the cat claw my couch and curtains, play little games with his tail, and bolt up suddenly to dash in hysterical circles around the desk. My wife, by the way, thought this was all "really cute."

There was one thing he did, though, that made me laugh every time it happened: When he was licking himself to clean himself, if a person did anything to get his attention, he'd look up, forgetting to put his lazy tongue back in his mouth. The pink tongue would just *hang* there against the black background of his body like a little pink fruit or something. Now that was cute, but you had to be there.

He was a smart cat, too. My wife would toss a toy mouse across the room, and Joe would retrieve it and drop it at her feet. It wasn't long before I was laughing and throwing the mouse myself, but then I thought of Erato. I was betraying her memory. I was frolicking and gamboling with her killer!

Watching Killer Joe claw the toy mouse made me think of how he must have clawed her, tortured her. Abruptly, I climbed from the cage and hurried from the room.

A few moments later, my wife approached me at the table downstairs. Her tone was conciliatory.

"Still can't let it go, can you?"

"No."

"Still plan on killing Joe?"

"Yes. In three days."

She sat and took my hand between hers.

"I really *like* this cat, Honey. Would you please at least consider sparing his life? At least for me?"

Rarely had I seen her so willfully subject and suppliant to me. I really wanted to honor her request, I wanted to make her happy, but I just couldn't.

"I love you so much, Honey." I said, "You are so beautiful and such a wonderful wife, but there's no easy solution to all this. I want to make you happy, but I just have to do what I feel is right."

She remained peaceful and respectful.

"Right? Do you really feel it's right to kill? Whatever your reasons might be, do you *really* believe it's right to take a life?"

"Yes." I said, "Sometimes, in the name of justice, we're forced to."

"You're afraid of the cat. Why don't you just admit that? It's affecting your judgment. You're letting your fear and prejudice force you to do something you might regret for as long as you live. How could you willfully destroy a life? You're not a killer!"

"I *am* a killer... because somebody has to, in the name of justice."

She turned her eyes away from me to hide the soft, pain-filled tears as she sniffed and spoke.

"You're wrong. There's no justice in it."

In that moment, she changed. She was no longer crying. She was sad, she was pensive, she was introspective. Looking up, she cleared her throat and spoke.

"You know, Honey, for all these years I took for granted that I knew you, that I really *knew* you. I would have bet my life on it."

She found my eyes with hers.

"But this whole incident with Joe has made me see that, in spite of being married all these years, there are fundamental differences in us, fundamental things we never talked about, things we *should* have talked about from the very beginning. We can't talk to or understand each other because we're complete strangers! I just don't know you anymore, and it hurts."

Seeing my wife so pained brought tears to my own eyes. I embraced her and spoke into her ear.

"It's frustrating for me, too. I can feel it. I just wish we could hear each other, understand and love each other."

I tried to turn the discussion in a hopeful new direction.

"But then, maybe it's just this issue. Maybe it's simply that we disagree on this particular issue."

She struggled to extract herself from my embrace and concluded before she left the room.

"I'd like to believe that, but there's more to it than that, Honey. It's not this issue. It's us. It's not just that we disagree. We are *not* the people we thought we were. We never really knew each other."

The next two days were filled with tension and uneasiness. Whispering, plotting, and conspiracy ran amok. I thought I was being a little paranoid about my staid positioning until I by happenstance discovered and foiled a breakout attempt by my daughter and son.

Troubled by bad dreams, I woke up soaked in perspiration at about midnight two days before the "execution" as my wife termed it. I could hear the poorly-oiled door screeching as it slid open and my son crying and quietly shouting. Turning on the light, I found my daughter at the back exit and my son and Killer Joe on the patio.

The door was wide open as the kids were trying to shoo the cat away. In a way I didn't understand, I was hoping the cat would run away, disappearing into the night, but he just stayed at my son's leg, unwilling to go. The boy looked up at me and then back to the animal.

"Run Joe! Run! You stupid cat! He's going to kill you! Run!"

As the cat neared him, rubbing against his leg and purring, I nodded to my daughter indicating she should pick the cat up, which she did, and I told her to take him back up to the room. Then I sat and hugged my sobbing son.

"I love you, Boy."

He cried even more.

"I love you too, Dad. But why? Why do you have to kill Joe?"

There was no easy explanation. I had painted myself into a corner. At that point, I wished I had ignored my wife's initial protests and smashed Killer Joe with the two-by-four when I first saw him. Doing that would have eliminated all the questions and circumvented me from being in the inextricable dilemma in which I found myself.

Even if I let the cat live, I was in a mess. Such an action would be interpreted, at least in subtle and subconscious ways, as *weakness* on my part, as a compromise to my perceived system of values.

Consequently, my position on any future difficult situation where there was extreme conflict of opinion would be weakened. I had absolutely no choice in the matter at that point. It was all too complicated for the boy to understand, so I just cried and held him.

"When you're a man you have to act on what you believe, Son. It's hard being an adult. You have to take positions and stick to them, even if the whole world says you're wrong. You don't understand now, but someday I hope you will."

He fell asleep in my arms, and I took him up to bed.

I put a padlock on the office door the next morning to prevent further breakout attempts and made sure I had the only key. Visiting privileges and meals were cleared by me. I hated taking things to such a level, but my family left me no choice.

As I sat, guarding the door, I was still uncertain about how I would kill the murderous cat, but then I remembered something I had heard from a person who no doubt didn't understand how profoundly political family life could be. She had said so self-righteously,

"This is the SPCA, not Animal Control."

Obviously, the people at Animal Control were more practical by nature and uncontaminated by the SPCA's petty activism. I called Animal Control and was encouraged to bring my animal over right away, but I told the nice guy on the phone that the killing would take place in the afternoon of the next day.

That evening, I worked on my calculator at the table downstairs as the kids fed Killer Joe a lavish meal of fresh fish, delicate chicken livers, and anything else he'd want to eat upstairs. My sulking wife sat directly across from me, steeped in a fiscal report she had brought home from work.

"Honey?" I asked. "How much did each of the kids cost?"

As she looked up from her work, she seemed both confused and annoyed.

"I don't understand what you're asking me."

Well, at least she was *talking* to me. I explained.

"Oh, you know: delivery, hospital stay, enemas, epidural, aspirin, Pampers, Chinese food, whatever—what was the out-the-door cost for each of the kids?"

She removed her glasses.

"Oh, I'm not sure. I guess above what the insurance paid, we had to put out maybe six hundred, seven hundred each. Why?"

I worked one last transaction on the calculator and looked up.

"Well, the way I figure it—between Erato, the keyboard, the birdseed, the food, toys, bribes, catbox, litter, and miscellaneous expenses, that animal up there has cost us more than the combined cost of the kids."

This was the first time my wife had ever resorted to violence. That spiral notepad bounced off the top of my head, but aimed a few inches lower, it could have put my eye out. Unnerved by such a close call, I gave her the bottom line.

"Sixteen hundred fourteen dollars and thirty-five cents!"

"There are *some* costs," she said, "there are some costs that can't be calculated, and I know you're not so naïve or foolish that you don't understand the cost of killing that cat!"

The day finally arrived. On that morning I stood guard outside the door as first my wife, then my son, and finally my daughter went in to say goodbye to Killer Joe. My wife made a final appeal for the cat, saying she would consent to having bells tied around Killer Joe's neck, bells that would warn birds that there was a cat stalking them, but, by this time, I was tired of the entire process and would not even consider the appeal. There were tears, wails, and much emotion so that I was relieved to see them go respectively to work and their schools.

Donning the protective gear my wife had purchased earlier, I entered the room, gingerly lifted Killer Joe, and put him in a cardboard box. Never once did he complain or put up a fight. He just looked at me with eyes that seemed to see right through me. I closed the top and hurried the box to the car.

Unfortunately, driving afforded me the opportunity to reflect, and, as I heard Killer Joe utter an interrogative *meow*, I wondered if I truly had a deep-seated prejudice against cats that caused me to be so bent against him. He really was a remarkable cat: handsome, intelligent, black, and sensitive to people.

Was I out to punish a cat who died perhaps many, many years ago, a cat who perhaps innocently pooped in a sandbox not knowing his emission would be discovered by and bring great shame to an impressionable three year-old? Maybe there *was* within me a sub-conscious prejudice that I did not want to confront. Not wanting to think any further on it, I turned on the radio.

My lean pet store friend was waiting near the front desk when I arrived at Animal Control, box in hand. I could tell he was excited to see me there, and, more specifically, the box containing Killer Joe.

"You're late," he said. "You got the cat in there?"

Still a little surprised to see him, I addressed the sadistic twenty year-old.

"It's nice that you came out, but I didn't mean for you to miss school. Why don't you go on back to your classes?"

"And miss the execution? No, I think I'll stay. Besides, I don't know when or if I'll get another chance to witness a *felinicide*."

"A felinicide?"

"A perfectly legal, government-sanctioned cat killing. This oughta be good!"

Just then, a very large, ugly, mean-looking man came up to me and forcefully took the box from my hands.

"So I hear those bleedin hearts over at the SPCA wouldn't *kill* your cat for ya?"

I resented having my box snatched from my hands and nearly said so, but this guy looked like he could beat me up. The bald-headed brute must have been 6'8" and he had the intelligence and disposition of a prime-time television wrestler. There was a wicked-looking bloody-mouthed grinning skull tattooed on one of his giant arms.

Looking up, I stuttered a reply.

"No. No, they wouldn't."

"The *wimps*! They want people ta think we're killers over here, that they really *care* about the animals over there, but they don't. We kill eighty a day, they kill about thirty-five, so what's the diff? Ya didn't buy inta any of their garbage, did ja?"

"No."

"Good. Cuz they kill just like we kill. They do the same as we do, Brother, but they disguise it so they can get donations from their damn bleedin heart, animal-lovin friends, that's all."

Then he opened the box and slapped Killer Joe real hard on the head. The cat shrieked in pain as he was jerked from the box.

"I hear ya wanna *watch*. Follow me."

By this time, I wasn't sure I wanted this particular man to execute Killer Joe, but fearing for my own life, I didn't want to upset so dangerous a man.

So we followed as the surly guard led us down a corridor lined with caged animals. Some stared viciously at me, while others, obviously mentally unstable, endlessly repeated erratic gesticulations and growled or hissed at invisible antagonists. As we neared the "termination chamber," I got a distinct and different feeling from the creatures; there was a definite sense of desperation in their eyes.

For a first and only time in my life, I could literally understand the language of animals. A little black and tan terrier mixture with sad eyes barked somberly toward me.

"They don't think we know what's going on here," he yipped in a fearful tone. "We *know* we're going to die!"

He whined and began to cry.

"I hear death, I smell death. It's all around me. I think. I feel. I want to live just like you. Please, please take me home. Take me *away* from this!"

My heart went out to that poor dog and others who agonized and called out from cages around him.

"Help me!" a tiger-striped cat on the opposite side mewed as it beamed an expression that seemed too human. "I don't want to die! Save me!"

The insensitive guard heard nothing; he only cursed to himself while sifting for the key that opened the ghastly room.

"When we're dealin with a mess of em, we *gas* em, but in your case, we'll use an injection."

"Of what?"

"Beats me, but it kills em pretty damn fast."

As he laughed, his malevolent grin was accented by a hideous rotten tooth that appeared opaquely gray lying in a row of off-white, plaque-encrusted, un-brushed teeth. At that very moment, Joe looked over at me and spoke, both asking for and granting absolution.

"I'm sorry I clawed you, but I was *afraid* of you. I didn't run away that night because I loved your family. They were the first and only people in the world who ever cared about me. I couldn't leave them. I know what's going to happen now, but in spite of what you are doing to me, I love you too."

The wicked guard slapped him hard again and ordered us to sit down. Joe had shrieked and urinated on the table. He cringed there, shivering in a fetal position as the guard verbally abused him while wiping up the urine.

This wasn't simply a system grown so accustomed to killing that it was done without thinking. This man *enjoyed* killing. He derived some morbid pleasure in the misfortunes of others.

"Well guys. Enjoy! But it won't last long."

I was amazed at how quickly and deftly so large a man could prep and fill a syringe. He grabbed Joe by the fur on the back of his neck, slapped him savagely to stun him, stabbed him twice with the sharp needle, pumped out its deadly contents, and slung him down hard onto the table.

"Not even *God* can save him now!"

I sat in horror as I heard my young friend burst into loud, uncontrolled laughter. To him, this was sport, and I was greatly disturbed because I had unwittingly provided this sport... at Joe's expense. And for what? Certainly not for Erato.

I looked back over at the guard who was laughing just as rancorously and then to Joe whose body spasmed as the death throes began. Ignoring the pain and laughter, he rolled his head and looked toward me, gave me a look that was at the same time disapproval, desperation, and pity, and he seemed to die.

Still laughing, the guard grabbed him by a hind leg and tossed him into a bin full of already dead animals.

Tears blurred my vision as I hurried down the corridor of doomed animals, all calling out to and condemning me. When I arrived at my car, I had to sit a moment to calm myself. I knew I'd be haunted by the last expressive look in Joe's eyes for the rest of my life.

My pet store friend tapped on the glass. Eyeing him with contempt, I rolled down the window. He was out of breath from running.

"Mind giving me a ride to work? I kind of caught the bus over here."

"Get in."

As I drove, I hardly spoke a word to him. All I thought of was the lousy job he had done clipping Erato's wings. He was at least partially to blame for her flying away from my wife in the first place.

A light rain was falling when we arrived at the mall.

"I hope you enjoyed the little show."

He bowed his head.

"Are you *mad* at me cuz I laughed?"

I had been deep in thought, so my answer was careful and directed.

"No. No, I wasn't mad. I felt *sorry* for you."

He seemed hurt and confused. Perhaps he really *didn't* understand.

"Do you know what you were *really* laughing at?" I asked. "Can you honestly say you *know* why you laughed, you, you crummy wing-clipper?"

I remembered his brick-bag method suggestion then. It probably wasn't as painless as he suggested it was. He started to speak, but I interrupted.

"Don't answer. Just *think* about it, okay? And the next time you laugh at someone's misfortune, think for a second about *why* you're laughing."

The sky had grown dark and dreary so that it poured rain. I could see lightning and hear thunder in the distance. I went to a bar for a beer because I dreaded facing my wife and the kids, but on arriving home, I noticed the house was dark.

There was evidence they had been home at some time since morning, but I couldn't imagine where they'd gone. To a movie maybe? No, we always went together, and on those rare instances that they went alone, my wife always left a note. In the downstairs bathroom I found a bad omen: all the toothbrushes but mine were missing.

As I, desperate, searched about to see how well they had packed, I found the note she had left me. It said:

"At least Joe, when and if he killed, he did it because killing was his nature. Whether or not you went against your nature to kill him you'll have to answer. If you didn't, then you're a killer too and no better than Joe. If you did, then you killed for spite, and that makes you worse. I think you and I are fundamentally different in our basic value systems. I don't know if we could ever understand each other no matter how much we talk. That's why I think we should go our separate ways. I love you, but sometimes love isn't enough. I'll call you tonight. Goodbye."

I hated being alone, especially when the weather was bad. I had no idea where she and the kids could have gone. I called her mother, her brother, her friends, but no one had seen or talked to her. I was miserable.

Streaks of lightning somewhere outside lit the windows in their panes. I feared going upstairs, so I found a blanket, grabbed a beer, and crawled onto the couch where I scanned the television channels with the cable remote. Drained, I fell asleep while watching a program on Darwin's finches.

I awoke screaming and soaked with sweat around midnight and realized I had a nightmare: in it I was being pursued by a huge black cat with razor-sharp claws and deadly white fangs. Then I saw the cat... on television. The Nature Channel was re-running a program on the black leopard of Ceylon.

Spooked, I turned off the television and picked up a book, *Dryden's Virgil*, and I read words to myself, words that held absolutely no meaning. Then it happened. I heard something that sounded like a hand or paw rapping on the window upstairs, the window in my empty office.

I threw the book down and immediately grabbed my son's little league bat. Maybe it was all in my mind. Maybe it was guilt, but then it happened again, this time louder and more urgent.

Slowly, nervously I climbed the stairs, not knowing what manner of creature I might find up there. The hand or paw knocked on the window one last time before I sprung into the room, ready to strike, but there was nothing there.

I opened the window, but there didn't seem to be anything outside either. There was only rain and the wailing howl of an unsettling wind. Suddenly, I heard the knocking downstairs. Only the racing of my heart rivaled my haste down those stairs, and I arrived at the patio's sliding glass door to find it slightly open, wide enough for a small animal to enter.

Then right there, just inside the door was a trail of animal footprints: fresh, small, amorphous, muddy. There was also a slight trail of blood. As I slammed and locked the door, I realized I was not alone. I felt like the victim in an Alfred Hitchcock thriller.

Bat in one hand, Bible in the other, I sat on the recliner in the living room and awaited my punishment or death, but then the many questions returned.

I thought about the note my wife had left, about the many arguments we had concerning Joe, about that last conversation with my son, and about the frustration of my daughter. Would I ever again be the way I had pictured myself, the way I was *sure* my family had always pictured me? A considerate, loving husband? A thoughtful, compassionate father?

Oddly enough, there came a coarsely whispered, froggish reply that harrowed me to the bone. The voice mocked me.

"Nevermore."

Quickly, I turned toward the sound and discovered the source of this profound commentary. Perched ominously above my head on the back of the chair, it seemed *less* like Erato, and more like Erato's specter.

Nearly all her feathers were gone exposing pale, sickly, white skin, reddened and cracked in places by sun and raw for insect pestilence. Her black beak appeared gray and slightly cracked while one wing was badly mangled and slightly deformed. She was gaunt, hideous, frightening, and dripping wet.

Aghast, I remembered the bird she was before, the bird I so proudly loved. What tribulation had befallen her in that cruel world out there? To leave her so stern, solemn and emaciated? How could I possibly feel the same love for this repulsive creature she had become? Would she ever again be what she formerly was? She answered.

"Nevermore."

Then I was struck with the most profound thought. Perhaps Erato had returned to show me what *I* had become within and in the eyes of my wife and children: not truly myself, but the specter of myself.

Was she a phantom created by unknown processes of my mind? A mirror of my inner self? Was this a cruel trick played on me by fate? It horrified me to think on it, horrified me to think of the ugliness my family must have seen in me. I was repulsed to look on this less than human side of myself.

Resenting it, I wanted to smash that bird with my bat, but I couldn't. I wanted her to go away, to disappear into the gloom whence she came. This was not my bird! I could not accept what she had become, and if she stayed, she would be a permanent reminder of what I had become. I hurried to and slung open the door, exposing the murk and abusiveness of nature outside.

"Get out, foul bird!" I screamed. "As far as I'm concerned, you're *dead*! I can't stand to look at you! Go back to wherever you were! Just get away from here!"

The bird answered grimly.

"Nevermore."

As I slammed the door, I stopped and thought to myself: *If ever I loved this bird, I would, in spite of its odious appearance, embrace it, heal it, love it and attempt to nurture it back to the health and beauty it had before.* There was at least hope in that.

Yet on that inspired note, I thought of Joe. Poor guiltless cat! He was dead. He had no hope. I realized that perhaps I was wrong about him from the beginning. I could admit that, but I was helpless to undo what I had done. I had killed him.

Ironically enough, it was in the death of a cat that I finally learned to respect and appreciate my own life and the lives of those around me. To me, the moment was an epiphany, for in his unceremonious and solitary death, Joe made me see all the ugliness in myself, all the ugliness in humanity.

Underneath whatever image we humans project, underneath our *feathers*, we are ugly all. Yet I would embrace that ugliness, attempt to change it, to heal and nurture it. I would always be ugly to some degree, but perhaps through love I could restore my world to what it had formerly been.

"Nevermore."

The phone rang. Certainly it would be my wife and I would have to tell her Erato had returned. Unlike me, she probably wouldn't point out the fact that she had been right all along. She was beautiful in that way. Could I possibly admit and accept my error and yet retain my damaged set of values, so opposed to hers? Did *rightness* even have meaning?

"Nevermore."

Never again, for I realized I was nothing more than a collection of values and beliefs, shaped by personal experiences and lessons which included all life's conflicts, all its pain, and a revelation on human nature learned in a sandbox a very long time ago.

How could anyone, except for love, accept me for all my contradictions, pride, stubbornness, flaws and ugliness? Except for love. The phone continued to ring. I would answer it, but neither apology nor answer could I make, for I had accepted my imperfection and ungainliness. Except for love. I *needed* my wife and kids, and they needed me.

Perhaps through life's misfortunes, through its pain, through the conflict of our differences, and even through our mistakes, we could restore through love and understanding that bright and beautiful world we once had.

"Nevermore."

The gore rose in the gruesome bird's throat. It heaved and vomited up a vile foul-smelling greenish mixture onto the chair, and somewhere in that putrid, repulsive and reeking emission I could barely detect the delicate little arm, then a leg, and then the broken head of a tiny kitten, the slimy, sickening indigestible remains of some innocent little black cat.

Relieved of this unpalatable burden, the grotesque bird reassumed her former grim mien.

"Nevermore."

DICK

IT ALL STARTED WITH A DREAM. As I remember, I was standing in a raging storm on the bank of some great old river. All around me, trees swayed and creaked as a violent gale wove through the grove on the edge of the water, uprooting the weak and cracking the hard and stubborn. The rain was so intense that, looking up, I could see nothing for the incessant assault on my face.

As I wiped the freezing water from my eyes to focus on an irregularity on the opposite bank, I noticed a clearing. As strange as the existence of such a clearing would seem when I awoke, within the dream it seemed natural. For even as the tempest savaged all around, within this clearing on the other bank the sun shone warm and bright. Tender grass stirred as it grew from dry earth and hummingbirds and butterflies flitted about the splendid scene.

But most attractive of all, a golden throne, bedecked with precious gems, shined brilliantly in the very center of the clearing. And seeing this, at once I freed myself of all my clothes and dove into the icy stream, struggling and fighting the motion of the current with eyes fixed on the warm wonderful sanctuary on the other side.

However, despite my intense efforts, I found that, upon reaching the opposite bank, I was a great distance downstream from the point I had sought to reach. As I stood shivering and befuddled on the bank, gale-force winds whipped and lashed my naked body with stinging rain and tiny daggers of ice.

Looking upstream, I could see the glimmering throne sitting there in the warm sunlight, but I could not get to it through scores of tangled trees and thorny underbrush that formed a barrier, barring me from paradise. Forced back to the frigid water, I waded in and tried to swim upstream, but the force of the river was too great. Only exerting enormous effort was I able to swim back across the river, only to find myself even further downstream though on the opposite shore. Eyes again fixed on my prize, I walked along the bank upstream and stopped at a place directly across from the peaceful clearing with the golden throne.

Without hesitation, I plunged into the stream and labored for the seeming oasis again even more ardently than the first time, but to my eternal frustration, I landed in the same place as before: within eyesight of the throne but precluded from reaching it by that abhorrent, antipathetic and thorny barrier.

I awoke from the nightmare with a start which shook the very foundations of the bed, realizing I had dreamed this particular dream before, had dreamed it many times over the years since my early childhood.

My wife hardly stirred next to me in spite of the highest Richter-scale jolt that had stirred that bed in years. I reached over and turned on the nightlight and looked at her as I debated whether or not to wake her up to tell her about this vision, which would certainly have some portentous consequence on me and by relation, on her. In the light I could detect that she had removed her make-up before going to bed.

She was actually one of the few women I had ever seen who was prettier *without* make-up. Her cream-coffee tone was smooth all over her perfectly balanced face and her eyes had a noticeable exotic appeal.

Sleep however, had a way of distorting even the most beautiful face: she had a way of sleeping with her mouth all twisted down in something of a sneer toward the mattress side of the bed regardless of whichever way she slept.

Then she snorted loud at random times during the night. Those snorts had nearly ruined our marriage in the early years. I never got any sleep. I just about went crazy. I remember lying in bed awake for hours, worrying about when the next snort would wake me up. With therapy and patience over about five years, I had learned to live with the snorts.

But the most eerie and disturbing thing about my wife at night was that she slept with her eyes open. Not all the way open, just cracked a little so that if you looked directly into her face, you could see them. I never knew if she was just pretending to be asleep at times, but she was definitely asleep that night.

Anyway, I shook her to wake her up, and after four callous insults and about ten minutes later, she was sitting up, her face struggling to overcome the fixed sneer that dominated her sleep.

"This better be really good, cuz it's four o'clock and I have to be at work at seven."

When it came to remembering dreams, I never did well under pressure. If she had just let me tell it, I would have had no problem, but when she told me, "it better be good," all of the sudden, I started forgetting the whole thing. I had to start in quickly.

"I was by a river. I mean, I was standing at a big river, and there was this throne, and I—it was on the other side, and I tried to swim to it, but I couldn't. I mean I missed it. So I swam back across and tried again and missed it again."

It didn't come out right, but I noticed right away that she was analyzing what I said. In truth, the reason I woke her up was because she had an uncanny way of interpreting dreams when she put her mind to it. She had taken classes in college for it and had done a lot of reading on the subject. Finally awake, she spoke,

"The river... was water. Even in sleep you subconsciously heard the tank running in the bathroom—the same tank you've supposedly been fixing for two years.

The throne... was the toilet. It's really simple. You forgot to go the bathroom before going to bed, and you've been trying to reach the toilet all night."

It was the silliest and worst interpretation she had ever done. No, there was another meaning and she wasn't telling me for some reason. Maybe she knew something that she didn't want me to know. I pressed further.

"What about me missing the throne?"

"Easy. You always miss the *toilet* in the bathroom, and I'm forever wiping up your little messes."

I was stumped.

"There was a storm. I forgot to tell you about the storm. What about that?"

"Bathroom fan. Once again, you forgot to turn it off. It's been running all night."

I studied her poker expression carefully, searching for the slightest flinch, the slightest indication of contradiction, but she was good.

"I'm gonna die! *That's* it, isn't it?"

Somber, she nodded.

"Yeah, you guessed it. You're going to die—someday, and hopefully with your life insurance policy in full effect, but your dream had nothing to do with death. None of the death symbols were there."

Finally, she smiled.

"Don't worry about it. You're going to be okay. That is, if you don't pee in the bed. Go on to the bathroom."

Considering it for a first time, I really *did* have to go. Relieved in a less-than-literal sense, I crawled from the bed and headed for the bathroom. My wife, then fully awake, called out.

"And Honey, don't miss the throne this time or you'll be cleaning it up yourself."

When I got back to bed I remembered there was something else I wanted to tell her. For years, the family had talked about getting a dog, but my wife had always been against the idea, that is, until the ugly, unshapely, sexually promiscuous, un-bred mutt next door had little puppies. Then she really wanted one. I however, was unwilling to allow her and my equally smitten children to bring one of those splotchy, mangy, un-papered, ignoble little mongrels into my home.

After all, my neighbor didn't even know who the father was, and his little she-mutt-slut probably didn't either. She was only two years old, only fourteen in dog years, and yet she had already had a litter of puppies.

Taking one of those illegitimate puppies in would be the equivalent of condoning teen-age pregnancies. So asserting my natural and divine authority as *the man*, I told my wife, my daughter and my son that not one of the baseborn issue of that teen-aged trollop next-door would be accepted in my house.

Naturally, as was the case whenever I cited "natural law and divine authority," they were mad at me, angry to the point of silent contempt. However, after a little more than a month of suffering their general disapproval and resentment, I was ready to strike a compromise. We would get a puppy, but we would buy it from a reputable source.

My wife suggested the city dog pound so that "for almost free" we would be "saving some poor dog's life," but I wanted a well-documented, purebred, high-cultured dog. Adjusting the creases in my well-starched pajama pants, I tumbled back into the bed.

"I've decided that we'll get an Akita. I hear they're an extremely protective, fiercely-loyal breed. They were ancient protectors in old Japan."

She sighed in disapproval as she put on her glasses and picked up a magazine.

"You know, when it's all said and done, a dog's gonna be a dog. There's no escaping that. All this so-called documentation by breeders is just so they can rip you off.

We can get just as good a dog at the pound, or next door. Probably better."

My wife was actually pretty smart about some things within her *little* area of knowledge, but she was clearly out of her league with me on this dog thing. I knew what I was talking about.

"That just shows how little you know about recognizing or appreciating fine breeding and quality."

She smiled, looking over the magazine.

"Ya know Honey, you're right. You know everything about recognizing and appreciating fine breeding and quality and I know nothing."

I couldn't believe it. It seemed she was finally giving me the credit and admiration I deserved, but I was suspicious. With her there was always a catch. I would know more.

"You really mean that?"

"Yes. You know everything and I know nothing. That's why you picked me and I picked you."

Well, it took me about three weeks to find a suitable breeder, and I had to fly over 800 miles up to Seattle to pick up the puppy from a specialized Akita wholesaler. In all, if you figured in the plane ticket, the rental car, the *puppy porto-condo* and the dog class airfare, it cost about fourteen hundred dollars to bring the completely white little whelp back home.

He was a cute little Akita that, despite the usual puppy clumsiness, carried himself with natural air of confidence and an unmistakable regal dignity. With no markings, he was white as driven snow.

That was it! I would name him Snow, and I called him Snow until I got him home. My wife and kids, as misdirected as they could be at times, thought the name was "too typical" and "lacked creativity."

They did not know, however, how long I had labored to come up with the name or even that it was my own idea. My pretty fifteen year-old-daughter smirked as she said it.

"Snow? You know Daddy, a two year-old could have been more original. You would think a breeder would have at least *heard* a good name or two over the years. The dog's white, so some brain-dead guy called him Snow. Isn't that the stupidest and cheesiest thing you ever heard?"

She was becoming more and more like her mother every day. I thought to defend the appropriateness of the name, but I wasn't about to tell them I had anything to do with it.

"Actually, the guy I *think* named him was actually pretty intelligent. I met him. Yeah, uh I think Snow was originally a popular name for dogs from a wise old Indian tribe. Yeah, from some tribe up around the Seattle area. It took a very intelligent person to research all that history and find the name. I don't know what the tribe of Indians was called, but actually the guy who named him was pretty smart."

My wife knew me too well, and she never passed up an opportunity to embarrass me in front of the kids.

"This so-called *intelligent guy* up in Seattle who came up with such a sophomoric, idiotic, ridiculous name? I think I've heard of him. Isn't he the same guy who, when he was growing up, had a goldfish named Goldie, a black pet rat named Blackie and a multi-colored parrot named Rainbow?"

I could not believe she had sunken to such depths! She was making fun of three of the best dead friends I ever had. No, Blackie was more like a brother to me. And I had confided to her about those guys only to have her turn some of my most poignant memories against me. Despite the pain of the betrayal, I had to set the record straight with the kids.

"There was a real guy up there. A real guy with a real beard and all. Real smart guy."

Looking at their faces, I could tell their mother had successfully led them to believe that I had chosen the name, so I thought I would defend it.

"Besides, what's so bad about Snow as a name for a white dog?"

My son answered.

"It's stupid, Dad."

He caught himself. Now the truth was out in the open.

"But that doesn't mean *you're* stupid, Dad. You probably just didn't put much thought into it."

I had put a lot of thought into it. Snow *was* a great name, but as always, it was them against me. I'd see if my son would be so smug if we traded places.

"It's easy to be a critic, Son. But you know, it's kind of different when you a *doer*, a man of action. Why don't we see if *you* can come up with a better name? Come on. I'll give you some time. Put some thought into it."

I caught him off-guard with my clever little ploy, and as he struggled to think of an unassailable new name, I readied myself to destroy him with sardonic criticism more virulent than he had ever heard in his nine years of life.

My wife and daughter seemed nervous for him. They were uneasy probably because they knew that when I was finished demolishing him, I rip them apart next. Finally, the seeming lamb spoke.

"I, I think we should name him Dick."

Suddenly I was the one caught off-guard.

"Dick? What do you mean Dick?"

At that moment, I realized my daughter was in the room and that she had heard me say what I said. I was embarrassed beyond belief. Maybe I had heard him wrong.

"Rick? You did say Rick, didn't you?"

Somehow the boy had grown more confident.

"No. I said Dick. I want to name him Dick. Dick, the dog."

I felt like covering my daughter's ears. Absolutely uncomfortable with the situation, I made myself plain.

"That name is out of the question! There is no way my nine year-old son and fifteen year-old daughter are going to have a pet named—I mean, with a name like that."

My wife sighed, laughing in ridicule.

"Honey, what's wrong with Dick? I think he came up with a *great* name. I like Dick."

I didn't exactly like the way that sounded, and then, there was the matter of possibly having to hear my daughter say that word... or name. Ironically, my sweet little daughter chimed in without thinking.

"I like Dick *too*, Daddy."

That was it! It was time to put my foot down.

"Never! We are not going to call him... not going to call him by that name! Not in this house!"

But whenever I thought to put my foot down, my wife had always found a way to wax the floors underneath ahead of time. She feigned docility.

"Oh Honey, we understand if *you* have a problem saying that name. The kids and I realize it's a real *macho* thing. Go ahead. You can call him Snow if you want to."

It was too good to be true, until she amended.

"But he's the *family's* dog, not yours. We're gonna call him Dick."

Well anyway, Snow doubled his size within two months. I had bought a series of videos on dog training/behavior and religiously worked with the dog at least two hours each day. Through a one-time only offer on television, I began purchasing a special formula dog food that cost about three hundred dollars a month, a savings of about two hundred dollars.

It was like having a new kid in the house, though my wife and the kids insisted that I treated the dog much more special than I had treated either of the children. Maybe it was, for a first and only time, that I had someone in the house that was on my side.

That puppy was loyal to me. When I woke up, there he was, and he followed me all over. He whined when I was away and yipped like crazy when I got home. It was great!

He slept at the foot of our bed until my wife ruined the arrangement. She insisted "all that expensive puppy food I was buying" was giving the dog gas and that I could sleep with either him or her.

She had a point. Snow surprised me with some horrendous gassers. Well, two days of sleeping out in the garage on an uncomfortable cot by the car enduring doggie intestinal fumes was about all I could stand, so I moved back in with my wife, reluctantly leaving Snow next to a heater out there for the night.

Because he was such an intelligent puppy, a young friend of mine who worked at a pet store suggested I enter Snow in a dog show or two for the prestige and extra money. It was such a great idea that, before I knew it, Snow and I were in a show at least twice a month. By this time, he was nearly the size of a fully-grown Akita.

While he won at a few of the shows, the fact that he had no markings (Akitas usually have brown to and/or black markings) handicapped him. But in those shows he won, the judges were impressed with his muscular physique, his incredible poise and posture and his apparent intelligence.

Before long, I was approached by an older provocatively dressed woman who suggested her dogs had too much color and asked if I would be willing to *sire* Snow out. I didn't know what she meant at first, but when I found out she wanted my dog to be the equivalent of a gigolo for money, I declined her four hundred-dollar offer with disdain.

"I'm not a doggie pimp! When my Snow does have puppies, it will be with a dog I approve of, a dog he has a substantial relationship with—you know, almost like a wife. Yeah, I'll buy him a wife when the time comes."

She laughed at me with a laugh that made me think my wife was standing there and then she said it, something my wife had said earlier.

"A dog's gonna be a dog. There's no escapin that."

Then this indecently dressed older woman told me I was being silly and that I'd only have to wait a few months for my dog to show me what he was. Leaving, she tried to put a curse on Snow and me.

"This one is going to teach you that you cannot fight something greater than you are."

And with an exaggerated sway in her hips, she left me standing there. I remember laughing to myself and thinking, *Yeah? Like age?* as I remembered I had bought an outfit just like hers for my daughter the week before.

It didn't seem like a big thing to anyone but me, but that's where it all started. Someone left the lid for the toilet open. I was upstairs in my office when I heard this strange sound coming from downstairs.

Thinking I was alone in the house, I picked up my wife's potted *Sansevieria* for use as a weapon and descended the stairs . When I reached the first bathroom, I saw Snow, his back facing the door, his head bobbing up and down.

To my utter abomination, my prized dog, my prized companion, was drinking from the toilet! Naturally, my wife and kids returned home to an emergency family meeting.

No one would admit it, but someone had left that lid up. I had my suspicions that it was my wife because I remember it seemed she was feeling some kind of morbid pleasure as she watched me ranting about the importance of closing the lid.

"Do you know what goes into those toilets?" I exclaimed.

I could tell the kids thought I was over-reacting. As usual they listened, but they had long since tuned me out. My wife minimized the significance of the crime committed.

"Honey, Dick was just bein a dog. All dogs drink from toilets when they have a chance."

Angry, I answered.

"Dic—I mean Snow, is not just a dog. Actually, I think he's some kind of dog royalty."

She whispered, nodding her head.

"Then by all means, find a way to gold-plate that toilet. That way, it'd be perfect for your dog to drink from."

Despite my strong warnings that anyone guilty of leaving the lid up would face severe punishment, I was often distracted from work or whatever else I was doing by the low, gurgling echoes of Snow slurping from the toilet. I figured my wife was leaving the lid up intentionally, but I couldn't prove it.

Anyway, I made a few attempts to change Snow's misconstructed behavior by flavoring the water in his bowl with first chicken and then beef bouillon, but with no effect. I even moved the water bowl into the bathroom next to the toilet, yet he still preferred the *e.coli* tainted water. It was around that time I learned how clever he really was.

One night as I hid on my knees peering around the corner in the dark, watching to see if he'd prefer a water bowl with tiny floating biscuits and won tons, I saw him do it. With his nose he pried up and lifted the toilet lid in order to begin drinking. He was a genius!

The solution was easy enough. I forbade everyone in the house to use the downstairs bathroom for any reason, even in the case of emergencies. It was set aside for Snow so he could drink from a freshly sanitized bowl. The family, after great initial resistance, established a comfortable continuity... that is, until the older, virtue-less, terrible little tart of dog next door went into heat.

Her infelicitous condition put me into direct conflict with a man I truly hated: my neighbor. Every experience I had with the man was both frustrating and execrable. First of all, *I* was in the neighborhood first. While it took me only two days to complete my move, this man was moving ugly furniture in and out of the house for over a month before it seemed he had finally settled down.

He wasn't grossly overweight, but he was a man most people would be frightened to look at with his clothes off. His general sloppiness, inattention and a certain lack of propriety were evident in everything about him.

His hair, even when he had just returned from the barber, seemed only *almost* neat. He face at best was *almost* shaven and he smelled no better than *almost* fresh. If designer Calvin Klein saw the way that messy man wore his fine creations, he'd have demanded my neighbor to take them off.

But my neighbor only wore suits on the three days a year he went to church, Easter, Christmas and the day after his birthday when he always had something embarrassing to confess.

He probably made good money at his job, maybe more than I made. But because he worked on some kind of cruddy and oily machinery, his hands never seemed clean. Worst of all, he never kept up his house or his lawn, but every once in a while, his wife would make him plant flowers along the weed-infested sidewalk in front of his house.

I first saw the disgusting and abhorrent display on one of the occasions he was planting purple and white pansies in the corner by my house. He was bent over and digging while his wife called out the orders.

Because he wasn't wearing a belt, the movement of his knees gathered his pants at the joint, dragging them off his waist and down his hips. It was actually scary at first. There, for the whole world to see was this large, sloppy man's hairy butt cleavage, literally larger than life.

I went to my wife after the police told me there was nothing they could do about it. She was just as useless, and as always, she reveled in exploiting my discomfort and frustration.

"To tell the truth, Honey, I think it's kind of sexy. I haven't been able to take my eyes off him all day."

It wasn't at all funny. I had a daughter who could be scarred for life if she accidentally glanced over at that hairy fissure. Then there was the hazard posed to unsuspecting motorists passing by who might have been so appalled that, who knows, they might have crashed their cars into my house!

Well anyway, after enduring five weekends of the torture, I decided I was going to tell him to cover that Grand Canyon up or else.

"Honey, don't go over there. He's bigger than you. He might beat you up."

And she *had* to say that in front of my son. Naturally, as a father I was forced to respond.

"He couldn't beat me up. He's fat and outa shape, but look at me. Besides, if you remember, Hon—I studied Karate when I was younger."

She laughed aloud.

"You watched Karate movies and made funny sounds while you chopped at the air. You didn't study Karate."

An explanation was in order.

"I did. I've just always been humble about it. You didn't see me fight a real person because I could have hurt someone. Who knows, maybe I woulda *killed* someone."

My wife wasn't at all impressed, but my son glanced up at me with a new level of awe.

"What color belt did you go up to, Dad?"

"I said it was when I was younger. It was a long time ago, back before they had belts, before they had *pants* even. Yeah, actually men wore, uh, robes back then. You see it in the movies all the time."

I walked past my neighbor's filthy Cadillac and along the oil-stained sidewalk up to the scratched and peeling front door. Glancing over my shoulder, I noticed that my wife and son were watching me from the yard. Intent on my purpose, my knocking was resolute and manly.

"May I help you? Hey! Aren't you my little neighbor from next door?"

I was glad my wife and son didn't hear him say that. He offered his grimy hand that I shook only reluctantly.

"Yes, uh, yes I am your neighbor. I was here before you. Uhm, I live next door."

"Excuse my manners. Wanna come in? Have a beer?"

Have a beer? He probably drank domestic.

"Uh no. You know, I was noticing you planting your petunias over by my house..."

"Yeah?"

"And I thought, and I thought, you know, I've never given my neighbor a housewarming gift. So I went out and bought something for you."

He smiled pleasantly.

"A gift? Awwh, Neighbor! Ya didn't hafta go and do that."

I spoke through my teeth.

"Yes, I did."

Then I handed him the package that he tore open like an eager five-year-old with a present under a Christmas tree. His reaction to its contents was serious and somber, almost fearful. He cringed.

"A belt? I don't like belts. No. My Dad used ta hit me with one of these things. I don't want this!"

"I've seen you bending over out in the yard. You really need it."

"No, he *really* used ta hit me with one of these things! I'll show you how."

Now this very large man had the belt in his hands like an ancient weapon. Before I could back away without losing too much face in the eyes of my audience, the man had grabbed me by the wrist and was holding my arm high above my head.

"Ya see, he used to hold my arm up in the air just like this so I couldn't move..."

I wiggled a little, unable to move. I don't own a gun, but if that man had hit me with that belt in front of his door with my wife and son watching, I would have found a way to have shot him. Just being in such a vulnerable position was humiliating enough.

"Okay! I believe you. Let me go. I'll take the belt away."

I spent the next few days suffering my wife's horrible sense of humor and explaining to my son why I hadn't used my lethal Karate on the man.

"I didn't want to kill him and hafta go to prison, Son."

Anyway, my next experience with this terrible man was just as frustrating. It happened when Snow was just a puppy. I like having my morning coffee out on the patio, enjoying all the fresh smells of a new day.

To that extent, I always picked up all Snow's poop at night so that I wouldn't have to look at it or smell it as I contemplated the day. I was curious however, about why he had been so prolific in depositing the pungent little piles.

Well, one morning as I sat, I thought I saw a tiny bird or something fly over my fence and land on my freshly cut grass. It never moved again, so I went out and examined it.

It was poop and someone was throwing it over my fence. After that, I began examining with skepticism all the poop I picked up. When I had gathered enough evidence, I again knocked on my neighbor's sunburned door.

"Somebody over here is throwing puppy-poop over my fence."

He called his son at once. The boy who came was a fat little miniature version of his father, only he lacked his father's refinement. His finger worked his nose furiously.

"Kid, have you been throwing puppy crap in our neighbor's yard?"

The boy paused, plugged the un-worked nostril, and blew the obstruction into the area behind him.

"Uh no, Dad. I would never do that."

My neighbor looked down at me in disapproval.

"There. He said he didn't do it. Ya know, ya really shouldn't accuse people unless you *really* know."

I had prepared myself for such an eventuality.

"I *do* know. I have proof."

"Yeah?"

"First of all, and you can check it yourself. Half the puppy poop in my yard is upside down."

" Upside down? How can you tell?"

"I studied it. When poop dries, the bottom is flat and the top can be dome-shaped or it might have another pattern, but the bottom is always flat and the top isn't. Half the puppy poop in my yard is flat-topped, with little grass patterns—upside down."

He was considering my words, but he seemed confused.

"Well, maybe you're kicking it over when you're walkin around out there."

"No. I never kick poop. Never. Besides, I never feed my dog whole kernel corn. Never! I think it's sick. I've studied the piles closely. Half the poop in my yard contains whole kernel corn. I even brought a sample."

I handed him the brown paper bag. Yet even before I could ask the damning question about whether or not he fed corn to his puppies, the boy broke down and confessed.

"Okay, I did it!"

While he didn't spank the kid because he said he didn't like the way his father spanked him with the belt, he did make the boy apologize, and the poop stopped flying over my fence. Nevertheless, it was on that day that I saw her for the first time.

Her name was Cleo. She was a kind of brownish blond with a small waist and long legs. Her face was angled and delicate, and her eyes, only seeming demure, held a hint of boldness and wild determination.

In an odd way, this temptress was both repulsive and enchanting. Our eyes met for a moment, and then she turned and sashayed away. Somehow I knew at that very moment that we were destined to cross paths again, and soon.

I had never heard anything so discordant and gut wrenching in all my life. Snow howled all day and night, scratching at the fence and rolling on his back in agony. My wife stopped me as I was pulling out the driveway in order to take him to the veterinarian.

"Don't waste your money! Our neighbor told me. Cleo next door's in heat."

I felt sorry of my best friend, who continued to whine as I shifted the car to *PARK*.

"Heat? What does her being in heat have to do with Snow?"

She sighed and leaned toward the open window.

"Dick's a dog. There's no stopping a male dog when a female nearby comes into heat."

She could see I wasn't *getting* it as she reached in and turned off the ignition.

"Her scent is in the air. He can smell it. He can taste it. It's driving Dick crazy."

I looked over at my whining, watery-eyed dog who drooled onto the seat.

"Isn't there anything we can do?"

"Yeah. We can keep him indoors until she's not in heat anymore."

The first time he escaped, he simply bolted out the door when my daughter opened it. She called him, my wife and son called him and I drove around the neighborhood trying to find him. He wasn't found until a day later when I opened my door to see my sloppy neighbor with Snow in tow. The very large man seemed angry.

"Now you either find a way to control your dog here, or *I* will. He's been after my Cleo for days now. I caught him just now scalin my backyard fence. Nothing personal against your pooch, but I don't need any more puppies. Just gave away the last one from the last litter!"

This Neanderthal had a nylon rope around my dog's neck and he cruelly yanked it from time to time in efforts at control. I resentfully took the rope from the man. By this time, my daughter had approached and was monitoring the escalating argument.

"He's not a pooch. He's an Akita, and he was just fine till your promiscuous dog went into heat."

My comment was not well taken.

"Don't blame my Cleo. You're the one who can't control your Dick there."

"My *Dick* is just fine!"

I could not believe I had just said what I had said in the heat of the moment. I stopped immediately, flicking my eyes aside briefly to see my daughter still standing there.

"No, uh, my... my Snow would be just fine if you'd put your dog up or something! Have her fixed! She's had enough puppies already!"

He almost butted me with his large gut as he neared to challenge me further.

"I'll be the judge of when my Cleo's had enough, little man! Get *your* dog fixed!"

Slightly intimidated by his bulk and lack of intellect, I backed a bit, but he continued.

"I just don't want her havin puppies by your depraved little hound-dog there?"

I didn't get it. Was this Cro-Magnon just saying these things *trying* to make me angry?

"He's not a hound-dog. Besides, he wouldn't *want* her. He's an Akita with papers. She's beneath him!"

He laughed sarcastically.

"That's the whole problem! He wants her beneath him, and I'll tell ya just like this, Neighbor. If I ever catch him in my backyard, you won't hafta worry about gettin im fixed. I'll do it myself."

It was a good thing for him he left when he did, because I never responded kindly to threats, and I suggested as much to my daughter as I dead-bolted the door and closed the blinds.

The entire family nevertheless, took the threat seriously. We all redoubled our efforts at keeping our ever-resourceful and indefatigable pet confined indoors. When he whined during the day, we just turned up the stereo. When he howled at night, we just put in our earplugs. When he humped our legs, we just pried him loose and pretended not to notice the fact that he continued humping even without the leg.

I lost a lot of respect for him during those days, but in the end, I blamed it on Cleo and whatever enchantment or spell she had cast in the form of this *heat* thing. I learned to hate her.

I remember getting in trouble with my wife for saying, "They have a descriptive little name for female dogs and now I know why!" Whatever Cleo was doing, she had my once wonderful dog, my best friend behaving like a brute, behaving like a beast.

Still, through careful planning and dogged determination, we had devised a system to keep him locked down. Within two days however, the entire family realized that this inexplicable force or magic that animated our dog was stronger and more formidable than we had ever imagined.

I'll never know exactly how he did it, but as best as I can figure it, he first went up to my son's room and climbed onto the windowsill. He chose that room for its approximation to a huge mulberry tree that I had thought about trimming the winter before, but never did. Balancing himself on the sill, he probably tapped the bottom of the screen with his paw to remove it the same way he'd seen my son perform the trick on the four days a month I had him doing windows.

Looking out, my keenly intelligent Akita spotted a branch roughly six and a half feet away (seventeen feet off the ground) and, closing his eyes, he leapt over and clung to the swaying branch until it steadied before inching down to a place where my son had tied a rope to assist his daily climb into the tree. Taking the rope in his teeth, Snow sprung from the branch and swung out over to the patio where he dropped onto the fiberglass roof and edged from there to the wooden-shake top of the garage.

Because it was Wednesday, I had moved the large hinge-topped garbage container out to the front pending a final move to the street just before I left for work. Spotting the garbage container, Snow then hopped on to the giant green bin, and finally from there, he scrambled to the ground. Once on the pavement, he was free at last.

It was my son who noticed the twisted screen and made the discovery that our dog was missing. While my son and daughter checked the house and backyard, my wife and I knew exactly where he'd gone.

Yet even as we stood at the neighbor's front door arguing about who would ring the bell and who would be forced to talk, we heard my son's panicked voice calling from our yard. I was certain I'd arrive to find my beloved dog dead, or worse at the hands of my neighbor.

"Mom! Dad! Hurry! It's Dick! He's back there with Cleo!"

Quickly, we rushed across the neighbor's weed-infested yard, over our lush green turf, through the gate and into our backyard to find both our son and daughter peering over the fence. I hopped onto the support beam and looked over to see Snow and Cleo standing back-to-back, connected somewhere in between.

"What are they doing, Dad?"

I wasn't sure how to respond without going into too much explanation and detail. Then again, maybe I didn't want him or his sister to know about such an unsavory activity.

"They're... they're dancing, Son."

His sister sighed and rolled her eyes, but he didn't buy it. His next question was spoken with typical nine-year-old curiosity.

"Then *why* was he humping her?"

I had no idea how much he and my daughter had seen, so I sent them indoors immediately. Climbing to the higher support 2 x 4, I had managed to fall over the fence into my neighbor's back yard and was trying to part the two dogs before I realized that the barbarian could have come out at any time.

In a near state of hysteria, I tried to reason with Snow, but it didn't do any good. Nevertheless, just as I was threatening him with severe sanctions, my wife informed me that the neighbors were not in the house. I sighed with relief.

"Finally! *Something* goes my way!"

She differed.

"They're not in the house. They just pulled into the driveway."

I heard the car doors slamming. The situation was not good. If that Troglodyte had come out and found Snow and me in his backyard, I didn't know what he might do. Fortunately, Cleo released her mysterious grip on my physically-drained dog at about that time and I, exerting all my strength, scooped him up and fled with him to the fence, straining to press his weight to the fence top.

"Hurry Honey! Take him, Fast!"

She backed away.

"*I* can't lift that dog."

I was stuck holding him there, my arms giving out. I thought logically. I could have done the responsible thing. I could have explained the entire situation to my neighbor, offered to pay for a doggie-abortion if such a thing were possible, apologized for all the disparaging remarks I had made to him over the two years he lived there and made an attempt at friendship with the man by sucking down one of his disgusting beers and burping on purpose.

Instead, I just let Snow fall onto the ground on the other side of the fence. His pain-filled yelp assured me that he was all right. In all the excitement I had never considered how *I* was going to get back over the fence.

My neighbor had the smooth finished side as all the support beams were on my side. My dress shoes were no great help as I struggled to climb the slippery fence, and the fact that my arms had been drained from lifting my struggling ninety pound dog for all that time was no benefit either.

I actually think I would have made it over if I hadn't heard the brute's sliding glass door slamming open. He shouted loud enough for the entire neighborhood to hear.

"Hey! What the *hell* are you doin in my yard?"

I stopped assaulting the fence and raised my hands slowly. Cautiously, I turned to face the disgusting and dangerous man. As I looked at him, his face contorted with anger, suspicion and probable envy, I distinctly noticed that he reminded me of another brainless big-mouthed bully I had encountered when I was a kid: Fred Flintstone. His filthy, overlarge bare feet only made the observation more acute.

He approached and gripped me by the left shoulder with his dirty though powerful hand.

"What are you *doin* over here?"

As a handsome, urbane writer with a very creative mind, I figured I'd have no problem outwitting the urban thrall. I initially thought to tell him my son and I were playing catch and that the ball had gone over the fence, but I knew I could do better than that.

"Well, you see. It was an opossum."

He probably didn't know what an opossum was. He just stood there dumbfounded as I continued.

"You see, I was cooking chicken on the grill, and this opossum that's been hanging around my yard just came up and took it. Last I saw, he was going over your fence."

The ogre was sniffing the air like a dog.

"So that's why I came over the fence."

Suddenly he stopped.

"I don't smell no chicken."

Double negative. He walked to the fence and illegally trespassed by sticking his head over onto my side.

"I don't see no smokin grill."

He looked at me suspiciously, and then he looked over at Cleo who sidelong, glanced back culpably, like a lipstick-smeared teen-age girl just returning from the prom.

I figured I knew the look because my teen-age pet store friend had told me nowadays *all* girls "put out" on prom night.

Then my neighbor looked at me again. Then he looked back toward her. Then at me. Then back at her. I didn't like the implication.

"Waitaminute, I hope you're not suggesting what I *think* you're suggesting."

He scanned the trees and around the yard.

"I never saw no possum round here. There aren't enough trees around here for possums."

The ruffian then grabbed the back of my neck with a huge heavy paw.

"I think you better leave."

As he, hand clamping my neck, escorted me toward the gate at the other side of the yard, I distinctly remember stepping in a gushy mass near the un-trimmed bushes along the house.

"There was a real opossum out here. A real opossum with a real hanging tail and all. Steals chickens."

I asked my wife to assemble the children in my office while I cleaned the mess from the bottom and sides of my shoes. We had discussed it and agreed.

Snow and Cleo's little spectacle in front of the kids deserved some manner of an explanation. I had feared it for years, but the time had come to have that talk with them about the "S" word.

Because talking comes easy for women, I let my wife begin the expository, and she performed wonderfully... until she became unduly graphic in front of the kids. She caught up with me as I descended the stairs.

"Why'd you walk out? They're still sitting up there waiting."

I could not believe that, after saying the things she had said up there, she had the nerve to ask me why I walked out.

"He's nine and she's fifteen. There is no need to be so, so sordid."

She twisted her face in an incredulous expression.

"What do you mean sordid? What did I say?"

Maybe she hadn't realized at the time that she was talking to kids.

"Well, well when you were describing female body parts, you said the 'V' word."

She seemed confused.

"So?"

I stuttered my reply in nervousness.

"Well, I just think that word is a little *much* for the kids."

She followed me into the kitchen and tore into me as I sat at the table.

"They know most of this stuff already. I was just trying to be frank with them. What was I supposed to say? The 'P' word?"

I bolted up instantly, absolutely astonished that she could be so gross, but she continued.

"Then again, I could have used the 'T' word."

I covered my ears with my hands and headed for the door, but she spoke loud enough for me to hear a final comment.

"Then again, I could have explained female anatomy using the notorious 'C' word!"

After I drove over to my parents' house to escape, my mother, as typical, sensed that I was disturbed by something. As usual my parents, after hearing my complaint about how my wife was ruining the kids' minds with the way she was discussing the "S" subject, told me that she was right and I was wrong.

They told me to go back home and help her. My father took it one step further. He said I should *listen* to her, that if I did I might learn something. Failing to elicit any sympathy from my callous parents, I was forced to return home.

I went back up to the room and listened while my wife explained to the children and me about where babies come from and about what grown-ups do. I actually learned a whole lot.

In any event, there was one thing in particular she said that stood out in my mind, something she strongly suggested to the kids over three or four times. She said the "S" word was something that should happen between married people. It was profound.

While I'm usually too modest to say it, I've always had this kind of incredible ability at making astute and acute inferences. I was struck just then with an absolutely brilliant idea. I didn't know why I hadn't thought of it before, that is, being the genius that people are always *saying* I am. I would find a wife for Snow, a good Akita from a good family with papers and all.

Thus I went out and searched and researched until finally, I found her, albeit fifteen hundred dollars was a little much to pay for a dog. But Muffin (a documented virgin) was gorgeous. She reminded me of my wife in an odd way though I would have never told my wife that. Discouraged by my family's reaction to the previous name I chose, I held off and let my daughter name the new addition to the family.

Anyway, after around three weeks of initial resistance, my wife and kids finally gave in and consented to going along with me about the ceremony thing. Although I had searched all the pet supply wholesalers in the city and in two cities nearby, I was unable to find a doggie tux large enough to fit Snow and surprisingly no one made formal doggie gowns. I was forced to settle on a silk black bowtie for him and I purchased her a petite white, lacy, formal, faux pearl-studded blouse from the women's department at Macy's. With a few alterations performed by a tailor, the blouse looked really nice on her.

Despite the fact that I sent invitations to everyone in my family and to friends, not one of my brothers or sisters or friends appeared on that Saturday afternoon. My own parents didn't even show up. At the last moment I thought to invite Cleo from next door, but I figured such an invitation might be taken as an insult.

Through painstaking efforts and a bribe, I had managed to get the official wedding ceremony text from a friend who worked at the Justice of the Peace department downtown, and with Bible in hand, I called the small assemblage to order.

Looking out, I noticed something I thought was really cute: my son's box turtle, Tabitha, was the flower girl. I had asked my daughter to tape a bouquet of flowers to the reptile's back and that shell just looked radiant.

Like my wife had done at our wedding, Muffin cried through most of the ceremony and she resisted as I tried to rub her nose together with Snow's nose in something of a kiss at the end.

I was very disappointed with her. Within minutes after I had announced them dog and wife, she had somehow managed to gnaw through the red rubber band which attached the ring to her wrist. I never saw that ninety-five dollar ring again.

The marriage was troubled from the beginning. Reflecting back, I don't think Muffin ever liked males, but it seemed she hated Snow most of all. She'd snarl and growl whenever he was even remotely near. She didn't like my son either despite his many and genuine attempts to befriend her.

Though if she hated Snow the worst, then I ranked a close second as an object of her scorn. I'd be sitting at my computer typing when all of the sudden, I'd hear these threatening growls coming from behind me. I'd turn to see Muffin glaring up at me, just daring me to in some way suggest that I had a problem with the distraction.

The strange part about it all was that she behaved like an angel whenever the *weaker* sex was around. When my wife and daughter were around, she pretended to like Snow and my son and even me, but the moment there was no female in sight she became some kind of red-eyed monster from a Stephen King novel.

Snow got the worst of it. Early on, he made an ill-fated attempt to consummate the marriage and paid for it with a torn ear and a bloody nose. I felt sorry for my poor dog. Nevertheless, I had friends who had told me they'd been in bad marriages like his. Some of their situations actually sounded worse.

While my wife and daughter just loved Muffin, they constantly ribbed me about my inability as a matchmaker. The two dogs just weren't a good couple. Muffin simply was not a good wife for Snow and probably wouldn't have been a good wife for any dog. After a while he lost interest. After a while he wouldn't even try to sniff her in that pungent area below her tail. Their differences were hopelessly irreconcilable.

I had just granted the divorce and sold her to some male-bashing women's rights activists for six hundred dollars when I was surprised with the most awful news. I woke up one morning to my corpulent neighbor's pounding on my door, his frazzled hair frightening my children so early in the day. Standing in my morning robe, I swallowed the mouthwash I had quickly gargled and opened the door. It was obvious that he hadn't gargled before coming over.

"Cleo's pregnant."

I was alarmed, but I pretended not to show it.

"That's nice. Thanks for sharing."

I tried to close the door, but Flintstone plopped a giant foot in the doorjamb.

"She's pregnant, and I wanna know what *you* are gonna do about it!"

Not since I was a teenager had I even considered anyone asking me such a question. I was at a loss for words.

"I don't... I don't know. Buy a shower gift? I mean, who's the father?"

He wasn't amused.

"Dick. That Dick a yours is the father. I'm sure of it."

He could never prove such an allegation.

"Dick is not the father. We kept him indoors the entire time she was all hot and heated up. Had to be some other dog, I mean, she's had puppies by two other dogs and no one knows for sure who the other two fathers are. I told you to get her fixed."

At that point he grabbed me by the robe and pulled me out the door, his actions bordering on criminal assault.

"I know Dick's the father. What about the time I caught you with Cleo in my backyard? Wasn't Dick out that day? Someone told someone I know that he *was*."

I remember thinking, "I haven't actually lied to this man up until this point."

Reluctant to cross the line, I deflected the question.

"Who is this someone who told someone you know? You're lying. You're bluffing. There's no someone who told someone you know."

He became threatening again.

"I don't appreciate bein called a liar, but if ya must know. Your daughter told my son. They've been talking on the phone a lot lately."

I was appalled! *My* daughter had been talking to his son on the phone? Why would she be talking to a boy on the phone whose family belonged on a daytime television talk show? He probably sensed the terror of my thoughts and sought to increase it.

"I think they're kind of *fond* of each other."

That did it. I was not about to stand there and let this big lummox get me all worked up, so I quickly dismissed him.

"Look! Dick is not the father. I've raised him better than that. Cleo's pregnant by some other dog and we all know it. And it's probably *your* fault she has no morals, so you can do whatever you want to do. Dick had nothing to do with it!"

Then before he could open his big fat mouth to respond, I quickly turned and slipped into the house, locking the deadbolt behind me.

Once inside, I went immediately to my daughter's room and caught her talking on the phone.

"Who's that?" I demanded.

"A... a friend," she answered, stuttering her reply. "Do you want me off the phone?"

"Yes. Now!"

As she whispered something and hung up, her mother, sensing a potentially major confrontation, left off painting in her studio and came in to defend her.

"Why can't she talk on the phone?"

Perhaps my wife knew all about her phone conversations. Perhaps the two had colluded to conceal them from me!

"Do you know who she talks on that phone to 'a lot lately'?"

My daughter sat there mute, turning the task of her defense over to her mother who answered in a seedy lawyer tone.

"She has a lot of friends."

I was unwilling to play games or mince words.

"I heard just now that she's been talking to a boy, something I've strictly forbidden. And what's worse, I heard it's the sonofa ogre next door who threw dog poop over into our yard!"

My daughter was quick to make the correction.

"That wasn't him! That was his bratty little brother!"

I had her!

"Ah ha! So you *have* been talking to him!"

Her failure to answer the charge was an admission of guilt. I sighed heavily. While I had a confession, I knew the situation could be tricky and even dangerous from that point on. My father always told me that I should never make a threat I couldn't or wasn't willing to carry out. I could have ordered her never to talk to the neighbor's kid again, though I wasn't sure how much good such a demand would do.

After all, I had already forbade her to talk to boys on the phone, but it was apparent that for some reason she had disregarded the order. Another such edict would probably yield the same result.

Then again, I could have threatened her with physical punishment, but in life I had seen many situations in which the threat and act of physically punishing teenagers backfired. Physically threatened people can exhibit extraordinary and bizarre behaviors. Besides, while I could threaten her with such discipline, I wasn't sure if I could or would follow through with it.

Then I thought I could modify her behavior by *harping* on the fact that she had disobeyed. I could have brought the subject up morning, noon and night for weeks—no for months at a time, always expressing my shock and disappointment and lamenting the way she had breached a sacred trust between father and daughter.

My wife always described the tactic as a "guilt trip." Yet if my daughter was anything like my wife, then the "guilt trip" scheme would have worked for a short time and quickly lost effect. Through a process of creative rationalization, over time of course, my wife could justify just about anything to appease tinges of guilt. My daughter, unfortunately for me, was too much like her mother, so the harping would do little good.

Finally, I considered reasoning with the girl. I thought of persuasively putting all the facts and all my concerns as a loving father on the table and letting her *think* she was making her own decision. In that moment I reflected that Mark Twain observed somewhere that "people are more convinced by discoveries they *think* they have made themselves rather than by the things we tell them." With that thought in mind, I began.

"You're fifteen now. As of this point I'm *giving* you permission to talk to a boy on the phone once a week, for no more than ten minutes. Now that being said, if you *have* to talk to a boy on the phone, why can't you talk to a boy whose father isn't a direct descendant of Attila the Hun?"

She took a deep breath and responded.

"His family is a little strange, Dad, but he can't help that. Our family's strange too."

I was shocked and insulted that she could fix her mouth to make such a comment.

"What are you talkin about? Our family is perfectly normal! How could anyone call us strange?"

She answered.

"Well, how many normal families do you know that have weddings for their dogs? And if that's not bad enough, our divorced dog has another dog pregnant, and you won't let him be responsible."

I considered her words for a moment. I was just about sure people had weddings for their dogs all the time. I was almost certain I had read it was a growing trend. Nonetheless, she had made a mistaken assumption.

"Cleo, if you remember, has already had two litters. She's a little trollop who just goes out and *gets* pregnant. There's no way of knowing whether or not she's pregnant by

Snow or just some depraved dog out there roaming the streets! She was in heat. She was putting it out there!"

She wasn't giving up.

"He had sex with her! They were *attached* to each other. Remember? In the neighbors' backyard? She probably got pregnant by him then!"

I could not believe such language coming from the mouth of my daughter! I had to change the subject.

"There's just no way of knowing. Besides, we're off the topic. Why don't you talk to some boy *other* than that crummy kid next door? There must be some nice boys in your class."

My wife who had been silent for a record time finally re-entered the discussion.

"Honey, the boy next door is a real young gentleman, and so polite! Just last week he volunteered and changed a flat tire on my car. Good thing too! He saved me from being late for work."

If anything, the junior barbarian over there was clever enough to win over my wife with grease monkey antics he probably learned from his filthy-handed father. She was susceptible to such bribery, but I was incapable of being fooled by mere obsequious displays. Un-derailed by the diversion, I reassumed the task of gentle persuasion.

"Look, his father's a fat slob. This kid might be in shape now, but what do you think *he's* gonna look like when he gets older? He'll be a porker too. Like father, like son. So what if he can change a flat tire."

My daughter ignored all my words and focused on the one new rule I had laid down.

"You said you were giving me permission to talk to a boy one time a week for ten minutes only. You didn't say you got to choose the boy."

I wasn't sure what she was getting at. Besides, I wasn't sure how to respond.

"Well uh. Yes and no."

She finished.

"Then I can talk to any boy I want? Just as long as it's one time a week for ten minutes only?"

Feeling a little cornered, I resisted.

"Nine. I think I said nine minutes a week."

She sighed and exchanged condemnatory looks with her mother.

"Okay, I can talk to any boy I want for nine minutes a week?"

"Well I... I think I said nine, but I really meant five."

It was worth a try anyway. Needless to say, neither my wife nor daughter was willing to settle for five. So there it was: in the presence of my wife, somehow I had agreed to allow my daughter to talk with this mangy, flea-bitten kid next door for nine minutes a week! I smelled a set-up. It was the only way those two could have conned a witty guy like me into such a concession.

Duly considering of my keen intellect, they had the entire scene staged days, maybe even weeks or months in advance. Notwithstanding, I was not beaten. I determined that I would keep a watchful eye on my daughter and an equally cautious vigil on the actions of the tire-changing teen-age charlatan next door.

An amateur in the fine art of espionage, I was a little bumbling and clumsy at first.

"Hang up the phone, Dad."

Nevertheless, I recovered smoothly.

"Oh! I didn't know you were on. Sorry. Just, just checking the time."

Click. She had a sort of sixth sense about my clandestine maneuvering.

"You hung up, Dad, but I heard you pick up again."

Click. I learned some sad things about my daughter during the first two weeks, and the most agonizing revelation was the painful reality that she didn't trust me, her own father.

Apparently, in a shameful display of her lack of faith in me, she had thoroughly searched her room and found an electronic listening device I had carefully planted. And without for once considering that perhaps her *mother* may have been responsible, she automatically blamed it on me. She got me in real bad trouble with my wife by telling on me.

My second discovery about her related to her body: she had been as tall as my wife was since she was thirteen, but for two years their bodies could not have been more different. She had always been flat in places where my wife was, well, a little less flat. She had always been firm or slight in places where my wife was soft and round. She was becoming more and more like my wife every day, though in some places where she was sticking out and up, my wife was beginning to stick down.

If the changes in her were noticeable to me, then they were glaringly evident to the teen-age boys in the neighborhood who began to suspiciously wander by my house for no apparent reason. One day some stupid kid even had the nerve to come by and knock on the door.

"Collecting for the newspaper, Sir."

He was grinning past me at my daughter the entire time he stood there. It wasn't till two days later that I remembered I didn't have a subscription to the paper newspaper. I got my newspaper electronically on computer.

It was then that I made the correlation. It was a combination of the parade of cars blasting loud music as they went by my house, the basketballs that somehow always went over the fence into my backyard and the *wrong number* and *hurried hang-up* telephone calls that brought me to the conclusion.

Locking the doors, I rushed into my wife's studio where she was swishing a brush in turpentine or something in one of my best crystal brandy snifters. I was so panicked that I ignored the transgression, panting as I locked the door behind me.

"Honey! We have to *do* something! Our daughter's in heat!"

Without even looking up, she responded.

"If we haven't already done what we were supposed to do and taught her what we were supposed to teach her in fifteen years of raising her, trying to make up for it now would be pointless."

My breathing was still labored.

"We could lock her up until it's over!"

She put the brush down and stared up at the large oil painting.

"I think she'll be all right."

For a first time I looked at the painting, when to my surprise, I was in it. There I was, with a grim, near-obsessed look on my face, standing in a threatening posture on a ship with sails and a furious ocean in the background.

I was screaming maniacally at another man who appeared calm and for some reason looked a little like my wife with a beard. Well, while I had always known my wife was a little strange, I hadn't realized the turpentine fumes had damaged her brain so severely. Swallowing loudly, I asked the logical question.

"Why?"

I had made a mistake by asking. I saw the wheels turning in her fume-demented mind as she began.

"It was actually inspired in part by that dream you say you keep having, the one with you at the river. It's called *Ahab and Ishmael*. As you can see, you're Ahab."

I didn't like the way I looked in the painting. I was all mean and ugly and one-dimensional, but then, I didn't understand why she had painted herself as a man. Perhaps there were some quirks about my wife I didn't want to explore.

"Ahab? Wasn't he the nice gentle ancient king who had the misfortune of marrying an evil, wicked, manipulative and bossy wife named Jezebel? Honey, shouldn't you be a *woman* in that picture?"

She ignored the comment and went back to swishing the tiny paintbrush.

"I'll just say this. Maybe you should re-read Melville."

"Melville?" I thought, and then it hit me. She had been holding out on me all along.

"Waitaminute! There *was* something else to that dream I told you about! Wasn't there? That dream when I'm at the river?"

Ignoring me, she had gone back to painting. After a while, she spoke without looking at me.

"Like I told you. Re-read Melville."

It was useless to try and have a conversation with my wife while she was painting, but unlike her, I was unwilling to abandon my daughter to those hormone-driven teen-age boys who were constantly hounding her.

"We have to manage that girl. I think I'm going to revoke her phone privileges."

My wife stopped painting instantly and looked up at me.

"No you won't. Look Ahab, I'm just as concerned about her as you are, but unnecessarily restricting her is not the way. It would only make things worse."

My wife's thinking was a result of typical flawed feminine reasoning. She always found problems with proposed solutions rather than solutions for proposed problems. I thought I'd just turn the tables.

"Okay Jezebel, what would *you* recommend since you're so smart?"

Disregarding the reference and implication, she responded irritated, while swishing the small, encrusted paintbrush in my expensive crystal again.

"We'll watch her closely, and we'll keep the communication lines open. Restricting her for no good reason would only make her rebel."

I watched as she painted another ugly furrow in my hard obstinate brow in the eerie scene on canvas. Smiling to herself, she concluded.

"Besides, she is allowed to talk to a boy for just nine minutes a week. What real harm can *that* do?"

Because I'm such a kind, thoughtful, considerate, empathetic and compliant husband, I followed my wife's admonition to re-read Melville. I had first thought to read Melville during my freshman year of college, but my English professor said I hadn't lived enough and suggested that I wait on reading him until I was thirty.

Intellectually challenged, I read him anyway and I made sure I understood every word on every page. Aside from a few subtly written demeaning racial stereotypes, I remember thinking the story was engaging.

Nonetheless, I thought fondly of my old professor on the day I turned thirty, but I never re-read the book because I thought I had gotten a good grasp of it at the wise age of nineteen.

Anyway, even as I re-read the first few chapters, I read the words and thoughts as if seeing and understanding them for a first time. As was always the case when I started a good book, I became completely absorbed in the work, forgetting my wife, the kids and myself.

I was standing aboard the *Pequod*, noting the grim aspect of Ahab as he stood upon his quarterdeck when my daughter came in, gently closed the book and sat across from me.

"I need to talk to you, Daddy. I need to ask you something."

Afraid she might tell me something that I didn't want to hear or didn't want to know about, I stood nervously, calling for my wife in panic. When she arrived, I sat her across from my daughter while I stood a distance away, hands in the pockets of my smoking jacket.

"She, she wants to tell us something. I, I thought you'd, you'd want to be here."

My daughter turned toward me carefully.

"It's something I need to ask *you*, Daddy."

"You, you can ask us both. What is, what *is* it?"

Her hands folded nervously, she swallowed a seeming resolution pill and began.

"I was invited to the junior prom and I, and I wanted to ask you if I could go."

While I sighed in relief, I felt a new ominous fear coming on. The prom—my teen-age pet store friend had told me what happens at those high school proms. I had to take control of the situation and nip the problem early.

"You, you want to go to the prom with a boy? A boy invited you?"

She smiled.

"Yes, a boy."

I looked over at her mother who didn't seem to be the least bit alarmed. She was actually smiling in that same silly doting manner. I knew then was on my own.

"You said *junior* prom? You can't go to that. You're only a sophomore."

My indulgent wife explained the rule.

"She can go if a junior invites her."

The two exchanged quick inside glances. Right at that moment I could tell that my wife and daughter had discussed this whole matter before. They had probably considered all my possible responses and had airtight rebuttals planned. While I hated to admit it, I knew I was no match for two well-prepared conniving female minds, so I gave a little ground.

"Who is the junior who invited you?"

My wife answered for her.

"Honey, you know him. He's the nice young man from next door."

It was the one answer I feared. I looked at my wife, muttering under my breath words she had uttered so irresponsibly,

She's talking to a boy just nine minutes a week. What real harm can that do?

There were however, a few defenses left. Yet by this time, my wife was completely carrying the argument for our daughter.

"She's only fifteen. She's too young to date."

"A prom is not a date. It's a sort of *social practice* for young people."

I didn't want that neighbor's kid or anybody "practicing" with my daughter, so I raised another objection.

"Prom's are expensive, especially for girls. I really can't afford to pay for an expensive prom right now."

"I'll make her gown, so you won't have to pay for that. And besides, do I have to remind you of how much money you spent buying your precious dog a wife, not to mention the untold amount you spent on that stupid wedding ceremony?"

I didn't want her to mention the amount. As I stood there vexed, I realized I had run out of extenuations, but there was one last hope. I could stall in order to think up a better excuse.

"This is all so sudden. I'm, I'm not comfortable giving my permission right now. I'll have to give this matter some thought."

And after saying that, I rushed out the room before they could pin me to a specific time for making a decision. Locking the office door behind me, I returned to and lost myself in the disturbing world Melville had created in print.

I didn't like Ahab, who was so monomaniacal and obsessive in his vainglorious though hopeless attempt to assert his will over the order of the universe.

The catholic Ishmael, on the other hand, became a friend to me, he became a voice that preached universal acceptance and caused me to reassess my thinking on many of life's important questions and themes. Never would I look at one of my favorite movies, *Star Trek II: The Wrath of Khan*, in the same way again.

Anyway, I finished the book in four days and was forced to face my wife and daughter again. It was only then I realized that Melville's work had somehow changed me. I relented without much argument and gave my daughter permission to go to this junior prom, though not without great reluctance.

"Well okay, you can go."

I continued as I slid from her excited embrace.

"When do you think I should get my tux?"

My wife and my daughter just stood there, wide eyes and mouths open in duplicate.

"Daddy, why do *you* need a tux?"

"Because I'm going to the junior prom with you two, as a sort of chaperon."

Try as they did, neither of the two could dissuade me from going down to that exclusive specialty store and renting that stylish tuxedo. Then I went right down to the high school and bought a prom bid. Before it was all over, it seemed my excitement about the prom grew while my daughter's seemed to wane. *How sharper than a serpent's tooth it is to have a thankless child!*

After all, how many fathers would be kind enough and willing to go all out so they could be a cool, hip chaperon at their daughter's prom? She was one of the lucky ones, and all she could say was,

"If it was my *brother's* prom, you wouldn't be chaperoning him."

What she wouldn't understand was the fact that chaperons were invented specifically for daughters in the first place, that the word derived from "*chaper*," meaning "the small pants of a daughter," and "*on*," meaning "on." Thus a chaperon was purposed to keep a daughter's small pants on. Both my wife and daughter thought I had made the story up, but I was just about sure I had read it somewhere.

In the meantime, my pesky neighbor knocked on my door almost every day demanding that I make Snow take some responsibility for Cleo's pregnancy, but I told him again and again that he had no proof. I told him a doggie DNA match would be the only way to know for sure, if he wanted to pay for it.

As the prom loomed closer however, I got the distinct impression that the hollow-headed ogre was actually trying to be nice to me. It was a disgusting display. He probably thought that we'd somehow become best friends since our kids were going to the prom together. He and his wife invited my wife and me over for dinner one night, but I refused to go. My ever-contrary wife went alone and pretended she had a great time. She said my neighbor's wife told her that Snow was over the fence and in their backyard with Cleo almost every day.

Disbelieving the claim, I began to watch Snow more closely. One day I even stayed home from work and, unseen peering out my bedroom window, observed him as he went across the fence. I quietly crept down the stairs, tipped into the backyard, and peered through a knothole in the fence only to see Cleo lying on the lawn in the shade of a tree. Snow was lying with her, his chin resting on her back. Needless to say, I went right over there and dragged him back home where, for a first time, I put him on a chain, a very short chain.

Snow had really disappointed me. I kept thinking, What had I done wrong in raising him? Had I been too easy on him? Too strict? I didn't know. He had been such a bright, intelligent, wonderful little puppy. We were so close to each other then. I remember how he used to study my eyes, just dying to do the things that would please me. And the shows! We were in the great shows together, man and dog, and everybody absolutely envied us for our relationship. At least a hundred people had come up to me and told me how lucky I was to have him while predicting great things in store for him.

He just had so much potential. And what did he do with it? Nothing! Absolutely nothing! It seemed that as he got older, he just got apathetic. When he was a puppy, I'd throw a ball, and he'd dash away after it and come pouncing back to drop it at my feet.

After he got older, I'd throw the ball, and he'd just look at me with an expression that insinuated I had insulted him by suggesting he should fetch a ball. He seemed offended that I had even attempted to initiate such an idiotic form of dyadic interaction.

At times I think he hated me as evidenced in gross and malicious behavior. Everyone including Snow knew I loved having my morning coffee on the patio, breathing in the fresh clean air of the new day. Well, two days after I got rid of his awful wife, Snow began a disgusting habit.

No sooner would I sit with my coffee, he would come over and stop intentionally, not more than four feet away from me. In short order he would squat in that way dogs do, and then he would grunt vulgarly like a bran-deficient old curmudgeon as he completely ruined the freshness of the air as well as my peace of mind.

And to imagine that he would treat me like that after all I had done for him! Then one day, he went out of his way to achieve the ultimate in disgust. As I sat there with my coffee and bagel, reveling in the beauty of the morning, Snow seemed to smile before pulling his lips way back off his teeth in that way dogs do. Teeth bared, he lifted a piece of his yesterday's poop, threw it to the back of his mouth, and swallowed it. I haven't touched a bagel since.

Anyway, his lack of control with respect to Cleo was the last straw for me. In that business he had behaved like a beast, like a brutish animal! While I wouldn't admit it to anyone, I thought that just maybe he had gotten her pregnant. In reality though, Snow had changed, he had fallen way short of his potential, and as a result we were no longer close. After all that had passed I don't think we even liked each other.

He didn't like being on a short chain and whined from dawn to dusk, reserving the dusk to dawn hours for intermittent pitiable moans. It was during that time that Snow and my son formed some sort of a boy-and-his-dog type bond. The boy would sit with that dog for hours brushing his hair, playing tug-of-war with him and teaching him tricks.

It was a relationship I kind of envied. I wished at times I could have been the recipient of the love either expressed for each other. When my son spoke, the dog understood as evidenced by nods, other non-verbal indicators and a sort of humming Snow would accomplish which at times seemed almost intelligible.

Of the two children, my son was the nature lover, the animal rights activist. From even the age of three he had owned a litany of pets which included tarantulas, snakes, lizards, crayfish, toads, rabbits, a turtle, a cat (for a few weeks) and orphaned birds. That is why I actually anticipated him coming to me to plead in Snow's behalf.

"Dad, it's inhumane to keep Dick on such a short leash. He should be free."

I was well prepared for his arguments.

"Why? So he can have puppies by every female dog in the neighborhood? He's fine just where he is."

He opened the blinds so that we were forced to see out into the backyard.

"Just look at him, Dad. There's something wrong with that picture. How long do you plan to keep him all tied up like that?"

I turned away from the window.

"Until he learns or you can teach him to control his, his urges and impulses."

In a serious tone, in a television lawyer type manner, my son closed.

"Dad, you're trying to fight something that's bigger than you, something that's stronger than you. It's a fight you can't win. You can't make Dick into something he isn't no matter how hard you try. We just have to try'n work with what we've got."

He didn't say another word. He just left me standing there. I remember staring out into space, impressed that my son, a mere nine year-old, had in the defense of a poor speechless animal, expressed himself so eloquently, so profoundly.

Of course, he had probably learned to speak so well by closely watching and striving to imitate me. Yet as I stood there, I felt for some reason a part of me, something central to my very being, start to unravel a little.

I remember feeling unnerved, uncomfortable and agitated for the next few days as I tried to sort through a distinct sense of confusion. Nevertheless, I made sure Snow stayed on the chain, and he stayed there right up until the time of my prom on that Saturday night.

I had it all planned. I vacuumed, washed and waxed the car early that morning, went to the specialty store to pick up my tux and drove across town to a special florist for my *boutonnière*. Fortunately, I arrived home in time to almost avert what I thought would be a near disaster.

There, standing on one of my best expensive upholstered chairs in the living room, was my daughter in, in what seemed to be an obscene, slinky, lacy black negligee purposed specifically for married women, women looking to get married, women looking to get pregnant, or both. I had no idea why my wife would let her wear something like that under her prom dress.

"You're back so soon, Honey. We wanted to surprise you. How do you like the gown I made?"

Unable to look directly at my daughter so nearly naked, I called back over my shoulder.

"I haven't seen it. Where *is* it?"

"Don't be silly. She's wearing it."

I peeked back at my daughter for a split second before modesty forced me to turn away. Painfully aware that my wife was never good about taking any manner of criticism, I thought for a moment and offered something careful and constructive.

"That's not a prom dress. That's a teddy. She can't wear that out of this house."

Luckily for me, my wife had the stick pins in her mouth she was using for tacking the hem of that thing my daughter was modeling, so all she could do was give me a hideous, evil, wicked *you're-gonna-be-sorry-you-said-that* glare.

She and my daughter exchanged another one of their underhanded, silent female-eye-language glances and my daughter understood that she should leave the room so she wouldn't be splattered with the blood my wife was intent on spilling. Yet, even as my daughter exited with her eyes bowed low, I began with a clever retraction.

"It's, it's a nice shade of black, though."

My generous compliment didn't matter, and my wife said things to me that would have shocked and surprised even Jerry Springer audiences. I was forced to sit like a kid in a principal's office while she went on and on about what she called "callous, irresponsible behavior."

She was like a crazy woman! Every time I said I was sorry, she countered with, "You're not sorry," and then later with "Oh, you're sorry all right." And if that wasn't enough, at a certain point, she tried to punish me.

"One more thing, I'm sorry you went out and got a tux and all, but you are *NOT* going to that prom."

There she had crossed the line. Now I might be a perfectly patient, understanding husband, but even perfection has its limits. Reaching back to my early childhood, I remembered something my father always said to my mother in heated arguments before she finally broke the power of the line. In a voice slightly deeper than his normal voice he would say,

"Who's the man, here?"

It was great, because at least for the initial few occasions he said it, it shut her up. It took her years to work her way into a good comeback. So, in a deep manly voice I said it.

"I'll go to the prom if I want. Hey! *Who's the man here*?"

Somehow, I think my wife had talked to my mother and my mother had insidiously warned her about the once-effective line.

"I thought *you* were—till you wanted to go to the prom. You tell me, how many men go to junior proms?"

Striving to remain in manly character, I continued in my best deep voice.

"How many is irrelevant. Besides, I'm going as a chaperon. Look, you might as well stop arguing with me. I'm the head of this house, and I say what goes, and that's final!"

My wife however, had no absolutely respect for finality.

"You're the head. I'll admit that, but I'm the neck. And you know, when the neck says turn right, the head turns right. When the neck says turn left, the head turns left. And right now, I think the neck is telling the head that he is *not* going to that prom."

At that point, I *knew* she had been talking to my mother. The three most important women in my life, all fiendishly plotting against me! I just couldn't understand such treachery.

Well anyway, it was pointless to argue with my headstrong wife, so after muttering a few things to myself intentionally unintelligible so she couldn't possibly have a comeback, I left the room. One thing had not changed though: no one and/or nothing was going to stop me from going to that prom.

I had made reservations for three at an exclusive four star restaurant that sat atop a glamorous hotel in a nearby city. The way I had it figured, we'd leave at four thirty, eat at about six fifteen and get back in order to make it to the prom by eight thirty or nine. Then after the prom, I thought we could maybe go out to breakfast, relax, shoot the breeze a while and head on home.

Initially, I was really flustered about the car seating arrangements. Now, there was no way I was going to let them sit in the back seat alone while I drove.

After all, my daughter was half-naked, and at almost seventeen, the neighbor kid's hormones were raging somewhere in the red zone. I could have put my daughter in the front seat and him in the back. But once again, my daughter was half-naked, and I didn't want to look at her.

Besides, if someone I knew who might have been driving by had looked into the car and seen a young female sitting there all bare like that, who knows what that person might have thought. I mean, that is if they hadn't known she was my daughter. So logically, I decided I would put the boy in the front and my daughter in the back, on the driver's side so I wouldn't have to see her in the rear view mirror.

I was standing in my one hundred sixty-two dollar-a-night tux outside the bathroom door badgering my daughter so she would finish getting dressed faster when my wife came out of her studio, glasses resting on the tip of her nose.

"Honey, you look so nice in that tux. Oooh! Can I get a kiss?"

Obviously, she grossly underestimated my immense intellect, because I knew what she was up to. She was trying to seduce me in order to buy more time for my daughter in the bathroom. They had probably planned it out weeks ago. I knew better.

"No. No kiss. We've got to go or we'll be late for dinner."

Her facial expression morphed to a perfect cast of genuine confusion.

"What are you talking about? It's only ten to four now. Dinner isn't until seven."

"Six-thirty, and we have to drive an hour and a half to get there."

"What do you mean drive an hour and a half? All we have to do is walk next door."

I didn't dare ask her to explain that last statement, but she would anyway.

"I mean, don't tell me you forgot that the plan was that both families would have dinner together next door before the prom?"

I looked down towards her feet; but that's a fable.

"How can I forget something that nobody ever told me?"

"I did tell you. I told you twice, but come to think of it, I think both times you were kind of sleeping."

"Then it doesn't count. You didn't tell me, but that's not the point! I want to go out of town for dinner before my prom, I mean the, I mean my daughter's prom."

She was playing with my bowtie.

"No, *you're* missing the point. Ask your daughter. She wants to have dinner next door. You do realize that it's *her* prom, don't you?"

Heavy I sighed, sadly surrendering my dazzling dinner plans.

"Besides Honey, that woman over there has been slaving over the stove cooking dinner all day long. It would be a lot easier to cancel reservations than hurt that poor woman's feelings."

As I, disappointed, trudged toward the living room and plopped onto the couch, I noticed she had followed me. I closed my eyes, commenting.

"You and the kids can go to dinner next door. I'm staying home."

She sat beside me, taking my hand.

"Does that mean you're not tagging along and forcing yourself on innocent high school students at the prom?"

"No."

"Well, if you don't care enough to eat dinner with your daughter on her prom night, then it wouldn't make any sense for you to chaperon her later. So you can go right ahead and stay home from both events."

Ironically, we sat at opposite ends of the table, my neighbor and I. I was in my glamorous tux while he wore bleach-stained, ugly cut-off shorts. Because it was Saturday, he was slightly sloppier than he was on typical weekdays.

His pretty wife, who sat next to me at my left, had never looked nicer. While my own wife would say later she thought the bare-in-the-back, black-sequined formal gown was a little much for the occasion, even she had to admit that it was stunning. My wife, in shorts and a loose pullover blouse, sat next to my neighbor, on his left.

At my wife's left sat the nose-picking, criminal, deceitful kid who threw dog poop over my fence, and next to him my son who sat at my right. My daughter, at my neighbor's right, definitely seemed nervous, but who wouldn't be nervous wearing little more than undergarments in public?

Actually, I guess the black gown would have been acceptable on any one else but my daughter. My wife described it as "a Rita Hayworth-style black satin, strapless, sleeveless ball gown re-created from a Vogue pattern with a few personal touches."

The unoccupied seat between my daughter and my neighbor's attractive wife was empty because her "date" hadn't finished dressing. His rude tardiness forced affected conversation at the table, though I was surprised and flattered that the lovely hostess knew so much about me, and about the family, of course.

By eavesdropping stealthily, I could hear my wife and neighbor discussing varying uses and applications for jigsaws through the chatter of my son and the nose-picker as they talked about school.

Finally, after about ten minutes, the neighbors' oldest son arrived at the table. Glancing over casually, I was suddenly frozen in shock.

That kid was wearing my tux! Right down to the black and white patterned bowtie and new Italian design shoes!

Embarrassed, my eyes darted about the table as I hoped no one would notice the similarity. To think that his parents would drive all the way across town to a specialty shop and pay one hundred sixty-two dollars so a sixteen year-old could go to the prom!

There was a moment of dead silence as everyone at the table looked from him to me, back to him, and again to me. My daughter, abruptly less nervous, broke the ice.

"Hey! You and my dad have the exact same tux! Did you notice that, Dad?"

I wasn't about to answer that question. It couldn't be. His was probably just a cheap imitation.

"They probably just look a little alike. Mine, mine is a special Nino Cerutti."

The boy broke in.

"So's mine. I got it at a place called 'The Cheap Man's Tux.' Is that where you got yours?"

Was he *trying* to insult me? My daughter, suddenly the social butterfly, answered for me.

"Oh no! My dad gets his tuxes at this expensive place called *'Le Gentilhomme,'* right Dad?"

Yet before I could answer, my wife interrupted in a deliberate attempt to embarrass me.

"He probably paid a whole lot of extra money for the exact same tux, too."

Her comment obliged the uncomfortable boy to divulge how much he paid.

"Mine was ninety dollars out the door. How much was yours?"

"Uh... Seventy-nine dollars, seventy-nine dollars and I think thirty-one cents. Frequent renter VIP discount and all."

In spite of the fact that I sat directly across from a man who ate like a farm animal, the dinner was very good. Unable to drink my neighbor's cheap, mass-produced, twist-off cap jug wine, I had made a quick trip home to supply two bottles of Sonoma Merlot and a wine opener.

I suppose it may have been the two glasses of wine, but sitting at that table, I got the distinct sense that I was in the river—not just any river, but the river from my dream. It was just a sense, a feeling. I remember feeling dragged along against my will by some great immeasurable infinite force. All my struggling against it was futile.

I looked across the table at my daughter, and for the first time I realized that she was quickly becoming a real person, her *own* person. No matter how hard I may have tried to assert my will and my attitudes on her, she would eventually be responsible for making her own decisions, and she would have to live with the consequences of those decisions.

I was comforted to reflect on something my wife had said earlier about our job as parents. She had said, "If we haven't already done what we were supposed to do and taught her what we were supposed to teach her in fifteen years of raising her, trying to make up for it now would be pointless."

Our daughter had been taught well, and as I looked across the table at her as she dug into her mouth with her little finger, at no time had her fine upbringing been more evident.

The wine also brought out the subtle attractiveness of my neighbor's wife. While I certainly wasn't lusting after her or anything, whenever she moved to stand up or sit down, the slit in the gown opened slightly to expose one of her incredibly shapely legs, a mere wisp of a black stocking between me and it.

I tried not to look, but ever since I was a kid, my eyes have always focused on movement. Thus whenever she moved, the motion just sort of caught my eyes. The motion of my eyes however, caught my wife's eyes. From across the table she said distinctly, without speaking a word,

"If you don't stop looking at that woman's legs, you'll be very, very sorry tonight!"

I immediately and intentionally raised my focus to an area above the table, but the gown really flattered those, those things she had in the front there between her shoulders a little further down on her body. Not that my wife didn't have those. I mean, hers were similar in a way, but I had already seen hers.

It was the gown. The gown just made this woman's things well, I guess, kind of interesting. Sometimes my wife was interesting too, depending on what she wore. Anyway, knowing I'd be in even *more* trouble if I looked in that area for too long, I stared directly into the woman's face as she spoke to me.

Maybe it was the wine, but her face—it really was exquisite. I was reminded of a smooth marble Greek sculpture. Oh, my wife's face was pretty too, but in all the time I had lived next door to this woman, I had never noticed how truly captivating she was. At one time, I realized that my breathing had grown shallow.

Of course, fearing my wife might be reading my mind, I didn't want to look at my neighbor's wife's face for too long either, so even as I continued to speak with her, I glanced slightly away.

Seeking to regain my attention, and for some reason unknown to me, she brushed my left thigh with her soft, beautiful, wonderful hand. Immediately, our eyes met and said an embarrassingly intimate *hello*. At that moment, I was certain that she was flirting with me.

Still, while it was a special moment that will live forever in my mind, like all such special moments, it was quickly, and perhaps divinely undone.

I don't know if anyone else at the table heard it, but I definitely heard it. It was something of a low, almost inaudible rumble that trailed off and ended in an ever-increasing higher pitch. The sound reminded me of the squeak of a clean butt in a wet bathtub, but I definitely heard it and I knew exactly whence it came.

It was hard to believe that this erstwhile attractive woman had passed gas (i.e. broke wind) right at the dinner table. I continued to look into her eyes, but her eyes refused to betray her petite indiscretion.

As I then scanned the faces at table, no one had reacted at all. Perhaps I was the only one who had *heard* it. Still, just when I began to believe my own ears had beguiled me, I caught a sulfurous aroma that absolutely could not be confused with any of those emanating from the food at the table. This woman was dangerous! Piquant! Ripe! I didn't know how to react or what to do.

However after a few brief seconds, the woman's unique intestinal aroma just got to be too much for me, so I invented the excuse that I had to go outside for some air in order to escape the uncomfortable situation.

Now, I don't know what happened at that table when I was gone, but I can only guess that the odor filled the room, because when I returned, it seemed everyone had smelled it. Dinner was definitely over, as no one would eat another bite. The hostess was even up opening the window.

What was worst of all, they were all looking at *me* like I had done it. I just stood there and once again, I could feel the river coursing all around me. Explaining who had really fouled the air would only make me seem like a louse, and even if I was believed, I would never be completely exonerated. It would have been impossible to put that genie back in the bottle, to un-think a thought, and I could tell the moment I returned they all thought I did it.

Embarrassed, I suggested to the teen-agers that we should head out for the prom. The typical picture taking ensued, I went to get my car, and just as we were about to leave, the entire gathering heard a horrible moan coming from my neighbor's garage. The sound brought on a general sense of panic so that everyone followed my neighbor as he rushed through the wobbly gate and into the garage.

There we found Cleo, lying next to a broken-down washing machine in an oval wicker-type basket, holding one leg up in the air, alternately licking at something down there and stopping just long enough to moan aloud. My neighbor seemed absolutely silly jumping up and down the way he did.

"She's in labor! The puppies are comin!"

While everyone crowded in for a closer view, I stood aside. I wasn't about to watch blood and guts come from that dog's most private parts. Instead I listened to the horrible, overly graphic commentary delivered by my neighbor and my wife. Nevertheless, before ten minutes had elapsed, Cleo had already delivered two puppies.

"Honey! Come see! This second one looks exactly like Dick!"

What was she doing? Whose side was she on, anyway? Still, I was pretty curious to see what the puppy looked like. I eased over, careful not to look at the area where Cleo was licking, and I peeked over my son's shoulder.

My wife was right. That second puppy did look just like Snow. He even reminded me what Snow looked like when he was a puppy. Next came another cute little puppy that looked like Snow in the face, but it had many of Cleo's markings and her tail.

We were just watching the last puppy being born when I looked around and noticed my daughter was missing. As I tried to contain a blossoming sense of panic, I noted that the neighbor's son was also missing. Had they gone to the prom without me? My wife would have known.

"Honey, where's our daughter?"

The neighbor's potent wife obviously heard my inquiry and answered, loud enough for everyone to hear,

"She and my son went back over to your house. From what I understand, she's over there gettin Dick."

It was the first time I had ever achieved a full sprint in a tux. Scenario after unthinkable scenario raced through my mind as I kicked open the front door and busted into the house. My daughter screamed in fright.

"Daddy! What's wrong with you? Why'd you kick the door like that?"

"What are you, what are you two doing over here?"

"I just came to get Dick, that's all."

She had taken Snow off the chain and had attached him to a leash that was wrapped around her wrist.

"Those are his puppies, Dad. There's no denying it."

I looked at the neighbor kid whom I had frightened perhaps even more than my daughter.

"I, I just came to protect her, Sir. I'm sorry, I'm sorry if I did something wrong."

He really wasn't a bad kid. No, actually I was beginning to think he was a nice boy. He was clean-cut; he had a job and was apparently a hard worker. My daughter said he was on the honor roll at school.

And while both his parents were boorish, it seemed he could transcend his ignoble origin. But best of all, I could tell that this boy feared me. Getting on my bad side was his worst nightmare.

At that moment I could have growled and he would have run right out the door. After all, I think the word had gotten around the neighborhood that I knew karate and all. For my daughter's sake, I had to preserve that fear in him, so while I wanted to warm up to him a little, I did just the opposite.

"You should never be in my house alone with my daughter when I'm not here. You understand that?"

"Yes, yes Sir!"

"Never."

"Yes Sir."

Stern expression, I dismissed the two so that they left me standing in the living room looking at Snow. I didn't know what I was going to do about him. The newborn puppies next-door were his. I knew that. Somehow he would have to be punished for his indiscretion, but I wasn't sure how. I seriously considered chaining him up for the rest of his life, yet there were other options.

I could have switched to buying a much cheaper brand of dog food so that I could give my neighbor the savings, which could be used to feed the puppies. That way, Snow would actually be paying puppy support for his little family. Then I thought of taking all the puppies off my neighbor's hands and making Snow share his backyard and the family's attention with the puppies. That option would have served him right.

But one day certainly Cleo or some other dog would come into heat again, and Snow would end up in the same predicament. Thinking that, I began to consider a final election: neutering.

I think he read my mind, because at the very moment I thought of neutering him, Snow began growling at me as he had never growled before. It may have been the wine or my imagination, but I could have sworn that his eyes glowed a little like Cujo's did in that movie.

Anyway, I cleared my mind of the offensive thought and gently escorted him to the backyard. After all, it was getting late. It was almost nine.

Just before I exited the house, my attention was drawn to one of my wife's paintings which rested on the fireplace mantle. It was her *Ahab and Ishmael*, and because she only let finished work out of her studio, I knew it was complete.

Years before in college, I read that there was enormous power in art. I never thought much of the statement or of my wife's art for that matter. But as I stood there, viewing myself in that dynamic scene, I thought about my life, I thought about meaning.

I was a little man on a small boat in an all-powerful, wide and endless watery expanse, a helpless soul whose will and opinions were completely insignificant in a much larger picture. Yet if I only wanted to, I could be a part of all that majestic greatness and actually benefit from it. Reeling in thought, I was reminded of something my son said to me earlier,

"You're trying to fight something that's bigger than you are, something that's stronger than you are. It's a fight you can't win. We just have to try'n work with what we've got."

The river. The dream. And then I thought I understood. Resolved, I grabbed up the leash, opened the back door and called my dog to me. Attaching the metal chain to his collar, I hurried with him out the door, across the lawn and over to my neighbor's house.

They were still huddled around Cleo in the garage when I re-entered. My dog barked aloud and dragged me toward the basket where the bitch stretched out, nursing four puppies. Cleo looked up, bared her teeth and growled at him.

It was a little funny, because she had the same expression on her face that my wife had when she looked up at me after delivering each of the children. Like me, he knew to stay away at a safe distance or suffer the consequences. I freed him of the leash and approached my daughter and her date.

"Prom's already started. You two better get going."

For a moment, I thought her expression showed a hint of disappointment.

"Dad? You, you mean *you're* not going?"

I sighed, putting the chain into my pocket.

"No. The prom's for you guys. I'll let you kids go and enjoy yourselves."

I didn't really mean it. I didn't want my daughter to think she could start doing these type things on a regular basis. But I figured as long as I was going to be nice, I'd just go all the way.

"As a matter of fact, I want you two to take my car."

I don't know why I said it, but I just felt magnanimous for some reason. Well, after establishing that the boy had a valid license and that his father would accept liability if he wrecked my car, we discussed a final consideration.

"What time do you want us home, Sir?"

"Let's see, the prom starts at nine, right? And it's over at about twelve? Okay, I want you two back no later than eleven forty-five."

My wife was the only person in the room brazen enough to challenge my demand.

"Why? They'll miss the end of the prom. The last dance is always the best thing about the prom. Can't they stay at least till it's over?"

Doggone that woman! Thinking as hard as I could, I was simply unable to find an excuse for making them return early. I pulled my wife aside, speaking under my breath.

"Why do you have to do this to me? Even Cinderella had to be outa there before twelve, and she was over eighteen! Our daughter's only fifteen."

My wife, as always, skirted the issue.

"How do *you* know Cinderella was over eighteen? I think she was fifteen."

I gave up, addressing the teenagers.

"Okay Twelve thirty. Twelve thirty or else."

Somehow my neighbor thought I was threatening his son.

"Or else? Or else what?"

I didn't know.

"Just be back before twelve thirty."

Just before they left for the prom, my daughter pulled me aside. With tears in her eyes she looked at me, smiling.

"I love you, Daddy. Thank you for trusting me."

After kissing me on the cheek, she and her date left for the prom. For my part, I started worrying the moment they drove off. I wanted to agonize in the comfort of my home, but my wife and my dog could not be persuaded to leave.

My wife and the neighbor's wife were sharing sewing secrets and a lot of other women nonsense while my dog was out there whining, trying to get closer to the puppies. My son was upstairs with the poop-throwing nose-picker playing video games. I was left alone sitting in a room with a man I didn't like and with whom I had nothing in common. We sat in silence for about ten minutes before he started with an icebreaker.

"Want a drink?"

While I wasn't in the habit of drinking with strangers and much less people I didn't like, I figured the drink would calm my nerves. After all, my daughter was out there alone, with a boy.

"I'll, I'll take a drink. What do you got?"

He ignored the question and simply pulled an almost-full black and white bottle from behind the couch, unscrewed the black cap and took a big swig. Contorting his face, he swallowed and said a loud *Ahh!* before thrusting the bottle in my direction.

Right away, he could tell from my expression I had no intention of taking the bottle and insisted.

"Here. Hit it. Take the damn bottle."

Afraid I might hear more profanity if I didn't accept it, I reluctantly took the hand-off.

"What're ya afraid of? I brushed my teeth this morning. Drink it. Alcohol kills any germs."

Abandoning any shred of dignity remaining, I slyly wiped the top, put the bottle to my lips and took a liberal sip. Right away I knew I had made a mistake.

First my throat and chest burned. Then I couldn't breathe. Then I wanted to cough but couldn't, and I finally lost my voice. As my eyes filled with water, he tried to hide it, but he was slyly laughing at me.

"Are you okay?"

All I could manage was a nod in the affirmative. I almost never drank raw booze. Anyway he took the bottle and swigged again only to return it to my trembling hand. Nonetheless, by that time the warmth and a general good feeling had spread to the rest of my body.

My second drink from the bottle was slightly less traumatic and the third was almost enjoyable. Needless to say, after about thirty minutes we were going on like we were old friends.

"Ya need ta gam with ol *Jack Daniel's* more often."

"Why?"

"Well right now, for the first time, ya seem almost as normal as the rest of us. Ya seriously need ta loosen up, you tight ass."

"You seriously need a belt."

Eventually we found ourselves out in the garage with our wives checking on Cleo and the puppies. Oddly enough, my neighbor was staring at my dog.

"He's never looked like a Snow. I don't know why you call him that. He looks like a Dick."

My wife agreed.

"I've always told him the same thing. That dog's not a Snow. He's a Dick."

My neighbor's wife chimed in.

"Definitely a Dick."

Swaying a little, I studied my dog as he continued to ease closer to the puppies, and for a first time I admitted to myself that he really did look like a Dick. Thus I determined from that moment on I would call him by that name.

Back in the house, my neighbor and I returned to the bottle. As a matter of fact, I had just put it to my lips when my daughter and her date returned.

I spilled a large quantity on my tuxedo shirt while attempting to hide what I was doing from her. My eyes then snapped toward my wrist where the ever-accurate watch displayed: 12:25. They had returned early. Upon hearing their entrance, the women rushed into the room, eager to ferret out all the details of their special little date.

Apparently, the kids had a good time. They danced, took pictures and just enjoyed feeling almost *grown up*, if only for a night. The nervous boy surprised me with unnecessary politeness by thanking me profusely for letting my daughter accompany him to the prom. He also thanked me for the use of my car and told me he had filled it up with expensive gas.

After stealthily examining my daughter's lipstick to make sure she hadn't kissed him, I breathed a gigantic sigh of relief and called the family together to go home. Thanking the hostess, I headed for the door only to be cut off by my large neighbor who, to my surprise and embarrassment, hugged me and kissed me right on the top of my head. I'll never forget the sickening smell of his stale shirt as I, face smushed into his fatty chest, struggled to free myself. I couldn't wait to get home.

My wife fell asleep as I wrote a short history on the events of the past month or so. Looking on her, she was so wonderful while she was sleeping. Always the perfect wife, that is, until she woke up.

Anyway, I turned off the computer and crawled into the bed next to her. The wine and those swigs from the whiskey bottle had relaxed me, so in no time at all I was asleep and dreaming.

There I was again. As I remember, I was standing in a raging storm on the bank of some great old river. All around me, trees swayed and creaked as a violent gale wove through the grove on the edge of the water, uprooting the weak and cracking the hard and stubborn. The rain was so intense that, looking up, I could see nothing for the incessant assault on my face.

As I wiped the freezing water from my eyes to focus on an irregularity on the opposite bank, I noticed a clearing. As strange as the existence of such a clearing would seem when I awoke, within the dream it seemed natural.

For even as the tempest savaged all around, within this clearing on the other bank the sun shone warm and bright. Tender grass stirred as it grew from dry earth and hummingbirds and butterflies flitted about the splendid scene. But most attractive of all, a golden throne bedecked with precious gems shined brilliantly in the very center of the clearing.

Yet unlike what happened in the many previous dreams before, I did not strip off all my clothes and dive, unthinking into the stream, striving in vain against the course of the powerful river to reach my goal. Instead, I thoughtfully watched the water course by, gauging its force, eyes forever fixed on my goal.

Because I had come to appreciate and understand the river and myself, I walked quite a distance upstream. Then wading into the water, I began to swim. Only this time, I swam gently. I swam in a relaxed manner toward the other side.

By realizing I just *had to try'n work with what I had*, I let the force of the river ultimately carry me right to that splendid golden throne. It was so easy when I worked *with* the river rather than against it.

Still however, I was not satisfied, for in the distance behind the throne there ran another river, a wider river, a faster river. And on the other side of that river there sat a slightly larger throne, within a slightly larger clearing. I could only guess that beyond that throne was still a larger river and still a larger throne.

The dream was alive. It was and had always been a part of me. It was a shadow of my own life in the enigmatic manner in which dreams reflect reality in that unknown realm called the sub-conscious mind.

The moment was both frustrating and inspiring, for within even the dream I realized that I could never stop striving, I could never stop dreaming, I could never stop learning. The dream was my life's lesson, the very reason I had come to be.

THE DOCTRESS

I'm not homophobic, really I'm not. It's just that somehow I've always confronted that particular phenomenon of human nature on somewhat shaky ground.

One warm Saturday afternoon as I passed by the state capitol while driving downtown on business, I noticed a huge gathering of people on the lawn who were engaged in what seemed to be the exchange of goods, i.e. buying and selling. Because I've always found it difficult to resist a bargain, I swerved into a street parking space right in front of the hostile driver of a Lexus or something and, after forcing two quarters into the meter, I half-walked/ half-skipped over to the area where the action was happening.

I went to a tented booth where this bohemian-looking man was selling these incredible hand-painted T-shirts. However, no sooner had I taken up the shirt to examine it more carefully, a photographer appeared from nowhere and, without asking permission, snapped my picture. This action was followed by the entrance of a good looking brown-skinned woman who I initially thought was trying to pick-up on me.

First, she gave me this slow, deliberate eyeing up and down my body, stopping ever so slightly in that area where women's eyes typically stop ever so slightly. Then she walked right up and introduced herself, asking my name. But I was thrown off-guard when she asked if I was gay.

Embarrassed that she had asked such a question in public, I forthrightly told her I was not and had never been, scanning people nearby as I hoped they hadn't heard her. Then suddenly I remembered I had read somewhere that some men enjoy putting on nice skirts and pumps like she had on and nice sexy tops like she had on and even suggestive make-up like she was wearing.

Covering my mouth to make sure no one could read my lips, I asked,

"Are... are you a man?"

Amused, she laughed.

"No, I'm a reporter covering the Job Fair."

Skeptical, I eyed her for some hint of masculinity, but she seemed all woman to me. As I began to take notice of other people in the periphery however, I discovered many of them had a sort of androgynous look. I mean a lot of them could have been either/or. Suddenly a little nervous, I continued,

"Are you *sure* you're, you're not a, I mean a man?"

First she seemed shocked and then she laughed aloud before whispering in an almost naughty tone,

"You know, you're kind of charming." Then she drew herself uncomfortably close to me, continuing, "No one's suggested I prove my womanhood since I was fourteen. It's an interesting thought."

Backing away and re-assuming a more professional tone, she winked, thanked me, signaled to her photographer, and the two headed toward a large booth hosted by a tall skinny guy with purple and green spiked hair.

Anyway, when I finally got back to the bohemian's table, the hand-painted T-shirts were almost gone. In fact, I got the last one. Then after I headed back for the car, for some strange reason I turned completely around and looked back toward the gathering.

That's when I saw it. That's when I saw the giant banner suspended between two tall thin metal poles. In bold, out-of-the-closet, flamboyant letters, the sign read, *Third Annual Gay Job Fair and Market.*

As I sped away, I was just glad no one had seen me. Anyway, my business downtown had taken a little longer than expected, so I didn't get home until after seven. I figured I wasn't really late because only my wife was there.

My sixteen-year-old daughter had gone to a slumber party with friends and my ten year-old son was at my brother's house visiting with his cousins.

The moment I walked in the front door though, I knew my wife was up to something. Whenever she burned our daughter's incense and lit candles in various places in the house, she was up to something. I went to the garage and checked the family car to see if she had wrecked it again, but it was fine. Then I went to my dresser to see if she had given any of my best stuff away to the Salvation Army again, but my collection of antique sweaters from high school was still there.

"I fixed your favorite dinner and I even opened a bottle of wine for you," she said as she stood in the doorway, her jeans a bit too creased, her make-up a bit too smooth, and her hair just looking a bit too combed. Suddenly, it hit me.

"How much money did you spend today?"

She answered as she led me to the table where a plate sat, steam still rising from the potato.

"Not a penny. I've been working really hard to curb my spending."

Well, it wasn't the car, it wasn't my clothes, and it wasn't money, so there was only one thing left.

"Waitaminute, are you trying to *seduce* me?"

She poured me a half glass of wine from the decanter.

"No. What kind of girl do you think I am? Do you think I slaved cleaning this house all day and sweated over that stove making you your favorite dinner and fixed myself up all pretty like this just to make you put out? You're not *that* good! You know better than that."

That's what I was afraid of. She had done this before. The first time was when unknown to me, she had volunteered me to be a sort of handyman for this women artists' collaborative. I spent eight months of weekends slaving for those picky, never-satisfied women dictators, parading as artists. Then there was another time when she forced me to deliver newspapers at six in the morning every morning for a month because she wanted to give the kids a vacation from the paper route. Turns out it was a paid vacation, because when money collection time came, they got to keep the profits and I didn't get one penny. I could go on, but I won't. I'm not petty.

Anyway, that is the sort of person I had to deal with as a wife. On the outside, she looked like a real wife, really, like any other wife out there. But it happened every time. The minute I started thinking of her as a real wife, she lowered the boom on me and I was stuck in some horrible situation I did nothing to deserve.

"I made your favorite desert and brewed some gourmet coffee just for you."

She had probably volunteered me to donate one of my kidneys to some television cause or something. Even as I ate the desert and swallowed the final sip of my coffee, I felt like a death-row inmate finishing his last meal. A dead man walking, I followed her down the corridor into the living room and took a seat in the armchair isolated in a corner.

"Aye-yie-yie!"

The chair had suddenly begun to vibrate. I quickly settled down upon remembering the chair I was sitting in was one we had purchased from a specialty store. She had turned on the electro-vibro massage.

"What's wrong, Honey?

"Nothing. Nothing at all. I just forgot about the chair."

"Can I massage your feet for you?"

"No!"

I could not take the suspense for another minute. Taking the chair remote from her hand, I ended the electro-vibes.

"*What* is it? You *have* to tell me. If you don't tell me what it is right now, I won't do this thing you want me to do no matter what it is!"

She was never direct.

"Did you hear about Merv Griffin?"

Merv Griffin? Waitaminute! She had always said she was going to sign me up to be a contestant on *Jeopardy*. Maybe she had finally done it!

"Hold on! Are you telling me that someday soon I'm going to meet Alex in person?"

I knew it was too good to be true. Her face answered even before she spoke a word.

"No. It was on the news today. He's got prostate cancer."

"Alex Trebec has prostate cancer!"

The less-than-direct way of talking which is consistent in *all* women has always made conversation with them difficult in my experience.

"No. Merv Griffin has prostate cancer, so I made an appointment for you to see a doctor for a complete physical."

I wasn't following her at all.

"I don't get it. What does Merv Griffin getting cancer have to do with me going to see a doctor?"

She took my hand between her two warm palms.

"Honey, I know you don't like hearing this, but you're getting to be middle-aged. And doctors recommend that middle-aged men should have complete physicals at least once a year."

Obviously her idea of middle-aged and mine were very different.

"What are you talking about? I'm not middle-aged! I'm still a young man!"

"You'll be forty next year. That's middle-aged."

Forty. I didn't like the sound of the word. Still, I disagreed.

"That's where you're wrong. Forty is not middle-aged. Forty is still young for men. Middle age begins for *women* at forty, but for men it begins at forty-eight and a half. I think I read that somewhere."

She ignored my astute assertion and moved back to the original issue.

"You're at risk. The family can't afford to lose you. I want you to go to the appointment and get this physical."

That's when I remembered. I had first started hearing the horror stories when I tried out for the ninth grade football team. Every boy who made the team had to submit proof that a physical had been performed on him. The coach knew a doctor near the school and recommended him to the team.

Anyway, the first few boys who went returned to the group with sort of uncomfortable expressions on their faces. Their uneasiness troubled the rest of us. We questioned them repeatedly, but not one of them would tell us what had happened. With the next group of four boys, the same thing happened, but no one was willing to talk.

The truth came out however, when the next group went. They had sworn in advance to us all that, no matter what happened, the rest of us would get a full report. None of us listening were prepared for the horrors they began to unfold. The absolute worst thing, the terror of all terrors, was the checking of the prostate.

In order to perform the test, first the doctor, described by them as a straight, professional, nice guy, had to put on these gloves. Then he would ask whomever it was to bend over, and finally, he would stick his finger or fingers up "you-know-where."

Describing the dreadful scene in full detail, they said the doctor then put the fingers of his other hand on that "you-know" that hangs under your "you-know-what" in the front and asked you to cough. That was all it took for a couple of the guys. They quit the team that day. I considered it, but I wanted to play football.

Nevertheless, I stalled and stalled until the coach told me that I had to show proof of a physical or leave the team. Startled from a nightmare, in which a demented German doctor from WWII was about to perform a physical on me, I devised a plan to solve my disturbing dilemma.

We had a family doctor who I knew and trusted, and after begging my parents to pay for it (he charged $20 more than the coach's doctor), I went to him. I told him I wanted a physical but that I didn't want the prostate check. In this way I was able to participate in sports throughout high school and in college.

But now, my wife was sitting there saying she wanted me to go to a doctor and specifically have that horrible test performed. I was skeptical. I've always been the person who's believed that *if it ain't broke, don't fix it*, so I answered her calmly.

"Thanks for caring, but I'm still young. I feel fine. I'll go when I'm forty-eight and a half."

Confident in her abilities as a motivator, she didn't blink.

"You're going to get a physical, and that's that."

I was awakened by the incessant ringing of the telephone at about 7 a.m. that Sunday morning. When I finally answered, my mother was on the other line asking if I had seen the paper. From the sound of my voice, the fact that I hadn't should have been obvious, but my mother was a woman, and therefore hopelessly indirect. Reluctant to get out of bed, I asked her what she wanted me to read, but she remained vague.

"There's nothing to read, actually. You just really need to look at the front page."

Five minutes later, my daughter called me from her friend's house.

"Daddy, have you seen the paper? I'm *so* embarrassed."

Suddenly an ominous feeling came over me as I probably made the connection on a purely sub-conscious level.

"Why? What is it?"

"Just look at the paper, Daddy."

Click. Tumbling off the futon, I stumbled toward the front door, but I was sidetracked by the phone that had begun ringing again. It was my brother. He was laughing uncontrollably, making absolutely no sense, but I was able to distinguish the words,

"Have you seen the paper?" and "I always wondered about you!"

Click. I went to the door, snatched up the bundle, slammed the door, snapped the stressed green rubber band and flipped the fully extended front page onto the kitchen table. A wave of numbness surged up my body as I lipped the word "NO!" knowing my life as I knew it would never be the same.

There, on the front page, under a headline that read, "Gays Rally at Capitol," was what seemed like a quarter-page picture of me. As I scanned the tiny words under the picture, my greatest fear was realized. I saw my full name in print there.

Flicking my eyes back up to the picture, I sighed aloud in revulsion. I don't remember exactly what I was thinking when that irresponsible hatchet man jumped out and took that picture, but for some reason I had what seemed like a "gay" look on my face. My face had never looked like that before.

By this time, I was a zombie, eyes transfixed. I couldn't tell if I was walking, but the hazy room and blurred hallway moved by on both sides of my face until I finally stood over my wife who was still sound asleep. Dumping the newspaper on top of her head, I collapsed onto the bed.

"Now you'll know if that new insurance policy you got on me covers suicide."

After over forty calls from people I once called friends, I unplugged the phone. The final straw had been the uncharacteristic call from my father. Now I had never in my life heard my father make fun of anyone, but to my abject incredulity, he smirked on the phone as he tongue-in-cheek told me he was proud I was finally brave enough to accept my feminine side.

The truth though, was that I had no feminine side. I had always been all man. Still, I felt challenged in a way. As the ribbing continued in the week or so that followed, I felt this need to make sure people knew that I just happened to be buying a T-shirt at what I thought was a legitimate stand and that if I had known the truth, I wouldn't have been there.

Nevertheless, it seemed that everywhere I went people were watching and whispering about me. Then one day as I sat in a coffee shop, I *knew* these two guys were looking at me. They just sat there and stared. I wanted to get up and leave, but they seemed definitely gay and I didn't want either of them checking out my butt.

As they got up to leave, the skinnier more dramatic one approached my table and introduced himself, telling me I looked really familiar. I told him I was a foreigner and that I had never been in the newspaper or at any rallies in this country.

Anyway, after that experience and another that was similar, I began carrying an exposed issue of *Playboy* magazine with me everywhere I went just so there was no confusion. As ashamed as I was to admit it, I even began wondering if I still had it—*it* being that manly sex appeal I know I've always had. I wasn't considering cheating on my wife, but I did want to kind of test it out to see if *it* still worked on someone who didn't wash my underwear.

With this in mind, there was a good-looking younger woman in my office in her late teens or early twenties. Well, I called her in one day and asked her what she thought of me, to which she answered, "You're a real nice guy." Pressing further (though not in any sexually harassing way), I asked her if she thought I was sexy in a manly way. Careful not to offend me, she responded,

"Well, I *did* see your picture in the newspaper, but I *know* you're not gay."

The *Playboy* magazine strategy had worked. I sighed with relief as she continued.

"But it's just that... you're kind of old and dweeby. It's hard for me to think of someone as old as you in that way. You're more like a father figure."

At least she didn't say *mother* figure. That was good enough for me. Still, I was amazed that anyone would think of me as old. I mean, thirty-nine is young for a man. The U.S. Constitution said a man has to be at least thirty-five to be president. That means thirty-nine is still young.

On the other hand, there was no such age threshold for women, meaning that what might be old for a woman might be young for a man. Therefore, that young woman who called me old was probably in actuality about my same age.

I explained all of this in great detail to my wife who refused to accept the fact that, while she was technically five years younger than me, in actuality she was about fifteen years older. In other words, thirty-four in women's years translated to about fifty-four in men's years. I thought everyone knew that, it seemed everyone but my wife.

But instead of thanking me for clueing her in, she told me that she had set up the appointment for the physical on my fortieth birthday and told me I had better go. Well, my father always said you should never argue with the person who's cooking your meals, so I said nothing. I just knew I wasn't going to make that appointment.

About a month before my birthday, I awoke with a strange crick in my neck that just wouldn't go away. While it wasn't debilitating, it was terribly annoying. Then strangely, a week later, both my wrists began to ache so that I was scarce able to carry anything over ten pounds without major pain. I thought the wrist pain was probably due to some carpal-tunnel problems as I had spent countless of hours with my wrists flexed at computer keyboards.

It was one day while I was standing at the urinal that I considered it for a first time. Standing there, I reflected to my high school years again. We had a wrestling coach who sometimes used the urinal next to the one I always used (that is, my favorite urinal). Anyway, I was always amazed at how long he stood there. Sometimes he'd stand there for five minutes or more. I considered him to be a kind of old guy, in his forties or something.

Listening to what he was doing, I could hear the steady hollow sound of the stream plowing into the water and then it would stop; then there would be a little dripping, and then the stream would start again; then it would stop again and he would stand there doing nothing for a half minute or so; then it would start dripping again; then there would be a stream again as he stood there patiently waiting to finally finish, but it would stop and he'd just stand there.

I was always able to get in there and, if I wanted to, blast the urinal clean with a steady, controlled stream. It never took me more than a half minute to finish. But in that month before my fortieth birthday, as I stood at the urinal in the bathroom at work, I found myself waiting for the stream to start again or drip or something. To my horror I had become just like my wrestling coach!

Thinking more on it, I thought I remembered hearing that he had died. It seemed I remembered someone telling me he had died of cancer or something. I didn't know if it had been prostate cancer, but I became concerned about my newly discovered condition. Maybe I *was* getting old.

On the way back to my office, I discovered I was victim to an even worse ailment—post-urinal drip. It was just a few drops, but their cold presence made me uncomfortable and self-conscious. I didn't know what to do, so I called my brother. Because he was only eighteen months younger than I was, I figured he must have been experiencing the same problems.

"No, not at all. *I'm* still young," he chuckled. "Maybe it's something you picked up at one of those rallies you go to."

Click. I had a friend who was a doctor, so I just kind of dropped by his house one night to pick his brain a bit. My wife had initially suggested that he complete the physical on me, but I wasn't about to let him begin any strange procedure on me.

After all, how would I have been able to look him in the face or golf with him without being affected by such an unnatural experience? Friends just don't do those type things to each other. Still, as I was sitting there, I asked the natural questions: "Do doctors use one finger or two?" and "Is there any permanent damage?" and "Can't they use *ultrasound* or *x-rays* or something?"

I also mentioned that I had heard about the fingers while I was in high school, suggesting that there must be some new technological invention, which rendered the finger thing a part of medicine's ugly past.

"We could use a baseball bat," he joked, "but you have to understand that we're trying to get information. Fingers are still the most reliable way. That way we can actually feel if there's something wrong up there." He continued, "As it is in a whole lot of medical applications, the old-fashioned finger works best. Fingers give us the biofeedback that's so important in these applications."

And to think I went to high school with this sicko. In any event, we both agreed that I should go to another doctor. That is, if I decided to go through with the physical. My manipulative wife, for her part, kept the pressure on.

Every night when I came home from work, there was a new article stuck on the beer refrigerator about some poor old guy dying of prostate cancer. I could never understand where she found those stories. Ignoring her scare tactics, I let my landmark fortieth come and go without public notice or fanfare and without going for the physical.

I paid for it. I paid every time I sat down to that bologna sandwich for dinner. I paid every morning when I had to sniff the underarms of my shirt in order to determine whether or not it was clean. I paid when my wife purposely decided to end her spending curb so that all around me I could see evidence that I was paying.

The yoga classes that the kids literally got sick to avoid, the $700 electronic programmable automatic power saw that sat unused under an expensive custom dust cover in the garage and the obscenely-priced make-over at the salon that made her look exactly the same (only about five years older)—all were evidence that I had paid for missing that physical.

Yet the thing that brought me around was not all the abuse and punishment doled out by my wife, but rather the news that one of my older cousins had been diagnosed with some prostate problem. I went immediately to my parents to find out how many of my relatives on either side had suffered from illness "down there."

To my chagrin, my father said one of his grandfathers had died from some agonizing complication relating to the prostate. My mother too had a story about an uncle who swelled up "down there" to the size of a basketball before he died a horrible death.

Shaken, I wondered if my parents had been talking to my wife, who wasn't above asking them to tell me stories that would scare me into some type of prostate paranoia. My mother, who was the family's holistic medicine guru, seemed to have some special knowledge on the subject, so I questioned her nervously.

"Why is it that certain men have uh, you know, problems 'down there' and others don't?"

Squinting her eyes a little, she seemed to look into the holistic past.

"Well, I don't think anyone really knows, but I've heard over the years that it's really a problem of men who are *oversexed*."

I could not believe my mother had made such a lewd statement! Still in shock, my discomfort and paranoia with the subject began to grow exponentially. Suddenly I thought,

"What if my parents thought *I* was oversexed!" and worse, "What if I *was* oversexed!"

I mean, how does a person know if they are or not? Undersexed, oversexed—what was the right amount? Not a minute after my father attempted to dismiss her suggestion as an "old wives tale," my parents began another one of their marathon arguments which typically lasted from about 10 a.m. until bedtime. Fearful of being asked to take a side again, I excused myself and hurried home.

By the time I crawled into bed, I was a nervous wreck: coaches catching prostate cancer, grandfathers dying, basketballs and stuff, five minutes to finish at the stall, and then that ever so slight post-urinal drip. I knew something was wrong with me down there.

Ironically, my wife caught me with the covers over my head as I peered down into the front of my boxer shorts. She said that what I was doing "kind of turned her on" and, to my dismay, she wanted to "do it." Oh she was sick all right, and probably oversexed! Rolling out of the bed to escape her groping hands, I stood my ground on that issue for the first time in our seventeen-year marriage.

"I am *not* just some plaything! I am not some boy toy for you to just use for a few minutes before rolling over to sleep. I'm a human being! With *feelings*!"

It was great getting those pent-up emotions off my chest. They had been building for years.

"You're just, I think you're just a *nymphomaniac*! There! I said it."

Her reaction was typical. There I had just poured out my heart to her and all she could do was laugh at me.

"Honey, look at you! You're a nerotic mess. If you come back to bed, your nymphomaniac wife promises not to molest you in any way, okay?"

Saying nothing, I turned off the lamp and crawled back into the bed. Thinking there for a few moments, I felt bad I had called her such a horrible name. I realized I had struck out at her in a reaction to my own insecurity. People really do that. I saw it on Oprah. Staring out into the darkness, I spoke.

"I'm sorry I called you that name."

She said nothing, so I continued.

"Tell me, do you think I'm oversexed?"

Incredulous, she chuckled again.

"You! Only if you're engaging in some kind of extramarital activity. Now go to sleep."

Most of us men, when we were boys, clutched a teddy bear, a blanket or a pillow in sleep in order to feel safe and cozy. But, as we got older, many of us somehow abandoned those inanimate artifacts of security and in our sleep began to latch onto something of a more personal/bodily nature.

Anyway, somewhere in the middle of that night, right after rolling onto my back in sleep, my warm hand discovered an irregularity.

"A lump!"

I bolted up from the bed with such great violence that my wife was sent tumbling onto the floor.

"I feel a lump! I have a lump down here!"

Crawling back onto the bed, my wife was awake and concerned.

"A lump? Are you sure?"

"What kind of question is that? Of *course* I'm sure!"

My hand continued checking.

"Waitaminute! I feel another lump! I feel another one!"

Sighing aloud, my wife grabbed a thick pillow and threw it savagely toward my face. I was aghast!

"Why'd you do that?"

"You feel two lumps down there, right?"

"Yes! Yes, I feel them!"

"You're *supposed* to have two lumps down there. Remember?"

When she rolled over, hogging all the covers, I was left sitting out there in the freezing cold with my hand down my shorts. I was embarrassed.

"Oh! Yeah, you're right. Never mind."

As I sipped coffee on the back patio the next morning, I decided for once and for all to get a physical, but since I had never been sick enough to go to a doctor in the previous ten years, I hadn't chosen one from my company's medical plan. After emptying a huge file-drawer of work-related papers and booklets onto the kitchen counter, I found the small booklet listing all the doctors in the state who were part of the plan.

In order to get a doctor, all I had to do was call one of the listed offices and find out if the doctor was taking new patients. The coverage would begin when I listed a doctor as my primary physician.

There were a lot of names in the book, so I began narrowing the parameters of the search with the hope of finding five "General Physicians" candidates in my county who I could interview in person before making a final decision. Still, one hundred sixty phone calls later, I proudly held the list in my hands. Wasting no time, I called work and took one of my vacation weeks immediately so that I devote could one whole day for interviewing each doctor.

On Monday I called the first doctor at 7:30 a.m., but the lady answering phones would not put him on the line. Instead, she took my number and promised he'd call me back. When I called back at 9:30, she asked me not to call again. When I innocently asked why, she slanderously accused me of calling back the office ten times that morning. If she had kept better records she would have known I had only checked back six times—twice the line was busy and the initial call technically wasn't a call back.

Anyway, I was determined to interview the doctor, so I just went down to the office and told the cranky woman at the desk that I had to see the doctor for an emergency. Looking over the tops of her granny glasses, the old wrinkly warden rudely pointed out that I hadn't made an appointment and tried to ignore me. I saw people come in after me who got called in immediately while I just sat there. Finally I grew frustrated with the discrimination I was being subjected to for not making an appointment.

There was an old guy sitting next to me who had trouble walking across the room. I astutely noticed his limping when he entered. I was just about sure I could beat him in a race to the door when the time came. So when the ogre buzzed the door to let him in to see the doctor, I rushed to the door ahead of him and I was in.

I would have had better odds trying to assassinate the president. Inside the door, I was instantly surrounded by a horde of ten ugly gray-headed nurses led by the rude queen insect from the front desk.

Somehow, she had managed to grab my arm and had twisted it behind my back. She was lucky she wasn't a man because she was really hurting my arm. Every time I moved in the direction of the doctor, she yanked my arm until finally I surrendered and allowed her to push me out the door where the violent old man stood, still waiting. Yet even as I rubbed my bruised shoulder, he glared down angrily at me.

"I should hit you with my cane!"

His eyes were bugging out and he was foaming at the mouth. I hoped the doctor was going to check his blood pressure. Anyway, I would have sat back down, but everyone sitting out in the lobby was staring at me like they didn't trust me or something. One old woman even growled like a dog. Gingerly, I tipped toward the door and eased out the office.

I was disappointed though not defeated. Although the day had been a waste, I decided to go on home and make an appointment with the doctor I had planned on interviewing the next day.

The smiling nurse called me in promptly at ten and buzzed the door so I could enter. The doctor was an older man, probably in his sixties, but he was very friendly and professional. He said my wife was right about me getting a check-up (especially since I hadn't had one in almost twenty years).

In a Marcus Welby-esque tone, he explained that many men encounter problems with the prostate because the gland, "which surrounds the base of the urethra," typically enlarges as men begin to age. The physical, he continued, would involve blood and blood pressure tests, heart, lungs, eyes, ear and throat examinations in addition to the prostate check. I was convinced he would be my doctor until the moment I looked down at his hands.

This man had the fattest fingers I had ever seen in my life! And there was no way he was going to put them in my— Well, there was no way he was going to check me with them. I explained I had a few other doctors to interview, told him I would call his office when I reached a decision, and bolted for the door. Two down, three to go.

There was something strange about the doctor I interviewed on Wednesday, something uncomfortable that I couldn't exactly explain. Apparently, he had gotten his doctoring degree in some other country, because he had a thick accent. Not that I had any problem with doctors from other countries or people with thick accents, but we had trouble communicating. I noticed the problem when I found myself unconsciously speaking in broken English.

He said the physical was necessary so that I "don't get dead or something," and I responded, "I not want that." He also told crummy jokes, if you could call them jokes. They were actually nonsensical one-liners that were apparently funny to him. He laughed maniacally as I stood there puzzled, struggling to comprehend what he had just said. Maybe he was a real comedian in his culture, but I thought he was a little weird. Anyway, we just didn't click. We just didn't make that connection necessary to a good doctor/patient relationship. Besides, I still had two other doctors to examine.

Thursday's doctor just seemed a bit too eager to get down to the physical. I had learned through experience that a man being a little effeminate doesn't necessarily make him gay, but the minute he mentioned he remembered seeing my picture in the paper I grew a little suspicious of the doctor. When he said it was a "cute shot" of me, I didn't need any further convincing. Not that I had anything against gay people, but I was uncomfortable with the thought of being examined by a person who probably did prostate examinations on people for personal pleasure.

Friday was my last hope, but according to pre-screening interviews with former patients, staff and a guy from the AMA Board, I had saved the best for last. Reports indicated that this doctor had been first in his undergraduate class at Stanford University and had graduated with honors from medical school at UCLA.

Yet instead of settling into a lucrative practice, he joined the Peace Corps where he volunteered two years in Rwanda before a life-threatening bout of malaria forced him to return to California. Within a month, he had been asked to be an instructor at the University of California at Davis, but after teaching classes for two years, he decided to put himself in a position where he felt he was more help to people. His office was known for regularly taking indigent patients on a space available basis.

Even as I walked into the office that morning, I was certain I had found my doctor. The girl at the front desk was pretty, friendly and efficient. I was called in right away. After sitting in cold sterile room for a few moments, the nurse came in and began asking some very personal questions.

"Ever had any STDs?"

I was in the dark.

"Look, I know STP—that's oil, I know TDs—touchdowns, KOs, TKOs, RBIs, HRs and even RSVPs, but I've never heard of STBs or Ds or whatever."

The nurse removed her glasses.

"STDs are sexually transmitted diseases. You ever had any?"

"No!"

If that hadn't been embarrassing enough, the nurse continued.

"Have you been sexually active in the twenty years you've gone without a physical?"

I was *not* going to answer that question!

"You know Nurse, no offense, but I think I'll wait for the *doctor* before I answer any more personal questions."

Closing the file with my chart, she smiled.

"I take it you haven't met the doctor?"

"No, but I've done a lot of research on him. I know all about his schooling, the volunteer work and just about everything else. I was pretty thorough."

This time the smile was a little more evident.

"Not as thorough as you'd like to think."

This woman had nerve. Insulted, I responded.

"Why's that?"

"Because *I'm* the doctor. Do you have a problem with that?"

I was overcome with a flush of embarrassment and confusion. I was just about sure I had read that she was a man—I mean that the doctor was a man. But then again, I guess I hadn't. I had just assumed she was a man because the doctor was so well accomplished.

And then, she was actually pretty good-looking. Women doctors were usually pretty homely—like women librarians, accountants, scientists and so-called women executives. No, good-looking women got *married* to doctors. They didn't *become* doctors.

And then, there was the question of competence with woman doctors. Doctoring just didn't seem like a women's profession. However, looking at the record, this woman doctor was the best-skilled, best-qualified, best-credentialed doctor in the entire booklet. Not that I was looking, but I caught a glimpse of her legs through the opening of the long white lab jacket, and oh boy, she had great gams!

That's when I thought that in order to have the physical done I'd have to get naked in front of her. What if?—

"I understand if you're a little nervous. Some insecure men have a problem with being examined by women doctors."

Insecure? I had been a lot of things, but never insecure. Still, I had to explain my discomfiture and confusion in a very *secure* way.

"No. I'm not insecure. It's just that it didn't say in the book that you were a doctress."

"A doctress?"

"Yeah, Actor—Ac*tress*, Host—Hos*tess*, Emperor—Em*press*, Heir—Heir*ess*, Duke—Du*chess*, Doctor—Doc*tress*. It saves on the confusion."

I was beginning to enjoy her amused smile as she opened the file again.

"Now *that* one is an original. Would you rather have a doct*or*, or are you willing to settle for this doc*tress*?"

Now I didn't want to say that *I* was uncomfortable with a woman examining me, but being quick on my feet, I figured I'd blame it on some outside factor.

"Well male, female—it doesn't make a bit of difference to *me* as long as the doctor or doctress is competent as I know you are."

I felt clever.

"But my wife! For some reason she's always been really jealous, and she might not take too well to, uh to me being checked-out by another woman. You know I, I'm kind of a worldly guy, and I can handle just about anything, but it's my wife! Uh, you know, she doesn't get out much, and I guess she's, she's a little naïve and insecure."

"Do you want me to call her for you?"

The unusual offer caught me off-guard.

"No! We don't have a phone!"

OOPS. I knew she wouldn't believe that one.

"I, I mean uh, you don't have to phone! My wife's away visiting her aunt in Milwaukee."

Returning the glasses to her nose, she seemed a little impatient.

"Well, I've got other appointments. What are we going to do? Do you need to get your wife's permission or what?"

Despite my appropriate trepidation, this doctress was my last hope.

"I don't need her permission. I'm just a really considerate husband, and I just want to see if she has any problem with you being a woman before scheduling the physical."

She extended her hand.

"Fair enough."

She grinned, almost flirting.

"And after you've gotten her permission, just call the girl at the front desk and she'll make an appointment for you."

"What do you mean you think this woman doctor has the *hots* for you?"

"I didn't say exactly the *hots* for me, but she was giving me this kind of, you know, ogle in a flirty way."

My wife seemed puzzled. She stared at me for a moment before she smiled.

"Well, if she's really *that* good-looking and she's really as hot for you as you say she is, then it should make for a really interesting physical. I say go for it. Can I watch?"

Here my wife could have been on the verge of *losing* me to this sultry doctress, and all she could do was make a joke about it?

"So you think I should tell her you want me to find another doctor?"

"No, I think she'll do just fine. As a matter of fact, I can't wait to meet her."

Apparently, my wife went by her office the very next day, because when she got home she went on about the woman for at least an hour. She even told me details of the doctress' stint in Africa among other things. I hoped my wife hadn't told her that I thought she *wanted* me. As we sat to dinner, she continued without even considering that the kids were listening.

"You know, Honey, she's every bit as good-looking as you said she was, and you were right. She said she did *ogle* you yesterday. She said you're really cute."

Here she was warping the kids' minds by suggesting I was having some kind of an *affair* with the woman! I could see my daughter's inner turmoil and emotion through her seeming unconcerned expression, though it must have been difficult disguising the pain the way she did.

When my wife said the doctress thought I was cute, my daughter laughed, but she must have been feeling equal parts of disgust, revulsion and reproach. My worried eleven year-old son, in what was probably an attempt to protect his mother's interests, launched an all-out attack on this would-be interloper.

"Dad, I thought you said girls can't be doctors. You said they make good nurses and even better waitresses."

He had invoked my wife and daughter's instant wrath. It was the wrong thing to say at the wrong dinner. We were having steak and they both had very sharp knives. Nervously, I made a clumsy attempt to repair the statement.

"No, Son. You got it wrong. What I *said* was 'girls make the best waitresses,' and they do. That's a compliment. I didn't say they couldn't be doctors. I said they could be doctresses (and some girls might make good doctresses). I just said that girls wouldn't be good surgeons. Too much icky blood and stuff. It's a compliment, really."

To his credit, my son corroborated the amended statement.

"That's right, Dad. That's what you said."

Maybe I was just being paranoid, but both my wife and daughter just happened to be clenching slightly bloody knives in their hands at the same time. I couldn't tell if they were insulted or angry, so I figured I had to qualify the statement.

"But I uh, I think I was quoting from a report or something. I'm just about sure I read that somewhere."

Later that night as I crawled into bed beside my wife, I carefully re-opened the subject on the doctress.

"You know, I don't get a really good feeling about this woman doctor, do you? Maybe she's one of those women who like to date married men. I, I saw it on Oprah. Someone even wrote a book about it."

She responded without turning over.

"She's perfect. I already made the appointment for you. One week from Monday."

In an instant I was standing in the middle of the bed.

"You what?"

She turned over, yanked me by my arm down onto the bed and pinned my neck to the mattress with an unyielding forearm and spoke in a firm voice.

"Look, if you flake on this appointment, you'll never be able to sleep with me in peace again. Because I'll just wait till you're sleeping, and then I'll perform a prostate check on you myself with one of those items women can order at parties from magazine catalogues."

Peering up into her eyes, I couldn't tell if she was serious or not, but I wasn't willing to take any chances. Gasping to breathe, I conceded.

"Okay! Okay, I'll go! I promise!"

Over the course of the next day, I began to consider the physical by the doctress more seriously. Now, she was a woman... and I was a man. In order to have this physical done, I'd have to take off my clothes and she would have to look at me with my clothes off. She'd have to look at me very carefully with my clothes off. I wasn't ashamed of my body or anything.

True, I had aged a little over the years. My waist wasn't as narrow as it was in high school, but I was still in pretty good shape. I didn't have a potbelly, even though my wife tried to say I did to make herself feel better about her poofy tummy. I still had pretty good definition in my chest and arms. My legs and butt had actually gotten a little better with the 10-15 pounds I had gained over time. None of those areas concerned me.

It was just that this doctor had probably seen a lot of people with their clothes off. She had probably seen a lot of men with their clothes off. Yep, she had probably seen maybe hundreds of men with their clothes off, and I couldn't help but wonder what she'd think of me when she saw my "you know what."

I mean, she'd probably seen hundreds of them in all shapes and shades and sizes. I guess I was wondering how I, you know, measured up. Size was never a constant for me. I wasn't sure if it was the same way with all men, but I had my good days and bad days. On a good day, I might look down and think, "Whoa, you animal!" but then on a bad day I'd just sit there staring, wondering what happened to it.

I hoped a week from Monday didn't fall on a bad day. Still, I had an expert on me at my disposal.

"Honey, what do you think of me?"

She was reading something, so she answered without looking up.

"You're neurotic."

I snatched the book.

"No, I mean *down there.* What do you think of me *down there*?"

She sat up immediately, smiling with glee. She sang her words in much the same way children do when they're teasing each other.

"You're worried about the physical!"

It wasn't funny to me.

"Just quit with all that. I just want to know what you think."

She settled down and tried to assume a reassuring manner.

"You're the perfect size. Not too big and not too small."

It sounded like a mixed review to me. Now, the *not too small* part was something I could live with, but the other part...

"What do you mean, *not too big*?"

She took care to be careful.

"Well, just that. Women don't want too big. That's why I said you were the perfect size."

And she had the nerve to think she was complimenting me. I wasn't buying it.

"Not too big? And I take it you've seen bigger?"

Her expression grew serious as she caught my eyes.

"Do you *really* want me to answer that question?"

"Well, yeah."

But then I thought about what I had said.

"No! No, I don't! Just forget I asked!"

I only had a week to get in better shape, so I worked out with my daughter and son in their daily exercises. One hundred push-ups in the morning, 100 push-ups before bed. I used to do sit-ups when I was in school, but the kids had these kind of politically correct sit-up things they did called "crunches." Despite the assertion that sit-ups were supposed to be bad for your back or something, I did them anyway, because I've always been the manly type.

Anyway, after about four days I felt I was looking pretty good (or at least a little better than before). But then one day as I stood before the mirror, sucking in my stomach while trying to flex my chest, I considered something I hadn't thought about up to that point. I wasn't sure if the physical would involve much touching, but this was a very attractive doctress.

What if while she was touching me *down there* something happened? Not with her, but with me. What if when I felt her soft, warm hand touching me, it became, you know, *aroused* or something? What would I do? What would she think?

She'd probably think I was trying to make a pass at her or something. What if the thought of me being aroused or something made her think less-than-doctress-esque thoughts? What if it made her make a pass at me? How would I tell her that, despite the fact that I found her very sexy, and despite the fact that other part of me had its own way of thinking, I just could never betray my wife?

I think I had read somewhere that it was a *mind over matter* situation, that I could never become aroused if I just thought of a brick wall or doggie vomit or something. But how was I going to think of doggie vomit with a very attractive woman touching or stroking me down there?

I grew more anxious with each hour that passed, so I sought desperate measures. A Japanese friend at work said that when he was going through his divorce, he was able to resist his wife's seductions through some kind of meditation, some kind of chant thing he did. For that reason, he came through the ordeal in pretty good shape. He only lost the house, the cars, his life savings, half his retirement and most of the rights to the children, but aside from those things, he got to keep everything else.

Without telling him why, I slyly managed to get him to reveal to me the technique he used and the sacred words that put a man in some kind of invulnerable state, able to resist anything. He told me I had to put an image in my head, a flame or an old tree or anything I wanted to create and focus on. He said he used a smiling dog, so in keeping with the Japanese spirit, I chose a frying koi fish.

Thus as I sat humming there with the image of the sizzling cornmeal-battered carp in my mind, he told me to assume a state of detached concentration, and he added that by my doing so, all emotion would pass and I would be able to resist anyone or anything. I practiced this meditation for two hours each day right up to the morning of the appointment.

"*Namuyo ho renge kyo, Namuyo ho renge kyo, Namuyo ho renge kyo.*"

Well, the day finally arrived, but despite the meditation and the subtle encouragement from my wife and kids, I was still a nervous wreck. First of all, I couldn't find my purple and gold paisley silk boxers. They were my best pair! I had painstakingly planned what I was going to wear six days in advance, and then on the morning of the appointment, my $28 piece of underwear somehow ended up AWOL. It was a bad omen, and still there were other problems.

I nicked myself shaving, I just couldn't get my hair to act right, and just when I thought things couldn't possibly get any worse, by accident I sprayed way too much cologne in that area "down there." First it burned like crazy. I started to take another shower, but I was running out of time. Then, when I was leaving ten minutes later than planned, as I bent over to wave the security key so I could start the car, I literally swooned upon sitting back up, drunk with the heavy designer-engineered fragrance.

I thought my wife and kids had just been giving me a bad time about my cologne when I left like they always did, but this time there was no mistaking. I reeked with Ralph Lauren so bad that I had to roll down the windows while driving. Undoing and unzipping my pants, I fanned furiously at every light until some rude, busybody, perverted lady had the nerve to roll down her window and ask if I was having fun.

I was already sensitive about the smell when I walked into the office, and it didn't help my confidence when the pretty little receptionist covered her nose with a handkerchief and held it there the whole time I was speaking with her. I headed right to the bathroom and began to wash myself at the sink, but I could not be thorough because people kept coming in. Still, I was certain I had removed most of the odor.

When I got back into the office, the receptionist told me that my name had already been called at least twice. Embarrassed, I hurried through the door and was led into the same sterile little room where I had first met the doctress earlier.

"Okay, take off your clothes and put on this gown. The doctor will be with you shortly."

I was a little disappointed. I had gone through great pains to get all dressed *up* for the doctress. I had put on my best seven hundred-dollar suit and all. I even bought a new tie. I thought I was going to be able send her into near-delirium by taking my clothes off in front of her, but instead the nurse tossed me a cheap five-dollar gown and told me to have it on when the doctor arrived.

Anyway, after I had taken off my suit, shirt, tie, socks and expensive shoes, I took the occasion to open my boxers to check everything out. It wasn't a good day. I think I was supposed to take everything off, but I just couldn't do it.

The gown was white with some tiny faded blue patterns or words at regular intervals. It was designed so that you put your arms in the two holes and tied it once behind the neck and once at about mid-back. If it had been a dress, it would have been a micro-mini, and if I hadn't opted to leave my boxers on, it would have been pretty breezy down there.

After I had donned the gown, I sat on the rice paper covered gurney and waited for the doctress. Sitting there thinking of that frying koi fish, I suddenly remembered that I hadn't done my push-ups that morning. Well, I didn't want to look scrawny in front of the doctress, so I dropped to the floor and began my vigorous and rigorous exercise.

That's when the doctress arrived, that's when I told her I was down there looking for my keys, that's when she went to and opened the windows because of an alleged allergy to strong colognes. She began by taking my temperature, blood pressure and pulse, looking in my ears, mouth and eyes. She was very professional and knowledgeable. She made me feel comfortable and answered all my questions.

Twenty minutes into the procedure, I remember thinking, "This isn't so bad. It's actually kind of fun. Me and her, her and me... *alone.*" Those deep, intelligent eyes behind those glasses, that soft, smooth, clear complexion and the wondrous angled contour of her face! Her low, calm, reassuring voice, and her warm, soft, neatly manicured hands! She was absolutely incredible! Sometimes you just can't help yourself.

But, just as I was getting into a really good groove with her, she called the nurse in and ordered me off the table.

"Lose em."

"Lose what?"

"The shorts. Take them off and bend over."

Just like that? She told me to bend over just like that? Sensing my discomfort and hesitation, she continued.

"If you're nice, I'll be gentle. But if you give me any trouble—watch out!"

Turning my back so she didn't see the front, I dropped the shorts at the very moment that the nurse entered. The older nurse giggled and she exchanged a sly smile with the doctress before saying something under her voice that I was sure sounded like, "Another virgin? Huh?"

"You may experience a little discomfort, but bear with me. I'll try to finish as quickly as possible."

When I turned back to the doctress, I saw that she had put on a rubber or latex glove and that the middle and index fingers of the glove on her right hand were covered with some kind of yellowish goop.

"What's that?"

"Lubricant. I could proceed without it, but I don't think you'd want that. Brace yourself."

If I had fifty lifetimes to do it, I could have never prepared myself for the absolute discomfort, agony and humiliation of what that woman did to me. In some kind of surrealistic slow motion I can still remember it. Her eyes held determination as she approached, her focus on the portion of my body that had become instantly vulnerable as I bent over. She placed her cold seemingly inhuman naked left hand in the small of my back, for support or leverage or whatever, and then I felt that horrible sense of intrusion and violation.

It was awful!—worse than having to eat liver sandwiches as a kid, worse than having my knee reset after I broke it, worse that my jaw fracture after my wife punched me when she was in labor with my son. It seemed to last forever. I couldn't comprehend what she was *doing* in there. I mean, how was that extremely excruciating probing going to help me. I had never felt such pain in all my life!

With tears in my eyes, I turned and looked toward the nurse who had this goofy smile on her face as she said, "You're doing great. It's almost over." I was doing great? How was I doing great? I thought I was going to die right there!

Well, after what seemed like three or four hours of her fingerwork, the pressure and pain finally relented. She was done, but the throbbing and burning had only begun. Still woozy from the shock to my system, I sank onto a hard cold chair where I collapsed not sitting, almost whimpering, hovering. The room seemed foggy.

"See, wasn't so bad after all, was it?"

She removed the glove and tossed it into a container listed as "Hazardous Waste" or something before re-washing her hands. When I looked back up, she held out a large portion of pink bathroom tissue. Pink!

"Here, I think you're going to need this."

But it wasn't over. The final examination was the test on whether or not I had a hernia. In doing this, she pressed pretty hard with her fingers down *under* there and asked me to cough. And to think I worried I might have become aroused by any of this torture! I half-cough/half-gagged and that was it. Because I could not sit, I just cringed there as she summed it all up.

"Overall you are very healthy, one of the healthiest men I've seen in here in a long time..."

I wasn't sure, but I hoped she was referring to a specific region of my anatomy.

"But I did notice some enlargement of the prostate. My best guess is that you have acute prostatitis in some stage, but it's nothing a few antibiotics won't cure. Thank you for being such a cooperative patient."

And with that, she walked out of the room. She just walked out of the room! Probably to the next guy she had to do! As I slowly put my clothes back on, I felt used. I felt cheap. There was no gentle "goodbye," no sense of closure. She just walked out. Abandoned and humiliated, I slinked out of the office.

Because I had to sit in order to drive home, the throbbing and burning seemed almost impossible to bear, and I had to constantly wipe my face so no one saw the tears. I had crossed a significant threshold that day. With that physical I had somehow crossed over prematurely into middle age. Yet somehow I knew that from that day on, my life would never be the same.

It was just little things in the first week. After all, I was a little bothered by the inured and clinical way she had treated me during the physical. I resented her for that. But still, I thought of her at various moments. I wondered what she was doing. At times I closed my eyes and imagined her smile.

At the beginning of the second week, I sent her a *Thank You* card with a note attached that complimented her on a job well done for "saving my life." I was hoping for a *you're welcome* card from her, but it never came. Before the week was over however, I found myself re-routing my path home so that I would drive right by her office.

The drive wasn't too bad. It only took about 35 longer minutes to get home. Nonetheless, I could see myself. I could see what I was doing. I didn't know what was happening to me. Why was I becoming so obsessed with the woman? I had to talk to her, so I made up an excuse. I contacted her by telephone.

"Tell me again, *what* seems to be the problem?"

"Well it, it drips after I'm finished."

"Are you shaking it?"

"Yeah, yes."

"Then shake it some more."

"Thanks. I never thought of that."

"Okay, but not too much. You don't want to have too much fun."

It was a wonderful conversation, but somehow it wasn't enough for me. I craved her attention. I craved some manner of intimacy with the woman, especially after what had happened between us. Not that I for once considered cheating on my wife.

The doctress was very attractive, altruistic, intelligent, professional, deep, and had great legs, but my wife had her good points too. She, she was very good with woodwork. As a matter of fact, she had just re-finished the cabinets in the kitchen, a real woodworking babe.

Yet, whenever I drove, I thought of the doctress, whenever I put my head on my desk to take my daily nap at work, I thought of the doctress, whenever I shook out those last few drops, I thought of the doctress.

One Friday evening as I was driving by her office, I saw her get into her car, a little red corvette convertible. Before I knew it, I found myself following her (inconspicuously, of course). Weaving in and out of traffic to keep up, I watched her drive up to an expensive restaurant where a valet, who apparently knew her, took her keys before she went in. On the next Tuesday, I followed her to what I could only guess was the street where she lived.

By this time, my wife was growing a little suspicious. All the signs were there: I came home late on a regular basis, my answers to direct questions on my whereabouts were vague, I was inattentive to both her and the kids, and I just seemed to be daydreaming all the time.

But my wife, since from the first day I met her, had for whatever reason considered jealousy and jealous behavior to be anathema. If she had ever been suspicious or insecure about an affair in the twenty or so years that I knew her, she never let me know it. There were a few times when I knew she wanted to question me about a woman I worked closely with, a woman who made it a point to dote on me in front of her, but my wife never said anything. She always dismissed any such discussion with the statement, "Hey, if you find something better, just let me know about it and go for it. Life's too short to worry about those things."

This time however, was different. For the first time in all those years, I saw it in her face, I heard it in her voice, I felt it in her embrace. She thought I was seeing someone else, and she was uneasy. No, she was afraid. I felt terrible. What had I done to her? What was I doing to myself? Why was I so obsessed with this other woman? The tension between us strained tighter with each day that passed.

One day, as I sat daydreaming at the kitchen table, she slammed her hand on the counter and almost yelled.

"Just tell me outright! Are you having an affair? Who is she?"

We had always promised to be honest with each other, so I answered, reluctantly.

"It's not an affair. It's, it's a kind of mild obsession."

"Who?"

"I thought you already knew. It's the doctress."

Taking a deep breath and then sighing in relief, my wife smiled and laughed to herself.

"Her? What? Have you been *out* with her?"

She was taking it all pretty well.

"No. I, well, I've just been kind of seeing her?"

"What do you mean? What? You go by her office and spend time with her?"

Tough questions.

"Well, yeah. I kinda go by her office."

"You're not being very distinct here. Do you go *into* her office and see her?"

Finally I had to come clean.

"No, I just kind of drive by every day, and sometimes I see her, sometimes I don't."

My wife took my hand and led me into the living room.

"Honey, this isn't good. Do you ever follow her?"

She took my non-answer as an affirmation of her question.

"Do you think she knows you're stalking her?"

My wife had gone too far; her thinking had gone overboard.

"I am NOT stalking that woman! I never stalked that woman! I just *followed* her a few times, that's all."

"See if you can get the judge to believe that. Stalking is against the law in this state. You could go to *jail* for what you've been doing! What is wrong with you?"

I didn't know, but there was something wrong. I wasn't exactly stalking the woman because I had no malevolent intent. I was just following her... helplessly. I could not for the life of me understand what made me crave contact with her, what made me so helpless to move beyond my traumatic experience with her. I wasn't in love with her, I didn't exactly want her physically when I hadn't had a drink, and I certainly hadn't enjoyed the close intimate personal contact that we shared during my physical.

Thinking, I realized why I had been behaving so irrationally. It was the *incomplete transaction* thing they talked about once on Oprah. According to studies done by the expert on the show, the doctress and I had formed a sort of relationship and, having other appointments, she had broken it off too quickly, leaving everything incomplete for me.

For me, there was no real sense of closure, and because of that, I craved some sort of intimacy with the doctress to complete the transaction, to end the relationship. That was it. My wife, having watched Oprah with me that day, understood at once.

"What you have to do is invite her to lunch or dinner or something and talk to her about what you've gone through. Maybe she has other patients who have had similar feelings."

But my wife had seemed so uncomfortable and even jealous ten minutes earlier, so I wasn't sure if inviting the doctress out to lunch was the best thing to do.

"Are you sure you wouldn't have a problem with me taking her to lunch or dinner?"

She laughed.

"None whatsoever. You just have to promise to tell me what happens... right down to the last detail."

I remember thinking then that quite possibly my relationship with my wife was just about to take off in some exciting new direction.

Now it became a matter of getting the doctress to go to lunch with me. I still drove by the office every day, but I never let myself follow her car. The very thought of myself as a stalker unnerved me. I had to invent an excuse to talk to her, whereby through that conversation, I could issue the invitation. I planned the moment carefully.

One day, as I saw her exit the office, I sprang from my car and sprinted in her direction trying to catch up with her. By the time I tapped her shoulder to get her attention, I was out of breath. Gasping for oxygen, I labored to speak.

"Ah Doctress! Is, is that you? I, I was just passing by and I *thought* I recognized you."

She looked over my shoulder at my parked car suspiciously.

"Nice to see you. Is that your car there next to mine?"

I glanced back.

"Well, if that red corvette's yours, yeah. Why?

"No reason. That car just looks really familiar."

I had to change the subject.

"Can, can I take you to lunch tomorrow?"

Smiling, she removed her rounded glasses.

"Let me get this straight. Are you asking me out on a date?"

"No! I mean Yes! I mean I'm asking you out to lunch, that's all."

She crossed her arms and appeared to be contemplating the question.

"Well, I've never gone out with one of my patients before. I've never broken that rule, but you're so cute I just can't help myself. Okay. Sure. I'd love to go to lunch with you tomorrow."

I couldn't believe it! It had been almost twenty years since I asked a woman out, but I never remembered it being so easy. Maybe it was just that I really *had* become cute as I aged. I didn't know, but I wasn't complaining.

Even though I was imbued with a definite sense of euphoria for the rest of the day, I played down my excitement when I went home to my wife.

"It's no big deal. It's just lunch and then it's on with the rest of my life, I guess."

I couldn't understand why, but she did her best to be supportive. She had picked up my suits and shirts at the cleaners and had gone to the bank so I would have enough money for lunch.

Unable to sleep because of my excitement, I tossed and sighed in bed all night. I got up at five a.m., shaved, showered, and got dressed so quickly that I was out of the house by about five-thirty. Only as I sat in the car waiting for my eight o'clock work start-time did I realize I hadn't needed to leave so early.

I told the front office that I wouldn't be returning after lunch. After all, how was I to know how involved my lunch with the doctress might be or what revelation she or I might divulge in that electric, intoxicating, tantalizing candle-lit space between us.

I had made reservations at a cozy restaurant downtown known for its intimate and romantic atmosphere. In a phone call that morning, the doctress had asked me to meet her in front of her building (she actually *owned* the building) at noon. I was there at eleven-thirty in order to give myself sufficient time for the necessary breath check, deodorant check, cologne check and underwear check.

I didn't want any of her employees to think there was any hanky-panky going on between us, so I just waited anxiously out in my hot car in dark glasses with a newspaper in front of my face until she came out. Peeking over the top of the paper, I must have watched thirty-six people go in and out that facility on that warm summer day.

But then, just as I was beginning to get over my initial nervousness, the doctress stepped out of the building, and she was so incredibly attractive that I temporarily lost the ability to speak. I mean, it was one thing to see her in a long white lab jacket but quite another to see her all dressed up like she was.

Her dark wavy hair, which I had only seen pinned tight to her head on every other occasion, was worn down in a full, relaxed style. The sleek, Italian-designed suit she wore was a stunning creation in my favorite color, red. I could never understand why, but the color red just "did something" to me, and red on a woman was even more intoxicating. The suit consisted of a smart, double-breasted jacket with a pleated skirt that fell to about an inch and a half above her knees.

Her silk stockings were black and almost wispy, gossamer on sculpted, contoured legs that no doubt tempted some married men to sinful thoughts. To me they were legs, that's all, just really good-looking legs. As my eyes gradually fell from her hair, to her face, to her suit, to her narrow waist, to her rounded hips, to her shapely legs, to her sexy ankles, and finally to her feet, I noticed she was wearing black silk pumps that were tied with delicate little black silk laces.

I was so nervous and anxious when I saw her that I, tossing aside the glasses and newspaper, locked the car and sprang from it without remembering to take my keys from the ignition. Locking the keys in the car would have been okay, but because it was hot and I needed to have the air conditioner on so I wouldn't sweat and stink, I had left the engine running.

"Hi, you look nice. Can we take *your* car?"

"Sure."

It was too easy. Initially, I thought she hadn't noticed, but right before we got into her car, she stopped and turned to me.

"Do you always leave your car running when you go to lunch?"

"Yes, I mean, No! I'm, I just have some problems with the battery. I just left it on like that because I'm testing if it'll charge. I didn't accidentally lock my keys in the car with the engine running or anything. I'd have to be pretty stupid to do that."

The size of her cockpit forced us to sit in close proximity in the fifteen-minute drive over to the restaurant. It was torture! I couldn't look at her without thinking she might be thinking that I might be thinking some less-than-virtuous thought about her legs or some other shapely area of her wonderful anatomy.

The truth was that my thoughts were wholesome, with just a few slight glitches, that's all. Her spicy warm citrus perfume wrecked such havoc on my already overloaded senses that, by the time we pulled up to the restaurant, I sat slumped in the seat with glassy eyes and an utterly blank face.

Somehow, the afternoon was not shaping up the way I had hoped. All I could do is think of other "tress" words like seduc*tress* and temp*tress*. I remember thinking, "What am I doing *out* with this woman? What am I going to say to her? What was the point of the lunch? What if she thinks I—"

"Are you ever going to get out of the car? I haven't eaten all day. I'm famished."

Per my request when I made the reservation, the maître d' led us to a little table tucked around a corner in the darkened area of the restaurant.

A satiny, pearl-white tablecloth was draped across the table and atop the tablecloth sat fine, golden-etched china place settings with matching gold-plated flatware. Two candles, on two delicate and intricate gold-plated metal flowers, flickered playfully, casting warm shadows out in all directions. Two glasses, filled with sparkling water and garnished with lemon, just seemed to appear as we sat. No menus were presented as the place served a pre-set lunch.

This was the kind of restaurant you went to once, maybe twice, every two years. I ordered a bottle of a fine California meritage red from an Alexander Valley vintner that complimented the caribou steaks served with spicy raspberry/guava chutney and white asparagus under honey-mustard pepper mayonnaise. About half-way through my first glass of wine, I began to loosen up a little.

"Do you know how much I think about you?"

"How much?"

"All the time, it seems."

She laughed sat back, sipping her wine.

"I'm complimented, but you're not the first patient I had who's somehow become affected with me after I've..."

She gestured with her fingers.

"You know, de-virginized him."

I had thought I was going mad, but apparently I wasn't the only one.

"You mean? Uh, it's *natural*?"

"Perfectly. It's much the same in women. Many women form bonds with their obstetricians that seem to endure beyond childbirth. They often become confused and uncomfortable dealing with many strange or awkward feelings they believe are genuine. In many ways, it's like ending a relationship."

I was already beginning to feel better, but still, how was I going to get over what I had been feeling for her?

"Okay. So what do I do?"

Sipping sensuously from the oversized glass, she deadpanned,

"Well, in my medical opinion, what you have to do is go out and have *another* prostate examination performed by someone else as soon as possible. You'll be over me in no time."

Not certain if she was joking, I just kind of stared into her serious, deeply wonderful eyes, hoping they would betray her queer sense of humor.

"Is that the prescription you've given to other patients?"

Finally, she broke character and laughed.

"Not at all. I've said it before—you are an original."

She reached over and caressed my hand as I poured the last few drops of wine into her glass. Then, to my extreme surprise, she leaned over and kissed me right on the lips and sat back in the chair.

"But tell me, aren't you glad that in the end you chose a doc*tress* instead of a doc*tor*? Who knows, you could have been having this same lunch and conversation sitting across from a man."

Withdrawing my hand from hers, I sat up straight in the comfortable armchair.

"Oh no! Never with a man! I'm not gay. I'm... I'm *normal*!"

I realized right away that what I said sounded, well, a little derogatory about those people who people had discovered alternative uses for the last six inches or so of the large intestine. Obviously sensitive about the matter, the doctress recoiled.

"Are you completely sure that you're not just a little gay? I'm mean you did develop this so-called attraction for me after I—"

I was not about to let her finish the suggestion.

"No! Not gay! Not even a little gay! Look, I am extremely attracted to you, but it has nothing to do with that painful, humiliating, disgusting prostate check you did. I like the person you are."

She took my hand again, caressing it.

"And what about your wife? You have a beautiful, sexy wife at home and you say you're somehow *attracted* to me?"

She was correct on both counts.

"Yes."

"Well, what is it that you want or need from me?"

Sitting there watching as the doctress rubbed my hand with soft delicate fingers, I realized that, while I had spent many minutes fantasizing about her and a moment like the one I we were spending, I really did have a beautiful, sexy wife at home, and she was the only one I wanted.

Still, though my wife was first with me, the doctress could have qualified as a close second. I mean, if my wife suddenly dropped dead or something, the doctress was the type of person I might look up. That is, after the appropriate grieving period. But my wife was healthy, a good driver and a woman, so a premature and untimely death was very unlikely. Thus dismissing any indecent suggestion by the doctress, I answered the question.

"Everything I want and need, I already have."

She smiled and winked at me.

"That's the right answer."

Despite the incredibly sexy woman across the table and the warming effect of the sensuous wine, I had passed the test, I had turned the corner. Feeling smug and perhaps a little bolder, I dared to delve into her life.

"And what about you? What do you need? Do *you* have somebody at home?"

Yes."

"Really? Well he's a lucky dog. I already hate him. Any man fortunate enough to have you is a very, very lucky guy. I never thought you were married because you don't wear a ring."

Holding up her arm and hand, she made the same gesture she had before when reminding me of the prostate check.

"People in my line of work don't usually wear rings. For one, patients find them uncomfortable, and two, we'd be losing them all the time, if you get the picture."

This time I knew she was exaggerating because she laughed as she finished. Pursing her lips, she continued.

"No, actually I don't wear a wedding ring because I'm not legally married."

"Not married?"

"Just living in sin, I guess. At least that's what my parents call it."

"How long have you been together?"

For the first time since I had met her, I sensed a deep sadness in the doctress.

"Oh, about six years."

By this time, I really did *not* like the guy, though I hadn't met him. He was leading my doctress on for sure. He was just telling her he'd marry her with no real intention to do so. I saw it on Oprah: *Wimpy Men Who Cannot Commit to Woman Professionals.*

"Do you want to be married?"

"Are you kidding? I'd *love* to be married?"

I wasn't sure, but I was certain I could see tears in her eyes. It made me angry beyond belief. Typically when I'm angry, I get my best ideas. I mean I could see this skinny jerk in a T-shirt, a wife beater, sitting on a sweaty couch, his hand down his dingy boxers. I could see him ordering the doctress to bring him another cheap beer. Placing the can gently in his hands, she'd get down on one knee and beg him to marry her only to be told "maybe next year."

I just couldn't let it go on year after year. She was too wonderful a person for that. My plan was to invite the doctress and him out to dinner where I could either talk some sense into him or expose him for the sniveling coward he was. Taking the doctress' hand, I began,

"What are you doing next Friday night? Because my wife and I would like to take you and your, your..."

"Partner."

"Yes, my wife and I would like to take you and your partner out to dinner at our favorite restaurant. *Our* treat. What do you say?"

"I might have to do some checking, but I suppose it's safe to say I accept for both of us."

Did I know how to enact a plan or what? But she began again.

"There *is* however, something that is important for you to know."

He was probably fat or goofy or old or bald or crippled or something weird like that. No, he was an illegal alien who didn't speak English.

"What is it?"

"My partner—"

"Yes?"

"He—"

"Yes?"

She paused and swallowed the last few drops of wine from my glass to build resolve.

"Well he, he—"

"Yes!"

"Is a *she*. I'm a lesbian. Do you have a problem with that?"

I recoiled so forcefully that my chair almost tipped enough to fall over backwards. Scanning over my shoulders and around the table to make sure no one had heard her embarrassing pronouncement, I managed a whisper.

"Oh no! No, I have no problem with that!"

"Does that mean you rescind your invitation for Friday night?"

So much for me and my great ideas. I couldn't in good conscience go back on the invitation. After all, the doctress *was* my ride back to the car.

"Oh no! It's a date! Me and my wife, and you and your, your partner, Friday night. Favorite restaurant. Our treat and all."

I quickly stuck my foot out, tripping the waiter who had been ignoring me.

"Check, please!"

"... and then she kissed me! *Against* my will! What was I supposed to do?"

My wife, evincing not even a hint of jealousy, pressed on.

"Well, what did *you* do?"

"What else? I kissed her back, I mean her lips back. I'm sorry. It was scary!"

She laughed.

"Why? She's a great-looking woman. Why would kissing a great-looking woman be scary? Unless you're gay and you don't know it."

I was growing tired of the insinuations and becoming more certain my wife and the doctress had coordinated their nearly identical insults.

"Very funny. She's not really a real woman. She's, she's one of those things she called herself."

"A lesbian?"

"Yes! One of those. And she kissed me. Do you know what those women *do* to each other?"

"No. Did she tell you? I'd like to know."

The kiss-and-tell session was over. Between my wife and me, we would have to come up with some ingenious way of getting out of taking the doctress and her partner out to dinner on Friday night.

"Here's what we're going to do. I'll call the doctress and tell her that you came down with the Russian flu and can't go out of the house."

My wife didn't like the idea. In fact, she didn't like any of the astute ideas I came up with and found fault in every suggestion.

"You can call and tell her that *you* have the Hungarian flu for that matter, but I'm just fine. I am *not* going to lie to that woman."

"Well, what are we supposed to do? Go out with the doctress and her girlfriend at our favorite restaurant where everyone *knows* us?"

"Yes! Loosen up, will you! I'll never understand why you're so hopelessly insecure!"

And that was the end of that planning session. Other attempts at resolving the problem met with the same result.

Anyway, Wednesday went by, Thursday went by, and finally on Friday morning I decided to take action. I called the doctress' office and told the receptionist to tell her that I was sick and that we'd have to postpone the dinner plans. I initially thought that canceling the dinner was the right thing to do, but I felt guilty about it for hours after the call.

There was really nothing *wrong* with going out to dinner with two other women and my wife. Who was really going to know that they, they licked each—I mean *liked* each other a lot.

Anyway, I went home feeling ashamed of myself for what I had done. I slumped on the couch and poured myself a large brandy. The doctress probably thought I was an idiot and homophobic, and my wife—my wife!

My wife was all dressed *up* and ready to go somewhere!

"What are you doing? Where are you going?"

She backed up to me.

"Zip me up. Don't be silly. Like I said earlier this week—I'm going to dinner with the doctress and her partner."

Uh oh! I forgot to tell my wife I had *canceled* the dinner.

"No you're not. The dinner's been canceled. I called the doctress this morning and told her I was sick and we'd have to postpone."

She didn't seem surprised. She only held the two ends of a necklace together at the back of her neck, intimating that I should fasten it.

"I know about your call to the doctress already. After your call, she called me and asked if *I* still wanted to go out to dinner, and since your Hungarian flu isn't contagious, I said 'yes.' Do you have any money? Never mind, I'll just get it from your wallet. She said you told her it was *your* treat."

I could not believe my wife was actually considering going to dinner with two women who, who did unspeakable, unimaginable things to each other's bodies. Who knows, maybe they'd want to do those things to my wife?

I walked down the hallway toward the bedroom wherein she was no doubt rifling through my wallet.

"Honey, I can't let you go. What if they try to make you into *one* of them?"

Leaving me only one dollar, she stuffed the rest of my hard-earned cash into a tiny purse.

"How do I look?"

That's when I noticed it. My wife was pretty hot, but she never got all dressed up like that for *our* Friday dinners.

"I forbid you to go. They're going to try to convert you."

Taking my hand, she led me into the foyer by the front door, and after kissing me, she concluded.

"Look, I trusted you to go to lunch with her. I think you can trust me to go to dinner with her."

"But!"

"Besides, why would I want anyone else... when I've got *you*. Bye."

I closed the door only after I heard her car pull away from the house. Sulkily, I returned to both the couch and my brandy. At first I was lonely, then I was depressed and finally I grew concerned. After all, on more than one occasion I had heard the doctress say that my wife was *sexy*, and on more than one occasion I had heard my wife say that the doctress was *really attractive*.

I think my wife probably knew the doctress was gay all along. I think that's why she suggested I go to lunch with her to tell her how I felt. And then the doctress called my wife even after I had canceled the dinner plans, leading me to believe that maybe, unknown to me, they talked on the phone about things.

Maybe my wife was curious? But just then I realized that she had always been honest with me and true to every promise she had ever made to me. Fidelity and honor were always premiums with her. They were virtues she demanded from herself and anyone in her company.

And yet, throughout history, even the most virtuous individuals suffered occasional moral lapses, so I couldn't help worrying about what would happen if my wife, being intoxicated with wine or for whatever reason, possibly suffered one while out with those two *you-know-whatses*.

In the end however, I realized what I was feeling was mere insecurity. Insecurity was always something I ran from, something I denied. My insecurity was a part of me that I somehow never accepted, in spite of the fact that it had been with me all my life.

When I was thirteen and skinny, insecurity made me begin a rigorous weight-training routine that resulted in a physique that made me proud; it had made me finally ask a rather plain girl to the junior prom only to find she was very nice, it had made me stay up for 48 hours straight preparing for the SAT; it had made me perform well in college; it had made me hold out for the best possible job for the best possible pay; it had made me finally propose marriage to my wife; and at last, it had shaped the course of my adult life as a man, as a writer, as a husband and as a father.

My insecurity probably had more to do with who I was than any other factor in my life. I was driven by it. As I sipped another mouthful of brandy, for a first time in my life I embraced that insecurity, for a first time I completely accepted it.

But it wasn't just me. My wife was insecure too, though she pretended she wasn't, and I think she was more insecure about just *having* insecurity than anything else. The doctress too, was insecure. She was insecure about not being able to be legally married and about whether or not I or anyone else *had a problem* with her gender as a professional or her chosen lifestyle.

Maybe I would always struggle with the fact that I *was* homophobic and xenophobic and agoraphobic and tridekaphobic and gynophobic, but I was finally ready to benefit from these insecurities rather than be limited by them.

For a moment, I thought to get dressed and join my wife, the doctress and her partner at the restaurant, but I decided to spend the time instead with my insecurity, enjoying it, reveling in it, learning from it, and being inspired by it. From that moment on, my distressing experience with the doctress took on real meaning, and from that moment on, I finally began to learn.

NERO

If there is any truth to Andy Warhol's suggestion—that we are all somehow destined to only fifteen minutes of fame, that we are all granted a mere moment of bathing in the limelight—then I got totally ripped off. Because I can't seek legal remedy related to such a claim (which a so-called friend and lawyer called frivolous) in any actual court, I am forced to simply tell this story.

It started on a wet, cold, miserable and foggy Monday night about an hour after a double-overtime football game. I had watched the game at my brother's house, which was roughly some three miles away from my own.

I can admit it now. I had two light beers while watching the game, but I was anything but intoxicated—just cold, miserable and tired as I navigated through thick curtains of fog which were impenetrable to my headlights. I drove slowly over the freeway overpass and by two obscured major supermarket shopping centers on the right before turning into my little neighborhood sub-division which was nested in a slight depression on the general terrain.

The fog was always much worse in my immediate neighborhood, so I had slowed to about fifteen miles per hour, or maybe twenty. As I was a little anxious to get home to relieve myself of that last beer, I mentally shifted to automatic pilot as I rounded the corner turning onto my street. That's when it happened, that's when the inconceivable happened.

All of a sudden, out of the gloom appeared this fat lady wrapped in a woolly blanket right in front of my car. I half-swerved/half-braked for an instant before I felt the impact of the grossly corpulent body on my left-quarter-side panel and bumper. Screeching to a stop, I turned off the car and buried my face in shaking, sweaty palms.

After about a half minute sitting there, I managed the resolve to exit the car. Stepping into the stilted illumination of the headlights, I knelt to check her body. Nervously, I grabbed the blanket and turned her toward me. Now I'm not the type of man who regularly screams out loud like a woman, but I could have never been prepared for what saw at that moment.

It wasn't a fat lady at all, but rather it seemed like one of those huge, ugly another-worldly beasts created by George Lucas for his Star Wars movies. The creature groaned aloud as a great billow of smoke erupted from its huge gaping mouth, causing me to fall back on the asphalt, which immediately imprinted its irregular pattern onto my buttocks. Around that time I realized that the massive, hairy behemoth sprawled before my car was of determinate earthly origin.

Mostly it seemed like the biggest Saint Bernard I had ever seen, yet I remember thinking it was at least partially mixed with the Mastiff breed. As it moaned again, I caught the sheen of bright red blood in the thick saliva that dangled from its mouth between the headlights and me. The dog was injured internally and externally, but I was unsure of both its disposition and its ability to inflict internal and external injuries on me.

Still, it lay there stretched out in the middle of the street. I couldn't just leave it there. Rushing back to my car, I grabbed up my cellular phone and started to dial 911, but I was stopped by a sobering thought.

If I called the police and they came out, and if while they were looking at the dog one of them asked me if I had been drinking, and if I answered *no* but they tested me anyway, and then if they became angry or irritated because I tried to deceive them about the drinking and decided to punish me for it, they could actually make a determination, however faulty, that alcohol was a contributing factor to the accident. They could then cite me for driving under the influence and utterly ruin my life. I looked over at the dog who, straining to raise his head, groaned again.

I felt bad for the poor animal, but in the balance, he wasn't worth a night in jail, heavy fines, higher insurance rates, and the social stigma of being cast as an uncontrollable and irresponsible alcoholic. Tossing the phone onto the seat, I grabbed the remote on the keys and popped the trunk.

The trauma of the impact had no doubt sent the dog's body in shock, so I covered him with a dirty woolen blanket I kept next to the spare tire for emergencies. It probably wasn't the right thing to do, because the dog began to wail. The sound was hard to describe, but it was something of a *plaintive* wail.

Tenative, I returned the blanket to the trunk and ducked into my car again to think. Nearing a state of panic, I pressed a button on the dash to illuminate the car's clock (which I always kept 15 minutes fast) which read 10:50 (meaning it was actually 10:35). It was too late to start knocking on random doors in any attempt to find the dog's owner or owners.

Besides, some people react violently to 1) being disturbed from their sleep and then/or when 2) being told, "I'm sorry, but I just ran into your family pet with the bumper of my car." I sighed out loud, not knowing what to do. Well, I knew I had to drag the dog out the street, lest some other unsuspecting person should speed along that way and cause further injury.

So easing behind the dog, I slipped my right hand under his right shoulder until I reached my left hand, which I had slid over his left shoulder and down its chest. Locking my hands, I did my best to drag the animal backward about three feet. Right about then, the beast yelped aloud and managed to nip the ring finger on my left hand pretty hard, drawing blood. Savage beast!

On my feet in an instant, I squeezed the throbbing finger that had begun to drip blood. Uncertain on the extent of the wound, I hurried back to the car and screeched my tires as I left the scene. By the time I approached my own house however, I realized that the business in the street behind me was yet unfinished.

My first impulse was to go into the house and dial 911, but 911 always made me nervous. I mean in my personal experience, the person on the other end of a 911 call always just knew too much about me right off—my name, my address, my social security number, my shoe size, the intimate details of marriage history and probably what I had for breakfast that morning.

And those calls were recorded. Anything I said could or would be used against me in the court of law or for any other purpose. I'm not sure if I heard it somewhere, but for some reason I believed in the back of my mind that the service was surreptitiously ran by the CIA. Truthfully, I just was never comfortable about calling 911 from my home for any purpose unless there was an emergency or something.

But as I had always been clever and resourceful, I contrived a way to notify proper authorities and yet remain anonymous. There was a coffee shop on the main street not more than about four miles from my house. I decided to call about the emergency from the pay phone there.

It was a slow night for coffee as the shop was virtually empty. There was a poorly-dressed man in one of the small booths who just kind of sat there, sipping coffee and engaging in a conversation with the empty seat across from him. Two highway patrol officers sat in a far corner, filling out reports as their static-ky radios squawked dissonantly beside them.

I took a seat at the counter and ordered coffee from a red-haired late teen, who had a large and rather noticeable zit right in the middle of her forehead. Careful not to hurt her feelings by staring at the red, encrusted growth, I focused on the area below her neckline instead as I asked about the location of the phone. To my astonishment, rather than showing me any manner of appreciation for my truly magnanimous gesture, she pulled her shirt closer together and fastened another button.

I thought to explain that I was not trying to look into her shirt, but I didn't think she'd buy it, so I paid my tab and ducked into the darkened hallway where I took up the remotest pay phone and nervously dialed 911. A woman agent answered.

"911— what is your emergency?"

All of a sudden, I didn't know what to say. I wasn't sure if I should have said I hit the dog or if I just ran across an already hit dog on my way home. Maybe somebody told me that they saw a dog get hit by a bus and I—

"Hello? Are you there? What is your emergency?"

"Oh!"

It wasn't my voice. My throat just kind of clamed up, raising my voice by an octave and more. I distinctly remember thinking the *Oh!* I said right then sounded like kitchen extraordinaire Julia Childs, so I just sorta went with it. I actually sounded just like her.

"I was on my way home, and I saw a very large dog down in the street. Apparently, he was hit by a car..."

"Was the driver of the car injured?"

"No. Just the dog, and I think he's hurt badly. Can, can you send an ambulance or something?"

"No, Sir. I don't think we could send an ambulance for a dog."

Sir? I wasn't sure if she was on to me or if she had made a mistake. Maybe the CIA had a camera hidden in a corner behind one of the tiles or something. I continued in the Julia Childs voice.

"Why not? If you don't send one, the dog might die."

"I'm sorry, Sir. Dogs die every day in the streets, and so far as I know, they don't usually have insurance policies. We can't send ambulances for every dog that gets hit by a car. Are you the one who hit this dog?"

Maybe they had a camera in my car!

"No! No, it wasn't me. I didn't hit the dog. I just ran across it."

"May I have your name please?"

"No! I've done my part. Just let the dog die if you want. I'm just trying to save its life!"

Click. I hoped I hadn't stayed on long enough for them to trace the call and send agents. Trying not to seem suspicious, I slipped past the officers seated just around the corner and exited the coffee shop.

I took an alternate route home so that I approached my house from the opposite end of the street, thus avoiding the dog where it lied about thirty yards from my house.

Only after the garage door rolled down behind me did I examine the car for damage. It was a mess as the moisture in the air caused the car to pick up masses of hair from the animal's coat. Brushing the fur away, I could see that there was a large dent in my left quarter-panel and that the left side of the bumper was ruined.

Feeling a little guilty, I filled a bowl and trudged out across the muddy backyard to feed my *own* dog who was snug and warm in his expensive little doggie condo. I still wasn't sure if I would tell my wife about the incident, so I covered the damaged area of the car with a blanket when I got back to the garage and I went into the house acting as if nothing had happened.

She asked the same stock question she always asked when I came back from my brother's house.

"You're late! It's almost eleven! How many beers did you have?"

"Two. Only two."

She didn't believe me.

"What? I only had two beers!"

She sighed aloud and continued in a lawyerly tone.

"You said *two*, right?"

"Yeah, two."

"How many fingers do you have up."

"Tw—"

I glanced at the raised fingers of my right hand in my peripheral vision. I had held up three. I folded and tucked my ring finger.

"Two!"

I wanted to tell her about the accident with the dog, but she'd say it was all my fault because I drank too much beer. Still, I think I saw an Oprah show where a doctor said husbands should be honest despite having wives who say they drink too much beer even if they only had two.

However, just when I had built the resolve to tell her about the accident and I had gone into the bedroom to explain it all to her, she had fallen asleep. So at that point, I decided I'd tell her about the event in a month or so.

After cleaning the wound and clipping torn skin, my finger looked much better. In fact, it was hardly noticeable once the 1-inch bandage was applied. Thus putting the horror of the night completely behind me and out of my mind, I fell into the bed and the rest was silence.

When I awoke, it was if nothing ever happened... until I went out to the garage and examined the car again. It seemed strange that the blanket had somehow fallen off somewhere in the night. I hoped my wife and kids hadn't seen the huge dent.

Yet, if they hadn't and I could get the car fixed before anyone found out, I could just pretend I hadn't hit that dog. The dog! So raising the garage door, I walked out to the curb and looked down the street. The dog was gone and all was calm, except for what appeared to be a van with a weird antenna or dish or something attached to the roof.

Maybe the dog wasn't hurt as bad as it initially seemed. Yeah, he probably got up and limped back home absolutely committed to look both ways the next time he crossed the street.

It was already 9:30, so the human-sized vultures that did body repair were well into their daily feeding frenzy. My cousin had a friend who scavenged at a dealership owned by an eccentric cowboy-type guy whose best friend was a real ape. Really! This guy went around with a hairy ape or chimpanzee or orangutan or something.

Anyway, I drove down to the lot and managed to find my cousin's friend in the body shop. I called ahead and had made an appointment for noon. I had never met the man before but she had armed me with a good description: she said he looked like a buzzard. For me, it was just a matter of picking out the right buzzard.

When I spotted his balding head and bulging eyes, his long thin neck with a big bulb in the front that moved up and down when he swallowed, his movements which were almost bird-like and the sense of greed in his eyes intently trained on the vehicle's wounds, I knew.

He was standing beside the car even before the engine died.

"Looks like you gonna be needin some hep (help) with that front end. What'cha do? Hit a big ol dog or somethin?"

"No! I mean no I, no I , I ran into a— I think it was a rock. What does it matter!"

"A rock?"

"Anyway, I was just wondering how much it'll take to fix it and how long."

Standing beside him, I caught whiff of a strange, sort of fetid odor escaping his body, so I backed away as he knelt beside the car, brushing away strands of dog hair from the bumper.

"An rocks are growin *fur* these days. Well, let's see. Take bout a week if we got all the parts."

"How much?"

He extended his long leathery neck around toward the front, measuring the damage.

"Now this ain't no formal estimate. I'll do that in a few minutes, but if ya wanna know in the ballpark, I'd say with damage ta the quarter-panel, bumper, grill, radiator, battery, labor and who knows what else—probably about twenty-five."

My cousin said he would cut me a pretty good deal, but to pay twenty-five dollars for all those parts and the work was almost the equivalent of stealing. While I had a new level of respect for the man, I couldn't let him do it.

"Sir, my cousin said you would be reasonable, but I can't let you do it for twenty-five. Why don't I just give you fifty and no one has to know."

The man almost swallowed the cigar butt he had been chewing on.

"Let me get this straight. You wanna pay me twenty-five on the side? Twenty-five hundred dollars?"

I instantly realized the error.

"Waitaminute, Ali Baba! You're telling me it'll take twenty-five hundred dollars to fix that little damaged corner of my car!"

The man had no conscience.

"I'm sayin twenty-five hundred is a low estimate cuz I know your cousin. Should I go head and do an itemized estimate an order the parts?"

There had to be someone else in town who was more reasonable. Yet there was no charge for the estimate itself, which I could use as a basis for comparison.

"Don't order the parts, but do the estimate. I'll be in the waiting room getting coffee or something."

While the strong gritty coffee only smelled four hours old, it tasted eight, like espresso made with beans that had been soaked in kerosene. Still, it was free, so I poured myself a large styrofoam cupful and took a seat on the sagging brown *pleather* couch, picking up a magazine that had been on the table for over two years.

I could vaguely make out the voice of the local afternoon news anchor in the background as I read predictions about a verdict in a criminal trial that had enthralled many in the country. However, my reading was interrupted by a distinct shift in the support structure of the couch.

A man, who must have been not one ounce less than three hundred pounds, had taken a seat on the opposite end. And if that hadn't been uncomfortable enough, his young teen-aged daughter, a seeming two hundred pound spitting image of the man, somehow believed she was narrow enough to sit between us. Plopping down, she made hot coffee spill onto the magazine and down the front of my pants.

As I stood in mild anger and disgust, I glimpsed an image on the television that changed my disposition.

"Turn it up! Turn it up!"

The oval man, with the remote in his hand, complied. There on the television was a nightmare image I thought I had all but forgotten. The big dog, the Saint Bernard or whatever, was lying in the street where I hit him. Then I heard the commentator's voice.

Dan, sometime last night, probably around midnight, a motorist sped recklessly around that corner, screeching his tires, and broadsided the poor animal, causing the broken arm and the other damage we saw to its face. Apparently the first impact initially stopped the car. And then, in an act of inhumane savagery and sadism, this monster revved the accelerator, threw the car into gear and deliberately ran the dog over, crushing its neck and causing other damage to the body.

The television cut back to Dan the newsman who seemed visibly shaken, almost in tears as he posed a question.

What are the police saying about who the killer might be?

Police? Killer? When the story first started I thought they were talking about a dog! The field reporter answered.

Dan, I think the dog was also stabbed in the face with a knife or something. They're saying it could be any one of a few things— devil worship, jealously, dog-hate or a berserker fit of rage. They just don't know anything for sure right now.

Dan's eyes seemed to be watering.

Were there any witnesses?

Witnesses? No way. I remember looking around. The entire neighborhood was dead.

Well, yes. There was a woman who said she heard tires screeching at about midnight. Apparently, she looked out and saw a white vehicle speeding around the corner. We'll bring you more on the story as it develops.

Back to a visibly emotional Dan.

This is a story that I will personally stay with. I won't stop until we find the despicable coward and black-hearted fiend who is guilty of this grave act of inhumanity.

While I was a bit shaken, I thought, "What's the worst that can happen to anyone who accidentally bumps into a dog?"

The midday news then detailed a related story about a drug dealer living in a remote suburb of town who was raising pit bulldogs in conditions of cruelty and squalor. A

Humane Society official said Animal Control had gone in and taken all the dogs, adding,

We're stepping up our efforts to seek prosecution and jail time for criminals guilty of cruelty to animals. Law enforcement and the courts have to let these heartless individuals know that animal cruelty will not be tolerated.

TV coverage then cut to the image of the drug dealer in handcuffs being led away by police and placed into a squad car. This was not good. I mean, I didn't feel sorry for the drug dealer or anything, and I didn't run over the dog like the reporter said in the story, but I was *there*. I did hit the dog. Putting down the coffee, I went back out to the buzzard.

"Order the parts. Fix the car."

He was just finishing up the written estimate.

"Well, I dunno. Ya bout had a cow when I said twenty-five. This come up ta twenty-eight an some change."

I wondered if vultures were on the endangered species list.

"I don't care what it costs. Just order the parts! Fix the car!"

Of course that meant I needed to rent a car to get around for the week, but I owned a distinctive white vehicle. If I was seen driving a different car around the day after the accident, neighbors might suspect that I hit the dog.

In a stroke of pure genius, I realized that I had to rent a car exactly like mine in every detail so not even my wife and kids would know. It took about four hours and a shuttle out to the airport before I finally had the car.

My ever-meddling twelve year-old son was waiting by the garage as I drove up.

"Hi Dad."

He thought he was being circumspect, but I could see him examining the car. I couldn't believe it! My own son viewing me as a suspect!

"Did you do your homework?"

"Yes, Dad."

"Chores?"

"Yes, Dad."

"What are *you* looking at?"

"Nothing Dad. Did you wash your car? It's never usually this clean."

At that point I knew he had either watched the news or that the entire neighborhood was aware of the story. I ignored the question, made sure the car was completely locked and went into the house. My seventeen year-old-daughter had just finished making seafood lasagna for dinner, and she and my wife were on the couch watching the local five-o'clock news. I took up the remote.

"Let's see what's on CNN."

The cacophony was instantaneous.

"Turn it back, Daddy. We were watching that!"

She had grabbed a secondary remote and within an instant, they were watching Dan again. I was insulted. After all, who paid the cable bill? Zip—CNN. Zip—Local news. Zip—CNN. Zip— Local news. Zip—CNN. Zip—Local news. Yet before I could turn it back to CNN again, my wife had snatched the remote from my hand.

"Look, we were watching the five o'clock news. You can watch what you want to watch when it's *over*."

I gave up. It was pointless to argue with two females. I started to leave for the bedroom, but I decided to stay and measure their reactions to the story. By this time, my son, a kid who preferred video games to anything on television, had sat on the couch, intently watching.

Basically, the story was the same one with words like "savagery, sadism, monster, killer, devil worship, white vehicle, black-hearted fiend and criminal" standing out most prominently. This time however, the station played an interview with the woman six houses down who said she saw a white vehicle. She was crying.

"Nero... Nero was such a nice dog. He would have never hurt a flea."

Oh come on! I thought. Who ever heard of a dog that would never hurt a flea! Nonetheless, this was the first time I heard the dog's name. What kind of name was Nero for a dog anyway? The woman went on to say she saw a white car at around midnight and that she was almost sure she had seen the car before... around the neighborhood or somewhere else. As the story ended and I looked up from the television, I distinctly noticed that my wife and the kids were staring at me with suspicion growing in their minds.

Just as it was with my father's dinner table before me, my dinner table was the focus of family discussion and debate. Not surprising, my officious son breached the subject.

"I think the killer, whoever he is, lives right on this street."

My daughter finished off an asparagus spear and responded.

"First of all, I think *killer* is a bit harsh. After all, it was only a dog."

"Nero weighed at least a hundred fifty pounds—that's almost as much as Mom—it could have just as easily been a person."

The boy wasn't winning points with his mother through his adept use of comparison. My wife was quick to answer.

"First of all, I don't weigh anything close to one fifty, and second, just what makes you think it wasn't a person just passing *through* the neighborhood?"

"It was midnight. The only type person who would be driving through this dead neighborhood at midnight on a Monday night would be a person who lives here, someone coming *home* from somewhere."

Could he have been any more obvious? My intelligent daughter, however, took him to task.

"What about a person *leaving* the neighborhood? Maybe it was a complete stranger who was visiting someone on this street."

To my utter surprise, he had prepared for the question.

"I don't think so. Maria and I went around asking neighbors if they had anyone visiting late last night, and no one said they had company. We talked to everyone on the street except at four places where no one was home."

He hadn't gotten my permission to knock on people's doors! Besides, what about this girl?

"Who's Maria?"

"Oh! She was Nero's owner. Her father is a news editor for TV. I thought you all knew. His name's always on the credits."

You'd think *Dan the newsman* was her father. I could not understand why the man had been so emotional on the midday news. It was as if he had some sort of personal relationship with the dog. But what about my son? Why was he so involved in the matter?

"You like this girl or something?"

"No, we're just friends. I'm sure you'd remember her if you saw her. We were in kindergarten together. We just decided together that we were going to investigate until we find the coward who ran over her dog and just drove away."

Coward? I could have confessed to my family, but after all the name-calling and cruel assumptions people were making about the person who drove the car, I wasn't about to subject myself to the abuse. No, better to remain silent and just let the whole incident blow over, but only if I could thwart the efforts of the two would-be-detectives.

"Look, I don't want you two knocking on any more doors around here, understand? Who knows? You could get yourselves kidnapped or something."

As usual my wife disagreed.

"Honey, I think it's good at their age for them to exercise their critical thinking skills to the fullest extent. I don't see anything wrong with letting them investigate during daytime hours as long as they're careful."

Actually, she was right. I mean, he was a twelve-year-old. How could he possibly trip up or outwit an accomplished operator like me with my obvious profound mental capability? I had nothing to fear from him. He was a kid, after all. What could he know about investigation?

"Okay Columbo—you and Nancy Drew can do whatever you want, but I want your schoolwork and chores completely done before you even think about knockin on any doors or asking questions, okay?"

"Sure, Dad."

But he had only just begun.

"Uh Dad?"

"What?"

"Well, I'm going to need the keys to your car. It's just a routine check. When Maria and I counted, there were only eight white cars or vans on the block, and you have one of them."

I was glad I had gone through the trouble to rent a car exactly like the one I was having fixed, but still, what if he discovered the car wasn't mine?

"Let me tell you something, Son. Normally, my keys would be yours for the asking, but if you're going to exercise your critical thinking skills like your mother said and investigate, you have to realize that you've gotta play by a set of rules that respects other peoples' rights to privacy. You can't just tell me *I'm going to need the keys to your car* and expect me to hand em over to you. That's not how it works in the real world."

"Dad, I already know that. In the real world, I would need a restraining order."

My daughter laughed, amused.

"No, you mean *subpoena.*"

My wife broke in.

"Actually, in the real world, he would need a *search warrant* issued from a judge predicated on just cause. But then, he could simply ask to search the car, and if his father had nothing to hide, he'd let him."

The boy turned back to me.

"*May* I have your keys please, Dad?"

"Sure... after you do the dishes and take out the garbage and feed the dog and mop the floor."

The additional chores kind of took the wind out of his scrawny sails, but shortly thereafter, even as he diced his red jello into tiny pieces, he rebounded. He even had a notepad.

"Do you know exactly what time you got home on Monday night?"

"What do you mean by *exactly*?"

Fortunately my wife answered for me.

"It was definitely before midnight. Had to be around ten-fifty. I know that cuz I always check the clock the moment he walks in the door. I got into the habit of doing it when he used to work nights."

I could see him scribbling something down, but I didn't have my glasses so I couldn't read it. Still, based on what the one witness had said—that she saw a white car screeching its tires as it drove away at midnight—he should have eliminated me from his silly little list of suspects. But just in case he wasn't quick enough to figure it all out, I thought I'd help him a bit.

"Now what time did the woman down the street say she saw the car leaving?"

My daughter looked up from her coffee.

"She said it was midnight. She said she was sure it was midnight."

Smugly, I looked back over to my son.

"Will you still be needing my keys?"

"Yeah I will, Dad... but don't worry. It's just routine stuff."

They weren't in any of my usual places when I checked the next morning, not on the computer desk, not on the entertainment center, not in my drawer. I couldn't find them anywhere. That's when I began to worry. The last time I remembered having my glasses on was Monday night as I started to drive home, and I couldn't recall ever seeing or having them since.

Maybe I left them at the coffee shop. That I could check. No, maybe they fell off when I was out there checking the dog! That had to be it. My first inclination was to go to the spot out there to check for them or for what may have been left of them, but I was too big a fan of Columbo and all the other television detectives: how many times did people get caught or entrapped because, for insecurity or for some other reason, they just had to return to the scene of the crime? I didn't even *drive* over the spot anymore.

Still, if someone found those *Giorgio Armani* frames out there, they could use them to link me to the event. The link to me would be inevitable, but not if I quietly and expeditiously replaced the glasses with an exact copy before I was ever questioned.

I was alone. My wife was at work and the kids were at school. I started to call our optometrist, but even as I searched for his number, I realized it was 12:15. The midday news was on! The TV screen and volume came up midway through a story on another White House scandal followed by the usual holiday commercials, but when the news returned, there was Dan.

In a follow-up to the story of Nero the dog, the victim of a cruel and vicious vehicular slaying, the family is asking the killer to do the right thing, to come forward and take responsibility for the horrible and senseless deed. In a recently released statement they say, "in the event that the morally-bankrupt, despicable little coward does not have the decency turn himself in, we are also asking the community to come together to find the killer." Anyone with any information or suspicion of who the killer might be is being asked to call the number listed below.

Despicable little coward? You would think the censors would disallow anyone from calling names like that on TV! But then again, I forgot they had been sleeping for the past thirty years. The coverage wasn't over. Next came a shot of a pimply-faced teen-aged boy who spewed spiteful virulence as a caption below named him, "Michael—Nero's owner."

It's wrong! And the ###hole who did it's gonna pay. It's not over. If the killer's out there watching, he might as well turn himself in now. We know who he is and he's not gonna get away with it. We're gonna prove it and make him pay!

Click. It didn't seem to be blowing over. I did realize however, that calling my local optometrist wasn't a good idea. If the glasses became a public issue, he'd probably feel compelled to come forward. However, I had to solve the dilemma with the glasses before my wife and the kids got home. That's when I decided to drive over the extra one hundred ten miles to the next major city located safely outside the local television market.

It wasn't a bad drive, actually. It gave me a chance to think about the whole situation that had so suddenly overtaken and overwhelmed me. Had I done anything wrong? I mean, I did hit the dog, but I literally did everything in my power to help him. Then why was I so reluctant to admit the truth to everyone?

It was because the public had already made up its mind. Even as I was filling up my gas tank before leaving, the attendant asked me if I had seen the front page of the newspaper. A large picture of Nero was featured above a caption which read "Nero the Hero." Apparently the story that followed detailed a supposedly true anecdote from years past in which Nero saved little Maria's life by pushing her out of the path of an errantly driven car.

"Nero knew traffic safety," the article asserted, "The driver was at fault. He ran over the dog intentionally. Nero would have never crossed the street without looking both ways." The gas station attendant, a twenty-something Gilligan look-alike, interjected a surprising comment of his own.

"They need ta find that idiot, throw him on the freeway at five o'clock and let us all watch to see how tough *he* is when he's up against a car. Oh to be the driver of that car!"

I halfheartedly tried to defend the *presumably innocent* driver.

"Maybe it was an accident..."

"Yeah, and maybe owners of this station'll decide to take a smaller profit to give me a big fat raise, and maybe they'll lower the price of gas cuz they think you're payin too much, and maybe..."

I had left him standing there spouting off an unending list of *maybes*, certain then that the public wasn't even willing to consider the possibility, however absurd, of the driver's innocence or non-culpability.

Beyond that, I could not begin to understand the hate and anger evinced from people who neither knew anything about the dog nor the reported details of the accident before Tuesday afternoon. Even as I was leaving town, persons calling into a local radio talk show were discussing the so-called *Tragedy of Nero*.

One woman said she feared for her children in a city where a "monster like that is running around free." Her comment was followed by a suggestion from a man with a Southern twang in his voice who called for "an old fashioned lynchin." The self-absorbed, hot-tempered female commentator, instead of being the voice of reason, only attempted to stir things up further.

I realized the station probably needed to sell advertisements and fight the never-ending battle for ratings, but the woman actually asked other callers if they thought a lynching was in order. That's when I stopped blaming the public who, whether they realized it or not, were also victims—only victims of the ignorant ilk—persons manipulated by self-righteous, seemingly good and fair-minded people who sat behind desks in editorial offices and newsrooms.

They could not excuse their degradation of the public by claiming an obsequious form of innocence and a professed desire to report the truth. Without a doubt, every one of them was aware of the awesome power in the printed, visual and electronic media. However, before I could ever make a public complaint, I had to prepare for the certainty of further investigation and questioning.

Once I got to that city out of the immediate media market, I found a phone book and located a *Get your glasses and be out in an hour* place where, after about three hours, I walked out with an Armani pair identical to those I had lost.

Worn out by the long drive, I took a nap when I got home only to be awakened by the sound of my son shuffling through my closet as he rifled through my clothes and shoes.

"What are you doing in there, Son?"

Startled, he tucked a black beanie cap and a pair of shoes under his arm.

"I, I was just going to borrow these things, Dad. You don't mind, do you?"

I eyed him suspiciously.

"You could have *asked* me."

"That's what I'm doing. Can I?"

What could I say? Then when I finally got up, I found out that he had invited a guest to dinner, a girl even.

So this was Maria, a twelve year-old who dressed like she was fifteen and a half, if not sixteen. It all seemed innocent enough... until we began to eat. Maria began the examination.

"Did you ever see Nero? Do you remember ever seeing my dog?"

"I've seen a lot of dogs. Can't tell one from another."

It was obvious she had prepared a whole list of questions.

"Haven't I seen you in glasses before? Don't you wear glasses?"

"Yes."

"Giorgio Armani's are my favorites. Is that the kind you have?"

"Yes."

She looked over at my son, beckoning assistance.

"Dad, do you know where your glasses are?"

"Yes."

"Where are they?"

I paused for a moment, toying with the two, before slipping my hand into the pocket of my shirt, pulling out the glasses and putting them on my nose.

"Right here. Why?"

They looked at each other in astonishment and then fell disconcertedly silent. In fact, ten minutes went by before my son challenged me again. He displayed a bright shiny dog tag, about the size of a silver dollar.

"You ever see this, Dad?"

"No, never. What is it?"

Maria broke in.

"It's the tag that was around Nero's neck. It was found in—"

Realizing he was treading dangerous ground, my son didn't let her finish.

"The tag was found in your car. It was under one of your seats."

I couldn't believe my ears!

"Waitaminute! What were you doing in my car?"

His face flushed. He stammered, struggling to mouth the words.

"I, my... You were sleep and I, my homework, I thought I left my language arts homework assignment in your car last week and I was looking for it."

I was trembling in an attempt to subdue my anger in the presence of our dinner guest.

"You, you *searched* my car without my permission?"

In spite of being shaken, he resolved himself to maintain the dubious premise.

"I didn't! I didn't search your car. I only wanted to find my homework. I had a paper due today. Why are you so mad? You let me go in your car all the time."

By this time, my half-embarrassed wife, always my son's surrogate, intervened in his behalf.

"He's right. You've never had a problem with him going in your car before."

It was time to dispense with the cloak and dagger business and the subtlety. They had already questioned me about the dog and the glasses, and we all knew why. Still sneering at him, I made an answer to my wife.

"Come on. Everyone at this table *knows* what he was after. I mean, what would his homework be doing sitting in my car? He thinks I hit that dog and he was in there trying to find evidence against me! Just like he searched my *closet* this afternoon!"

Hearing this, my wife looked over at my son in disapproval.

"When you searched his car this morning, did you do it because you thought he was the one who hit Nero?"

He stuck to his story, though he seemed a bit less confident.

"I was looking for my homework."

By this time, Maria was ready to resume the interrogation.

"What about Nero's dog tag? What was it doing in your car?"

"First of all, I've never seen that tag before, and second: it wasn't in my car. I could bet my life it."

I could be so definitive because I knew something they didn't. Even if the tag came off when I was trying to help the dog, even if it stuck to my clothing and fell off in my car and rolled under my seat, even if I hadn't seen it when I searched my car Monday night, the tag would not have been in the car they searched Wednesday morning.

Unknown to all of them, it was a *different* car. I was the only one who knew I rented it. If the tag had somehow stuck to me that night, it would have still been in the original car.

"Dad, the only way that tag would have gotten in your car is if you were there at the scene that night and you accidentally carried it away with you."

It didn't make any sense. It seemed absurd, but it was the only reasonable explanation.

"If it was in that car, you put it there."

The suggestion prompted an immediate protest from my wife.

"Honey, let's not be so distrustful. Maybe you don't know how it got there, but you can't accuse your own son of trying to *frame* you!"

"He had to put it there. That's the only way it would have been in there!"

Maybe I shouldn't have been so adamant. As I looked over at my son across the table, his feelings seemed genuinely hurt. In fact, he was almost in tears. I wanted to apologize, but apologies in such situations usually resulted in emotional outbursts, and I knew he didn't want a girl to see him cry.

My daughter however, who had been carefully listening through all the questioning, was ready to explore the car search further. Her questions were directed toward my son.

"When you searched the car this morning, where you alone?"

"Yes. I was alone at first."

"What do you mean by *at first*? Did someone help you later?"

He looked over at Maria.

"Well, Maria and Michael came over to pick me up for school, and they came out and helped me at the last part."

Michael, now why did that name sound familiar? She wiped the milk mustache and continued.

"Michael's Maria's brother, isn't he?"

Maria answered.

"Yeah, he's my brother. He's the one who found the tag."

"Well, isn't he the same kid who used to always leave his bike out in the street about four years ago till it got run over by a certain *no-drivin-grown-up* who lived further down?"

I knew what my daughter was getting at, but Maria didn't, yet.

"Yeah, I think I remember when his bike got hit. I was eight."

"Do you remember that your brother egged the grown-up's house and said that someday he'd make that grown-up pay for smashing his bike?"

While my son was already on board, Maria was still paddling fast to catch up.

"Yeah, I think I remember that."

"Good. And do you remember who the grown-up was?"

Ship ahoy! She was there! And there was no need for her to answer. *I* was the no-driving grown-up who crimped her brother's bike, and it was very possible that her brother Michael—the same ugly kid who said he knew who the killer was on the midday news—had slipped that dog tag under my seat to subject me to public condemnation and reproach as payback.

Notwithstanding, nothing could be proven, but it was enough to shed doubt on the one piece of evidence that would have placed me at the scene of the accident. Thus with the dog tag matter and the concern about the glasses behind us, the family plus Maria were able to finish dinner in the spirit of peace and facility.

It wasn't until shortly before the eleven o'clock news that I began to feel apprehensive again, but I was almost certain that, in all the time that had passed since Monday, public interest had diminished and the story was old news. No one cared about that dog anymore. More of the White House scandal, please!

But five minutes before the news was over, even as my little family crowded around the TV, ol biased-for-whatever-reason Dan the newsman found a way to dredge up the stale old story again.

Just this afternoon, the family of Nero the dog, the tragic victim of a drive-over, asked the community for whatever they could muster to help find the killer, and tonight a woman has come forward. Unwilling to give her name for fear of repercussions to her own pets, she is a 911 operator who claims the killer called her Monday night to boast about striking the animal with his car...

Dan paused a moment, apparently distracted by an electronic device in his ear.

This just in. Reportedly, the station has a copy of the tape that we'll be broadcasting momentarily. At this time we'd like to advise our audience about the nature of the tape which may be graphic and may contain objectionable language. Parents with young children are encouraged to excuse them to another room for the duration of the broadcast. I believe we're ready. This is the 911 call from Monday night at 10:45:

"May I have your name please?"

"No! I've done my part! Just let the dog die!"

A printed transcript of the call appeared at the bottom portion of a screen covered with a warm family portrait of Nero, and yet when the cameras cut back to Dan, he was daubing his eyes with a white handkerchief.

I'm sorry, but I... I just wasn't prepared for such cruelty without the slightest hint of remorse.

The female news commentator broke in.

And he's still out there at large, and that's why we here at the station join the family in calling the community together to bring this cold-blooded killer to justice.

She was interrupted by a call from the mayor who said he was willing to provide limited services from the city in an effort to bring about justice.

That's when I just turned the TV off. Lights flashing through the living room window caused me to go out the front door and glance down the street where no less than four news vans were in front of Nero's house. There were also two city police cars parked as the officers had cordoned off the street with wide yellow emergency tape.

"We've got a circus out there! You wouldn't believe how many idiots are out there!"

My daughter peeked from the corner of the window, agreeing.

"This is stupid! All this over a dog! You'd wish they'd put so much effort into solving all the unsolved murders of *people* in this city!"

My son, who had watched the news broadcast, opened the door and scanned down the street.

"They're late. The trail's already cold. If anyone is going to solve this crime, it'll be me. I'm the only one who can put it all together."

I didn't watch the noon news the next day in protest. In fact, it was only by protesting in this manner that I regained a sense of normalcy. Somehow I had blocked the entire incident of Monday night out of my mind, and by doing this, I could stand or sit by dispassionately as I heard whiners, sickos and would-be know-it-alls discuss the person who must have run down the dog. I could even lend an opinion of my own if the commentary went too far awry.

"I think she probably would have come forward if it hadn't been for all the negative publicity."

"Are you kidding? That voice was a man's. A homosexual, probably with AIDS, and he's taking out his frustration on poor helpless animals. I feel sorry for him, actually. He needs mental help."

"Did you read the paper this morning? Just yesterday three more dogs were hit, and four cats. That brings the total to almost twenty in the last week. I don't know why they can't catch this guy."

It seemed people were talking about Nero and "the crazed animal assassin" everywhere I went. While it was disconcerting, I was absolutely astonished at how quickly and how completely the news media could villainize a person.

Certainly someone involved in the process, certainly at least one person, had to consider the grave impact the story would have on a real person's life for no other reason than the manner in which it was reported. By the same token, they had made a hero out of a big, sloppy dog who didn't have the good sense to stay out of the street when he saw car headlights coming.

Perhaps there was a time when news reporting was a responsible and respectable profession, but that was before technology, cutthroat competition, politics and sensationalism robbed the industry of its conscience. As might be expected, before the day was over, my cool, detached dispassion yielded to smoldering anger.

"She should sue him when they find him. That was the worst impersonation of Julia Childs I have ever heard."

And that waiter thought I was sneering in agreement as I wrote in that ten percent tip with great satisfaction. Criticize *my* impersonation, would he? Anyway, I arrived home to find my family crowded around the TV awaiting the six o'clock news. Click.

"Hey Dad! We were *watching* that!"

"Not anymore. I'm tired of the news. There's just too much news in the world. Half the stuff we don't need to know, and the other half doesn't matter because it's biased and irresponsible. For those reasons, this family is going to boycott all news from this day on."

My daughter may have gone along with it without a problem. My son, after I threatened him with bodily harm, would have initially resisted on principle and would have acquiesced. But my wife, probably a direct descendant of Lot's wife, was addicted to the filth. She turned the TV back on with the second remote.

"*You* can boycott the news for whatever your reasons are, but I don't have a problem with it. Go read or something until dinner, but we'll be watching the news in here. Just don't ask us what happened."

As I rolled peas with my fork, examining them, I was dying to ask if there was any more news on the Nero story, but I wouldn't. After all, I was only thirty minutes into my boycott. Still, being the clever and resourceful guy I was, I had but to pull a few strings to discover anything I wanted to know.

Sometimes I felt a little guilty about being such a master of manipulation, but while my wife and daughter had their beauty and my son his youth, I had the power of my mind. My buddies over the years had always admired me for my silky smoothness.

"So... see, it's just like I said. Same ol stuff on the news. They report the same stories day in and day out. There wasn't anything new or interesting on there at all, was there?"

My wife smiled mischievously, almost seductively.

"Oh yeah... there was something new, and it was very interesting."

"You're just saying that. I don't wanna know."

I was dying to know. Maybe I should have made it a silent, private boycott and kept it to myself. What if there was something incriminating on there? Just then I noticed that my son was staring at me, had been staring since he sat to dinner.

"What are you looking at?"

"Your finger. How long has it been cut like that?"

I quickly returned my left hand to my lap, answering curtly.

"Bout a week. I cut it doing yard work."

Uh-oh, I had lied. I had always detested lying, opting instead to be something less than precise in situations where the truth was incriminating.

"Or maybe it *wasn't* yard work. I don't go around documenting every time I get a scrape or a cut. What does it matter, anyway?"

He opened a thick manila folder and pulled a leaf of notebook paper covered with writing and scanned the page. Then he pulled another page with a Polaroid picture attached. Unclipping the picture, he gave it to me.

"I have stuff not even the police have. Whoever the killer was, somehow he had a cut on his left hand."

Now how could he know that from a poorly angled picture of a third or half footprint?

"You see the partial bloody footprint of a left shoe?"

"Yeah, so what?"

"Look to the left about a half inch over. What do you see?"

"Nothing."

"Oh, I forgot!"

He handed me a 3-inch magnifying glass that had been in his front pocket.

"Do you see the blood drops to the left of the footprint?"

"Yeah, I see something, but it still doesn't tell me that the killer had a cut on his left hand."

He handed me another picture.

"This one shows a trail of blood drops leading away from the scene. The car had to be parked in the spot where they end."

Then he offered a third photo.

"And there are the black marks in the spot where the car screeched its tires. I'm still trying to match the marks to the tire patterns of one of the white cars on the street and to the one on Nero's body."

The kid was thorough if nothing else.

"So?"

"So the killer had a cut on his left hand just like you have on yours. Maybe the dog bit him or something."

I didn't have to look up to realize that my wife was staring from my hand to my face and back to my hand with this *I don't wanna know—don't tell me you hit that dog!* look on her face. Nonetheless, I did have *some* of the facts on my side.

Little Iscariot had turned on me, had made me a hostile witness, but I was prepared to play hard ball with the kid. After all, when I played little league, I hit a guy with a hard ball once, on purpose.

"So Sherlock, tell me something: If some horrible, irresponsible, devil worshiper really did hit that big ugly dog with his or her car and then drove over him, don't you think the car would have sustained any physical damage?"

Closing the manila envelope, he seemed stumped. Strike right down the middle.

"That's the only part I haven't figured out yet. If you had hit him with your car, you would've needed a new front end."

"But as you can see, my car's just fine—which means it wasn't *my* car."

He was beginning to back away from the plate.

"Well yes, but—"

"And then there's the time line. A woman says she hears tires screeching and sees a car speeding away at midnight?"

"Un-huh."

"Well, your mom's my witness. She was here and she distinctly remembers me coming home at about 10:50. So your timeline is shot to bits."

He thought for a moment, but instead of re-gripping the oak, he grasped at straws.

"Maybe the woman's clock was fast. And maybe Mom says she remembers 10:50 because you told her that and it stuck in her head. A wife is never a reliable witness. Maybe you changed the clocks."

I had the count at full, but it was my daughter who pitched for the strikeout.

"Why don't you just give it up and go back to acting like a regular twelve year-old boy? All you've got is a folder full of useless junk. No solid evidence of anything. I mean, where's your dented-in car? Where's your eyewitness? If you don't have those, you have nothing!"

Suddenly his eyes lit up.

"Waitaminute! You remember the girl on TV tonight? The one who said she was working in the coffee shop the night Nero was killed?"

Apparently, this was a critical little piece I missed while boycotting the news. Awkward in my rare moment of ignorance, I sued to know more.

"What about her?"

"Well, she said she thinks she remembers the killer when he came in the coffee shop that night and used the phone. The 911 people said the call came from there."

It's no wonder I was uneasy about that secretive 911 service, and you would think details of emergency calls should be classified and kept in Washington or in Area 51, away from unsavory newshounds like Dan.

"Did she remember the woman coming in the shop?"

"She said it was a man. She said he wasn't good-looking or anything because his face was just too average to remember. All she said she remembered was that he was a *disgusting old sex pervert*, that he leered at her and tried to look in her blouse."

She said I was old? That's what I got for being nice and not looking directly at the big zit on her forehead! Well, at least the description Polyphemus' daughter provided pointed *away* from me. I wasn't old, after all, and I wasn't a disgusting sex pervert. I just couldn't understand why my wife was staring at me again with growing suspicion. My son however, hadn't finished. He swung for the center field fence.

"Dad, I'd like you to go over to that coffee shop with me when she's working. That way she could say whether it was you or not. If she says it wasn't you, then I'll scratch your name from my list of suspects. And I promise I won't bother you again."

The nerve of that kid! But now I was mad!

"What *list*? How many names are on that list? One! *That's* how many! You've thought it was me and only me from the start! That's not how you run an investigation, Son. If police in the *real* world kept little one-suspect lists like yours, they'd never catch any criminals! The trails would get cold and the real criminals would be getting away!"

He answered.

"Your name's not the only name on my list. There's another name on there."

"Oh yeah? Who?"

"Can't tell. Can we go to the coffee shop after dinner?"

I suddenly realized the boy was behaving in a manner that was unhealthy for a kid. His sister was right. It was time for him to go back to being a regular twelve-year-old again. He was obsessing over this road kill thing. While I appreciated his dedication and all his hard work, it was warping his personality, so I had to put an end to it.

"No, I won't go to that coffee shop with you, and as a matter of fact, because I'm the master and head of this house, which makes me something equivalent to police chief and district attorney, I'm calling an end to this investigation, closing all the files and labeling the case *unsolved*. From this moment on, I don't want to hear another word or question about that dog murder, that dog incident down the street. Do I make myself clear?"

He seemed crushed, but he would get over it in time. My wife on the other hand, decided to take up an appeal in his behalf.

"I'll give it to you. You're the master, the head, the police chief and the district attorney, but let's just say I'm the judge hearing the case. Now, the police chief and the district attorney can't just up and close a case once it's gone to trial. Only the judge can do that. And by the way, instead of taking this whole thing so personal, I think you should be proud of your son. He's done a very thorough job. That's why I think we should let him give it his best shot to solve the thing."

I gave her one of my mean, evil, *I'll get you back for this* looks, but she ignored me. I remained firm.

"I'm not playing this little game. I am *not* going down to that coffee shop to stand in a line-up for some drug addict, spaced-out teenager."

By this time, my wife was scanning through the documents in my son's manila folder.

"You don't have to go if you don't want to, but I'm sure you realize that your refusal to go to the coffee shop does make it a little easier for someone to believe that it was *you* who hit that dog."

I had a friend who was a lawyer, or at least he said he was. All *I'd* ever seen him do was hang out in a downtown restaurant and shake dice at the bar. All the regulars called him "Santa" because they could always take him for enormous amounts of money. He was tall, brown-haired and in relatively okay shape.

In spite of being in his early fifties and looking in his late sixties, some of the women regulars actually thought he was good-looking. I wasn't sure, but I think he did probate and divorce, a regular legal lamprey. We usually debated the news of the day during the time I used to frequent the place, but I hadn't seen him in a while. Anyway, I went over there, thinking I could butter him up in order to get some free legal advice.

I started out by letting him take fifteen dollars from me at dice, and then I let him win an argument, the first he had ever won against me. And just then, just as he sat there with his eyes rolled back savoring the counterfeit victory, I hit him up for a legal opinion.

"Have you been following that story on Nero, that Saint Bernard?"

His face ignited with intense interest.

"Are you kiddin? That's a very fascinating story! What's your take on that?"

I could tell that, intoxicated by his only victory in five years, he was ready to launch into another debate. Still, I couldn't believe how easily he had been hooked as I went after the advice, only indirectly at first.

"Well, I think there's a whole lot more to the story than what we've seen on television."

"Are you crazy? That nut's been on a killing spree! According to the last numbers I saw, it's something like 48 dogs and over 30 cats. No, I think it's more like 65 cats."

"What if this guy hit Nero, but he didn't hit any of the other pets? What would you say then?"

He sipped the chardonnay as he considered the question.

"He's still guilty. He hit Nero, then he backed up and ran him over. He'd be guilty even if he had nothing to do with any of those other incidents."

"What if he hit Nero and left the scene and then maybe someone *else* ran over the dog as it was there lying out in the street?"

He raised his eyebrows, cocked his head slightly, pursed his lips and nodded.

"That could've happened, but then if it had happened like that, then why hasn't the coward come forward and explained his involvement limited to just initially hitting the dog?"

"What if he didn't want the negative publicity? I mean, did you hear what they were saying about him early on? I think they called him a monster and devil worshiper."

He smiled with a degree of sadistic satisfaction. That's when I knew he knew.

"Who knows, maybe that's what he is. Guilty, guilty, guilty."

He laughed and continued.

"He should have come forward and taken his lumps. At least it'd be over by now."

"Well, I'm sure he had his reasons. Anyway, what about the negative television stuff? Can't he sue for slander of defamation of character or something?"

"Did anyone say his name? Did anyone specifically call him a devil worshiper by name?"

I had to reflect on the telecasts for a while. While no reporter had actually mentioned me by name, the broadcasts had prejudiced the public against any person who might have thought to confess his involvement. I couldn't put my finger on it, but it seemed the news people had injured me in some way.

"No, but if this guy had come forward to explain, he would have already been convicted by the media and everyone would doubt his innocence and think he was a devil worshiper and a killer and monster and all those other things they said about him."

When I looked back toward my predatory friend, his eyebrows were furrowed as he gazed up toward the ceiling. Then he answered.

"I don't remember the exact verbiage, but reporters are usually pretty careful about not saying things that'll get them or the station into trouble. A lot of them tiptoe along the edge of legality. I think it'd just be pretty tough to prove any kind of malice or actual injury. I mean, you're a nobody. Who knows you?"

Thanks a bunch. Waitaminute! He said *you* instead of *him*. Now I could be more direct.

"What do you think? You think if I just lay low this thing will blow over?"

"With over a hundred people screaming vengeance for their loved pets that they think you *killed*? I wouldn't count on it."

"What should I do?"

He ordered more wine for both of us and continued in a whisper.

"First of all, can you absolutely prove that you *didn't* run over Nero?"

"Yes. My wife knows what time I got home that night."

He frowned.

"Wife's a lousy witness. Anything else?"

No, nothing. A lot of good it did talking to a lawyer. He probably *wanted* to see me in trouble anyway. That way my wife would divorce me and he'd be in business, and then some grieving nut out there would shoot me and he could double-dip by doing my probate as well. As horrible as it sounded, it was the natural thought process of the depraved and devious legal mind.

Of course, by this time I was onto him and I had to fight with him in order to obtain and pay the bill. I wasn't as conniving as a lawyer, but I wasn't about to let him sell the story to the *Enquirer* either. Throwing down a crisp fifty, I put him on notice.

"Of course you know that, because I paid the bill, I'm entitled to attorney-client privileges. You can't say anything about what I told you."

He laughed, amused.

"I'm bound by a code of legal ethics. I've already heard too much. I couldn't have said anything anyway."

Hearing that, I snatched the fifty and the check back up just before the eager bartender could grab it.

"On second thought, why don't we just split this one right down the middle, even though you drank one more glass of wine than I did."

My daughter phoned me on my cell phone as I drove home.

"Daddy, the garage called. They said your *car's* ready?"

The idiots! I told those scavengers at the lot not to call my home phone number!

"Oh! Thanks. Just getting a little tune-up, that's all. Thanks, I'll go right on over."

Click. I wondered if she had figured it out. I had asked those dunderheads on three separate occasions specifically not to call me at home. I had even given the buzzard's boss a tip to ensure discretion, and now they had blown the whole thing!

I tried to call my daughter back in an attempt at damage control, but the line was busy. She was probably on the phone with Dan the newsman even then. Or maybe she was on a conference call with Trial TV or the newspapers. Maybe the flock at the shop figured it out and beat her to the punch. And to think she betrayed her father only to have been scooped by buzzards!

Feeling a little tentative and self-conscious as I pulled onto the lot, I drove through the roll-up door of the body shop without slowing or stopping, at once sending the disorderly flock squawking in protest and scrambling in all directions.

My repaired car sat in a corner, the numbered triangular cube which designated it car "97" still resting on its roof. My cousin's ancient avian friend was the first to wobble over after I exited the car.

"I s'pose ya heard the news. There was a break-in at this garage a night ago yesterday. And it look like someone was up in your car all up in your glove box."

He bit the tip of the pencil-thin cigar and lit the end.

"Far as I can see, nothin was broken and nothin was missin, unless ya had some important papers I don't know about or somethin'."

Skeptically, I walked over to my car and peered into the lowered front window on the driver's side. Everything appeared normal, but it was too good an opportunity to forego.

"I don't understand it. How could you guys let someone break into the garage? I, I feel *violated*."

Then I played my hand.

"Doesn't that mean I'm entitled to a discount? I think I read somewhere that break-ins are a 25% reduction? On my bill?"

For a moment, I thought he was going to hit me. I mean, I was sure I could have beaten him up if it came to blows. He was probably in his sixties after all, but he had this real mean look in his eyes as he closed on me, foaming at the mouth and chomping that smelly cigar.

"Full price."

"Okay! Okay, I'll pay. Full price."

I counted my blessings as I drove away. At least no one at the garage suspected me, and they even made arrangements for the rental to be returned. However, my worries about my daughter's suspicion resurfaced as I neared the house. Surely she had pieced the whole night and the events that followed together in the hours since the garage made the disclosure about my car being fixed.

What was I going to say to her? She probably thought I was an iniquitous, unrepentant and unapologetic killer. Certainly she had shared the discovery with my son and wife who were no doubt just as condemnatory. I walked into the door leading from the garage braced for certain assault.

"Hi Honey! How was your day?"

My *Stepford* wife was even cooking a full meal in an apron.

"Fine. Where's the girl?"

"In her room on the phone. She made the couscous."

Maybe my daughter hadn't been suspicious at all. Maybe I had worried myself sick for nothing.

"Where's the boy?"

"Skateboarding. He did all his chores."

Finally, it seemed my comfortably boring life was returning to normal. As I sat at the dining room table, discretely scanning articles from the front page, I noticed a distinct anomaly.

"Why the extra setting? Who's coming for dinner?"

"*You* remember Maria? The girl from down the street? She denies it, but I think she has a slight crush on our son."

I remembered Maria all right. Nero's owner. Somehow, I didn't think it was just my son and dinner she was after. I was sure she and my son were up to something, a notion that was confirmed the moment they sat at the table, each with a microcassette recorder. We had barely begun dinner when Maria resumed the questioning.

"Sir, what kind of tennis shoes do you wear?"

It seemed direct enough.

"Nikes, but I'm sure you two already know that. I saw him checking my closet."

"Yes, I was just wondering if you knew that the bloody shoeprint at the scene was made by a Nike shoe about the same size you wear."

I was still at odds about the credibility of a bloody shoeprint in the first place.

"Look, the dog wasn't shot or stabbed. How would there be any blood for a footprint anyhow?"

She opened a manila folder she had placed in her lap.

"Well, when Nero was first hit, the car cracked his arm and the bone broke through the skin. He bled a lot there and from a deep cut on the side of his head. The killer must have got out the car and went near to kick Nero or something because that's where he picked up the blood on his shoe."

Just then, as a complete surprise to me, my daughter came to my defense.

"Well, when you checked his shoes, was there any blood on the soles?"

My son responded.

"Not exactly. But that's because he probably walked through one of those muddy puddles in the back. The mud could have mixed with the blood and made it impossible to see."

I couldn't resist.

"Impossible? Well, you know what they say—blood's thicker than mud."

No one laughed. My son broke the uncomfortable silence.

"I *did* find one little brown spot on the shoe, one that could have been blood."

By this time, my daughter had taken up the argument in earnest. She leaned across the table in cross-examination.

"What do you mean, *could have been*? Was it blood or wasn't it?"

Recalcitrant, he answered.

"I said what I said. It looked like the spot coulda been *blood* on Dad's shoes."

"But then it *could have* been something else, right? Like ketchup or chocolate ice cream or radiator rust or something, maybe even something from the dog he stepped in out there?"

Turning away from her, he just ate another chunk of lamb, but she was only just beginning.

"Oh so you're gonna try'n ignore me? Well, here's something you *can't* ignore. Just before dinner, I talked to one of my friends who works at the coffee shop down the street. Well, she told me you and Maria were in there today. Why don't you tell Mommy and Daddy what you were doing in there?"

After a moment of silence, she turned to our dinner guest.

"Maybe *Maria* can tell us what you two were doing in there. Maria?"

Maria seemed a little irritated with my son despite of the so-called *crush* she was supposed to have on him. Her answer was almost angry.

"I told him it was a bad idea."

They exchanged sneers before she continued.

"He borrowed a photograph of your dad and took it down there to see if the lady who was there that night recognized him. I told him—"

My daughter didn't let her finish.

"What she say? Did she say our dad was the man who came in that night?"

Maria squirmed in the seat as she tried to formulate a good response.

"That picture didn't look anything like your dad. It was probably taken ten years ago when he was still young."

"*What* did the girl say? Just tell everyone what the girl said. Did she recognize him?"

Maria looked from my wife's face to mine and answered.

"No."

"Not did she just *not recognize* him. Didn't she say she had never seen him before in all her life?"

Maria bowed her head.

"Yes."

Completely satisfied with herself, my daughter concluded,

"If it ain't his face, then you've got no case."

As we enjoyed our chocolate mousse for dessert, my son started up again, this time asking a ridiculous question.

"Do you hate animals, Dad?"

"No."

"Do you hate dogs?"

"Of course not. I love dogs."

"Do you have a dog?"

He was headed somewhere, but I was beginning to lose my patience.

"Get to the point! You *know* we have a dog named Dick. I bought him myself. Paid a lotta money for him."

He dropped his spoon onto the table and turned toward me.

"Okay, have you ever beat Dick? You ever beat our dog?"

"No! Never!"

Never as far as I could remember off-hand, though I had screamed at him a lot lately. As my son thumbed through the manila envelope again, I just wanted to grab all that stuff he had and throw it into the fireplace.

"Do you remember what you did on April 4th of last year?"

I had no idea. What had he been doing? Keeping a *file* on me?

"No. Do you remember what *you* were doing on April 4th?"

He ignored the question and continued his line of inquiry.

"Do you remember planting tomatoes that day?"

I still couldn't understand where he was going.

"I remember planting tomatoes last year, but I don't know what day."

"And what happened within thirty minutes after you got your tomatoes in?"

Uh-oh! It was then that I remembered.

"I, I watered them, I guess."

He paused, almost smirking at me, before continuing.

"And you don't remember anything else?"

"Well, I don't know. I'd have to think about it."

He closed the folder.

"Didn't Dick go around and make it a point to dig up each of your tomato plants and tear them to pieces one by one? Do you remember that, Dad?"

"Well, yes. Yes, I guess that happened if you say so."

By this time, my wife, my daughter and Maria were hanging on his every word.

"You put a lot of work and money into those tomatoes that Dick tore up for no good reason. You were pretty mad, weren't you, Dad?"

"I, I was mildly upset, in a *controlled* way..."

"Well, what did you do?"

Using my napkin for the first time, I blotted the sweat on my forehead.

"I, well I had a few choice words for him, and I told him not to do it again in a loud voice."

"Weren't you so angry that you beat him?"

My wife, raising her eyebrows, sighed, appalled.

"Don't tell me you beat that poor dog!"

"No, I never beat him. I don't beat animals."

I couldn't believe this was my own son accusing me in this way. He was relentless.

"In your fit of rage, didn't you pick up a weapon, maybe a newspaper or something?"

"Fit of rage?!" Apparently, my daughter didn't like the way the whole conversation was going. Since my wife had appointed herself a kind of chairperson or judge over this dog matter, my daughter appealed to her mother.

"Mom, before we go any further with this (and because we have an outside dinner guest at the table), I need to talk to you in the kitchen."

Nodding, my wife agreed.

"Excuse us. We'll be back in a minute."

My son followed his mother and sister into the kitchen, leaving me sitting out there with Maria, a girl who I could tell hated me. Anyway, when the three returned about ten minutes later, I could tell my daughter wasn't happy. Obviously, my wife didn't buy her argument. No sooner had he sat did my son start at me again.

"Didn't you pick up a weapon or a rolled up section of the newspaper?"

My wife looked at me in my reluctance.

"Answer the question."

"Okay, okay! Yes, I picked up a newspaper."

Pleased with himself, my son continued.

"And didn't you beat Dick over and over with that newspaper?"

"No."

"Didn't you in anger strike him again and again and again?"

"No, I barely hit him once, and that was only to scare him."

"Didn't you threaten to *kill* him if he ever dug up any of your plants again?"

"Yeah, but it was a figure of speech like I might *beat* eggs or I might *whip* cream."

"Or you might *kill* a poor animal?"

He paused and returned to the alleged beating.

"On that day, did you ever hit him with that newspaper?"

"No."

He sighed, frustrated.

"Then what did you do?"

"I touched him. I touched him with it."

This time my wife intervened, again raising her eyebrows.

"You were mad, so you *touched* him with the newspaper?"

"Yeah, I didn't say how hard. I touched him kind of hard with it."

My daughter, who had been sulking about whatever happened in the kitchen, finally found her way back into the discussion.

"What I don't understand is: what does any of this have to do with whether or not Dad is the one who ran over that mutt in the first place?"

My son recoiled at the sound of the word.

"Mom! She said it! She said the *M* word! She shouldn't be saying that. You said just a minute ago she couldn't say it! It's an insult!"

Yet before my wife could respond, my daughter defended herself.

"What's wrong with *mutt*? I'll say it again, mutt, mutt, mutt. Nero was a mutt."

He looked back toward his mother.

"You said in the kitchen she couldn't say the *M* word just to be saying it. You said she'd need a good reason to use the *M* word. And she'd have to get your permission."

My wife looked toward the girl.

"He's right. Don't just say the *M* word to be saying it."

Smug and satisfied for having upset her mercurial brother, my daughter conceded.

"Okay, but I don't know what any of this has to do with whether or not Dad hit that mongrel in any case."

Maria responded.

"Don't you *see*?! He beats dogs! He hates dogs! And *that's* why he did it!"

My daughter laughed to herself.

"That's the stupidest thing I've ever heard. I don't think even *you* two believe that! You don't know what really happened, so you're trying to make everything fit into this little fairy-tale about Dad you dreamed up."

She scoffed at my son.

"And you! I can't believe you're trying so hard to pin this thing on your own father and not looking anywhere else!"

He glanced toward Maria and then back at his sister.

"Hey, I'm just trying to find out what really happened. Dad's just the number one suspect."

He sat back in the chair.

"Don't hate me. I'm only the messenger."

My daughter also sat back, rolled her eyes, sighed and then took another tack.

"Look, don't pretend you two don't know about all the awful things Nero did around this neighborhood. And the news is calling him a hero?"

The implication brought an immediate response from Maria.

"Nero *was* a hero! He saved my life!"

My daughter wasn't pulling any punches.

"I'll tell you what he was. He was a dog who should have been on a leash or locked in a backyard. Yeah, he got hit by a car, but what was a two hundred pound dog doing running free in the first place?"

"He got out that night. We didn't know."

"Don't give me that story, Maria. Nero ran the streets every night and we *all* knew it. Your grandfather has everyone who watches television believing Nero was such a great dog, but around this neighborhood they're saying something different. Nero was a *zero*! He crippled the Chihuahua across the street last year, last month he rammed the paperboy's bike, breaking the poor kid's arm, and then he knocked down the fence and got our next door neighbor's purebred Fila Brasilio pregnant—twice. He was no hero."

Maria just trembled there, biting her bottom lip, her composure dissolving.

"No one in this neighborhood even *liked* that dog. It was like the lawn lottery. We woke up every morning wondering who was going to have to clean up a giant pile of Nero's poop. We're all glad he's gone. If you're looking for someone to blame, blame yourself. Face it—Nero's *dead* because you and your family let him run wild in the streets. It's *your* fault."

That's when Maria lost it. Throwing first her arms and then her head onto the table, she wailed more pitifully than Polonius' daughter did, her shoulders shivering between discordant refrains. My son glared at his sister, his eyes expressing malice aforethought. Finally, he looked over to my wife who was at a loss for what to do.

"Mom, I think the three of us need to have another talk in the kitchen."

And so the three went, leaving me at the table with a volatile, hysterical twelve year-old who despised me. I didn't know what to do. Still, I was confused by something my daughter had said, so I hoped Maria could settle the matter.

"Maria?"

"Don't talk to me! I hate you! I hate your daughter!"

The little angel. Now just *where* was that rolled up section of newspaper I "touched" my dog with last summer?

"Maria, honey, I'm sorry if she upset you, but I was hoping you could tell me something."

"What?"

At least she had stopped crying.

"I thought your *father* worked for the news as an editor. Why did she say your *grandfather* made everyone think Nero was a hero?"

She still hadn't raised her head.

"*Both* of them work at the station. My father's the editor, and my grandfather's Dan the newsman. He's the one who bought Nero for me as a puppy."

There it was! At that very moment a climacteric connection was made for me. Answers to questions that had vexed me since that tragic Monday night became utterly perceptible. Finally, I understood why the irrelevant story aired in the first place.

Further, Dan's gushing performance when he first brought the story and his teary eyes after the 911 call fell into context. I understood at last, why a story about an ordinary dog that had been hit by a car hadn't died after almost a week and a half.

I understood the profound influence that not only the media, but individuals in the media, have in shaping public perception, in shaping public policy, in assigning public priorities and determining criminality and legal pursuit.

Yes I understood, but as I considered the haunting image of my tiny being standing in opposition to the media, as I saw myself in the shadow of an ever-advancing, monolithic, unconscionable machine with the heart of a beast, a composite charlatan with virtually unlimited access, intelligence and resources, as I considered the abject futility of resistance, I hung my head in recondite chagrin.

"Wake up, you two!"

My wife and children had finished their little conference and had returned to the table. Clearing her throat, my wife began.

"Maria, I think someone at this table has something to say to you."

Maria snapped up as my daughter, squirming a little in her seat, hesitated a moment before speaking in a quiet, non-modulated, resentful tone.

"Okay Maria, I wasn't trying to insult your family. I'm sorry if I hurt your feelings."

Maria sneered.

"You *should* be."

My daughter wanted to say something or come across the table, but she restrained herself in the glare of my wife's stern expression. Suffice it to say, the dinner was over. The moment was uncomfortable.

As far as I could discern, my daughter was mad at Maria, her brother and her mother; Maria was mad at me, my daughter and my son; my son was mad at his sister, me, and the girl at the coffee shop; my wife was mad at Maria, my daughter and me; and me—I was mad at the world, the manipulated American public, and the media.

While I was as big a champion of the First Amendment as anyone, I felt strongly that there was something fundamentally and ethically wrong about the new reporting process in my city, and indeed in cities all across the country.

So anyway, as Maria excused herself from the table and prepared to go home, I was the one person thoughtful enough to offer a polite goodbye.

"Maria, thanks for coming for dinner! It was fun! We hope you'll come back to have dinner with us again soon!"

"I'd rather kiss a pig."

Apparently, she wanted to follow in her mother's footsteps. I'd seen her father at shared school functions, after all.

Needless to say, acrimony was the theme during the next day. As neither my wife nor son would speak to me or my daughter, she and I became natural allies. And to think I had worried that the disclosure about my car being repaired would have made the girl suspect me!

Anyway, my daughter told me she was convinced that I hadn't run over that dog and that she was dedicated to helping argue my case. Like me, she was disgusted about the way the media had handled the event, and so she urged me to *go after* Dan the newsman, after Maria's father and after the rest of them. I certainly wanted to, but it seemed hopeless.

And yet I felt there was something basically wrong about a man and his son-in-law working in such influential capacities at the same news station, let alone the most-watched station in the market. Beyond that, while they had made Nero's incident a feature story, they had never disclosed publicly that they had hidden personal motivations, interests and agendas relating to the matter. It reeked rotten, but what was I going to do about it?

Well, I could have tried to ignore the irritation and bided my time as public interest waned, but someone out there was keeping a tally of animals killed in the streets and blaming the deaths on the driver of a white car curiously dubbed, *Piso'd Off*. There was even an Internet website listing dates, times and animals killed according to kind and breed.

And then I could have gone to a rival television station and launched a negative publicity campaign against Dan and his son-in-law, but that would have involved a public confession, and I didn't want to subject myself or my family to the persecution of notoriety under those circumstances. Besides, it would have appeared inconsistent if not foolish to use the media in an attempt to attack the media at large on ethical grounds.

Finally, though after much deliberating, I determined what I would do. I was going down to that station and I was going to have a showdown with ol unethical Dan, man to man, face to face, eyeball to eyeball. Initially, the telephone appointment secretary said Dan was too busy to meet any time in the next month, but when I identified myself as *Piso'd Off*, she put him on the line. Within a minute, we had scheduled a meeting for the next day in an obscure sandwich shop downtown.

Dinner that night was uncharacteristically quiet with all verbal exchanges limited to requests for second helpings of kiwi chicken and extra servings of artichoke salad. On the right side of the table sat my brooding son and on the left my smug daughter while my wife sat contemplating something at the tail of the table—naturally I was seated at the *head* of the table.

The tension in the room made breathing difficult for all of us despite the whirling of the overhead fan. Finally after thirty minutes of silence, my frustrated wife spoke out.

"Okay guys, this Nero business is wrecking our lives around here. Here's what we're going to do: tomorrow night at dinner, each of us will have a full five minutes to say whatever he or she wants to say about whatever happened to that dog or who did it, and that will be the last time any of us mentions that dog at this table ever again. You guys got that?"

My daughter and I were quick to consent, but my son hesitated.

"How about the day after tomorrow and ten minutes?"

"Five minutes tomorrow. Take it or leave it."

He took *it* right away from the table and into his bedroom, slamming the door behind him. My daughter provided the editorial.

"He's pretty smart for a twelve year-old. I have to admit that, but he's too hot-headed to ever solve anything."

It was the first time I was thirty minutes early for anything, but instead of going to the sandwich shop, I sat at a sidewalk table outside the coffee shop next door. The dark glasses were a perfect disguise, except they made it difficult to read the newsprint. Boycotting the news at home had made me realize my acute media addiction.

Since I began the boycott, whenever I was out of the house, I fiended for a media fix in the form of broadcast news, newspapers, newsmagazines or the round-the-clock loop newsreels. I didn't blame myself. I was the victim of an insidious new addiction predicated on the media-generated need to be constantly informed and updated about local, domestic and world events, events which would have meant nothing to me or anyone else fifteen years ago.

The general fixation all started with one news pimp from the South who had been enormously successful in developing the public obsession, and the rest of the mainstream media followed. I had never before considered the media's responsibility or culpability until I became a victim, and I was in the midst of all this cogitating when I noticed Dapper Dan standing out by the street, fifteen minutes early. He was talking to a couple of overweight cameramen who had a newsvan parked around the corner behind a hedge.

After giving them animated instructions, he pointed to the sandwich shop and went inside. Under those circumstances, I wasn't about to follow him. Instead, I went to my car and drove to a site about a mile away from the studio, and then I walked over to the station and disappeared into a shadow as I waited for him in the parking lot.

The dark glasses and a black beanie hat were an effective disguise. I actually scared *myself* as I walked past a large mirrored window.

Anyway, I watched him pull into the lot and park almost an hour later. Inconspicuously, I followed him right to the back door and waited for him to enter his access code before grabbing his shoulder.

"I'm sorry I stood you up, Dan, but I didn't want to be on the five o'clock edition."

He knew who I was. I could see him sizing me up. He was already writing the intro to the breaking story.

"I'm sorry you didn't trust me. I can assure you I went to the sandwich shop alone. There were no cameras. Won't you come in? We can talk in my private office."

I balked.

"Give me your word, for whatever it's worth. I don't want to be on any camera today."

"Scout's honor."

Some pledge. He probably was never a scout. Still, I followed him through a labyrinth of corridors going upstairs and downstairs, along narrow hallways and around corners until finally we sat in an upscale, modern room with a shiny mahogany desk and light jazz playing in the background.

Dan sat behind the desk and urged me to sit across from him in a comfortable leather-upholstered armchair. Sitting back, he squinted and spoke.

"So *you're* Piso'd Off?"

I took a deep breath and answered.

"If that's what you want to call me."

"What is your real name?

"I can't tell you that, not yet."

He smiled in an attempt to disarm me.

"So why'd you come here? I suppose you *want* something from me?"

"Yes, I do."

"Well, what is it?"

Sternly, I began.

"I want you to let Nero die. Let the story die."

"And why should I do that? Why should I let his killer go undiscovered and unpunished?"

"Because one—I didn't kill him. I hit him initially, but I never, never ran over him. And two—nothing you do is going to bring that dog back to life. I don't understand why you're doing this!"

He crossed his hands, steepling his index fingers.

"Because I have the *power* to do it. I have the power to reach out and punish Nero's killer."

By that time, I was becoming frustrated.

"Haven't you heard anything I've said, you idiot. I did *not* run over that dog!"

"That's what *you* say. I say something different, and fortunately I've got a hellava lot more power and credibility in this town than you do."

He picked up the phone and dialed a four-digit extension.

"He's *here*."

I knew the expensive cameras weren't coming in that office where I might damage them. The cameramen would be waiting outside the station, filming me as I left. I wanted to slug Dan. I imagined myself pounding his face over and over with my fist. I mean, really—what did I have to *lose*? The man would ruin me if he could. Yet despite thoughts of sanguinary retribution, I held myself back.

"You're a piece a crap in a suit! That's all you are."

Dan laughed.

"Is that the best you can do? I'll tell you what, little man. *You* talk, I'll listen. Give me one good reason why I should seriously consider anything you say and I'll call the cameras off. I promise."

Somehow that's when I forgot the philippic I had been rehearsing over the past week. The tortuous trip through the station, the posh office and the oh-so polished Dan in all his haughtiness—they had all angered and intimidated me, made me forget my well-planned vituperative speech. Knowing this, Dan laughed again.

"You've got your chance. I'm listening."

Trying to pull my thoughts back together, I began.

"Well, first of all, I have no respect for you. You are a liar and an unethical person. You—"

He interrupted.

"That's quite a comment from a man who drives his car over the bodies of animals for the thrill of it."

I stood.

"I didn't run over any dog and you *know* it! If you had checked the facts, you would have known it from the start! But you don't care. It's just a personal thing with you!

A power trip! You've *used* the news to advance a selfish personal agenda for you and your family!"

He seemed apprehensive. Perhaps he sensed I had a plan.

"I don't know what you're talking about."

"Oh, I know. I know it all. I know Nero was your *granddaughter's* dog, I know you bought him for her, but how many of your viewers out there know it? And what would they think of you if they knew you failed to tell them about your personal involvement in the story from the start?"

Speechless, the newsman knew how to maintain his cool under pressure, but I continued.

"And what if they knew that your son-in-law, the man who owned the dog, was the news editor at this station? What would your viewers say if they knew that? You see, Dan, you've *used* your viewers, you've manipulated the people of this city and your position at this station for your own personal ends. What would the owners of the station say if they knew *that*?"

He smiled.

"Nothing. Just what makes *you* think the people who own this station care about anything but ratings and the advertising dollars spent here? They don't even live in this town! What most of you out there don't realize is that this is a profit-motivated *business* here, not some benevolent group of do-gooders who give a damn! I'm not running for office."

I couldn't believe it was Dan talking! The same Dan who the whole city admired and trusted. Where were the cameras now? The *public* needed to hear what he had said. Taking another deep breath, I continued.

"I think you've been in the business too long. You've sold your soul for advertising dollars! And ratings! You've lost it. You and your ego need to get out to make room for someone who cares about reporting the truth."

When he laughed and cleared his throat, I realized that Dan was one of those people who loved hearing himself talk.

"You're so naïve. Do you think it's the job of any of us, anywhere all over the world, to tell the truth? Do you think that's what we're reporters of? The truth?"

"I always believed you guys *tried* to report the truth."

He sighed, shaking his head reproachfully.

"This is almost pointless with an idiot like you. We report *news*—that's what we do. Truth is a separate issue we leave to philosophers and the clergy. But at the bottom line, we sell news for profit. Ultimately, we *do* control public perception. We create the news, develop it, package it and sell it to you morons, for a profit."

He continued.

"What does the public know? What does anyone care?"

Satisfied with his bare-knuckles speech, he concluded.

"We attempt to be accurate on the facts where we can, but rumor sells, innuendo sells, scandal sells, stories with shock value sell. And stories about *sickos* like you, who run over people's pets, creating public hysteria, those stories sell very well."

His arrogant demeanor made me more than a little uneasy. It seemed he was *getting off* on the idea of it all. I was almost afraid to challenge him further.

"You have to answer to someone."

He gulped the shimmering golden liquid.

"Not really. The President of the United States has his checks and balances, and he has to answer to the voting public, but all news editors have to do is turn ordinary, even trifling events into news for profit, which sometimes means pandering to the lowest common denominator. If they're making money and getting the numbers, they're untouchable. Lawyers are bound to a code of ethics by the

State Bar, the doctors are regulated by the Medical Boards, but so long as we turn profits, we have a First Amendment-guaranteed freedom to do what we want with no interference from you or anyone else."

He was comfortable and secure in what he was saying, his very comportment lending an unerring sense of credibility to everything he had spoken. I was disgusted.

"Hide behind the First Amendment if you want. But this country's going to pot! And you guys are to blame!"

He stood again and called out as I turned to exit.

"Now hold on! Don't blame *us. Who* do you think is the force that drives us? Who do you think really dictates what we put on as news? It's idiots out there like you. The whole ratings and profit system is based on what you morons out there turn on and buy. You complain about tabloid TV, but someone's obviously watching it. You're the same lamebrains who zip right past *The McNeil Report* and *National Geographic* on your way to *The O'Reilly Factor, Glen Beck* and *Jerry Springer*. You've got a lot of nerve condemning us."

Glancing furtively through the door I opened, his demeanor changed. The arrogance was gone as he poured on the false charm.

"What's the rush, my friend? And you still haven't told me your name."

All I had to do was walk out that door and away from the station and I was home free. Dan knew neither my name nor anything else about me, and he wouldn't have known what I would have looked like outside the disguise.

As for the cameras outside the station, I'd peek out the door to spot them, then I burst out and make a dash for the first building corner, and that's all they'd get of me. I had slowed over the years, but I figured I could still out-sprint a couple of fat men with cameras on their shoulders. I'd dart around another building, along the fence, across the bridge, back to my car, and I'd disappear.

It was the perfect plan, but I wasn't through with Dan. I hadn't risked so much to stand there just to listen to his stupid speech. No, I had come because he was either going to drop the Nero story or get a taste of his own medicine.

"No, you're not getting my name. But you know, just maybe we morons you call the public aren't as idiotic as you think. I'm going to take my chances with the other stations and the newspapers in this town, your competition for profit. I'm going to tell them just what a pompous jackass you are, and if they're as slimy as you people are at this station, idiots all over town will be glad to know newsman Dan is no different than the rest of us."

I took the recorder from my pocket and showed it to him.

"I've got it all on tape!"

Again I turned to go out the door.

"Wait! Please!"

His voice had lost its confident air. Cracking, it seemed panicked, almost vulnerable. I spun to observe his face that appeared desperate as he nearly pleaded.

"We, we don't have to make this whole thing ugly. You've got it. I'll drop the Nero story."

I couldn't believe it! I had gone up against Dan the newsman and won! The little nobody had taken on the mighty media machine and brought it to its knees! I wanted to smile, but I didn't. I wanted to kick up my heels and slap someone a high five, but I knew I had to keep a low profile until I was safely away from the studio. With that in mind, I set additional terms.

"Now I'm going to walk right out this door and away from this station, and when I do that, I don't want any cameras following me, and I don't want to see another story about Nero. Do I make myself clear?"

He seemed eager to comply.

"Crystal clear. Perfectly clear."

That was how I wanted the story to end, right at that moment. And yet within an instant, I stood there facing utter defeat and destruction.

"Dad? You okay?"

Standing right before me was Maria's father, Dan's son-in-law, my porcine neighbor from down the street. I held my breath and tried to distort my face, hoping he wouldn't recognize me.

"What's going on in here?"

Dan tried to cover.

"Oh, nothing. Just a quick chat. This gentleman was just leaving."

Thankful, I tried to slip out the door past the balloon-shaped man, but he abruptly threw his arm across the door.

"Waitaminute! Don't I *know* you from somewhere?"

"Excuse me."

I ducked under his arm, hurried down the hallway and out the building. Once outside, I looked around. Not a camera in sight. Breathing a sigh of relief, I half-walked/half-jogged to my car, hoping all along the way that Dan's Sumo-wrestler-sized son-in-law hadn't reflected on the shared school functions and made the connection.

We had never met formally, and I had only seen him from a distance. If I hadn't established a context when he referred to Dan as "Dad," I wouldn't have recognized him. So I hoped that, outside the context of the neighborhood, Dan's doughboy son-in-law wouldn't know me from Adam. Yet I knew that if he *had* recognized me, it wouldn't be long before I'd know it, me along with the rest of the city.

We were all silent during the first fifteen minutes of dinner as we had come to the final deliberations in the Nero saga. Each of us would have a turn to speak, and then it would be over forever (with any luck). But who would be first? At last my wife, stacking her plates and sliding them to the center of the table, began nervously.

"I talked to Maria's mother today. She said she met with the vet yesterday..."

We all stopped eating in order to attend her every word.

"Anyway, she said the vet told her that poor Nero had been tortured. She said his face had been cut with a knife or something either right before or right after he was initially hit. He also had a couple of irregular bruises on his body. The vet said, according to canine CSI, Nero could have lived after he had been hit if he had gotten some kind of medical treatment. The impact that put him down in the street at first wasn't fatal. But when he was run over afterward, and he said that could've happened up to an hour later—that killed him."

I was surprised.

"Really?"

"Really. And whoever ran him over apparently stopped deliberately, got out and kicked him or something before finishing him off. He said he could tell that because the front and back tire tracks are out of line. He was kicked or somehow moved in between. The CSI person said it was no accident, that someone deliberately cut the dog, hit him, beat him, tortured him and then killed him."

She sighed in disapproval.

"It's disgusting, and all I want to say is that if anyone at this table had anything to do with it, he should admit to it and come clean. This is the last chance he'll ever get."

Upon that cue, my son began.

"Well um, okay, I'll go next. There's something I haven't told anybody yet. I was kind of hoping I would never have to tell it..."

If my wife had captivated us all, then my son had just one-upped her.

"I didn't want to play the chase card, but I guess I have to now."

My wife, my daughter and I responded in unison.

"The *chase* card?"

"Yeah."

He hung his head shamefully.

"It was around 10:30 that Monday night. I wasn't supposed to be outside, but I was. I was out down the street talking to Maria until about 10:15. I remember it was really foggy that night..."

He paused to take a sip from his sparkling cider in a wineglass.

"See, I had these metal scissors in my hand that I found when I was coming home, and I was just sort of... playing with them. But then when I got to the hedge between our house and the neighbors', just when I came around the corner, Nero was right there and he growled and jumped at me. I found out later that he was there taking a poop and that he growled because I surprised him when I whipped around the hedge."

His eyes were fixed as he replayed the lurid scene in his mind.

"I didn't know it was him. He scared me. I thought it was a monster or something. So before I could even think, I punched him in the face with the scissors. I can still see it now, in slow motion. I can see the scissors cutting across his face and the blood."

He stopped, momentarily returning to the present.

"I had no idea it was Nero, but when I saw it was, I threw the scissors down and tried to help him. But by that time he was running away. I chased after him, but every time I got close, he ran away again. Finally, I gave up and started walking home. That's when I thought I heard tires screech and then a bumping sound. I would have gone back, but I was trying to get home before Dad came back from watching football. I felt really bad when I found out that he was run over. He was probably in the street in the first place because I was chasing him. I felt like it was my fault."

He struggled to stay dry, but his eyes were becoming liquid.

"That's why I have to know what happened. That's why I've been trying so hard to solve this thing!"

After listening to the boy, I was moved. It had taken a lot of heart to come forward with such a painful confession. For the first time I could ever remember, I admired my son. At that moment I knew that finally, after all that had happened, the time had come for me to come clean.

Not that I hadn't wanted to admit the truth from the beginning. Dan and his son-in-law and made the truth irrelevant and difficult at best. But this was my family and they deserved nothing less than honesty from me on this final night of Nero.

Besides, as I scanned their faces, it became obvious it was my turn to confess regardless of whether or not I wanted to. Patting my son on the shoulder, I smiled.

"It wasn't your fault, Son. It was mine. I must have ran into Nero that night just seconds after you did. I was coming home in the fog and I didn't see him. The car smacked him pretty hard. I heard a crunch and he went down, but I swear I didn't run him over."

Confessing actually wasn't so bad. I couldn't understand why I hadn't come forward before.

"I was going to tell you guys that night, but your mom fell asleep, and then when I saw the news and the reports were saying I hit, shot, stabbed and ran over the dog and a hundred dogs afterward, I couldn't do it. I *did* hit Nero. I *did* get bit on the finger when I tried to pull him out of the street. I *did* call 911. I did lose my glasses. I did all those things, but I didn't run him over. I did not kill that dog."

My son interrupted, eager to understand various details.

"You *switched* cars, didn't you? You rented a car just like yours to drive while you had someone fixing the dent you got from hitting Nero, right? And you got new glasses?"

If I was surprised by his conclusion, my wife was equally incredulous as she broke in.

"No, that's impossible. Your dad wouldn't go to all that trouble just to—"

I stopped her.

"No, he's right." And then to him, "How'd you know?"

He opened the file and glancing down occasionally, he began.

"Well, when I searched your car the first time, it was clean, except for the dog tag which I'm sure now that Michael planted. I saw no dog hairs, no dirt, nothing. Then when I searched again yesterday just to be sure, I all of a sudden found tiny blood drops... on the carpet, on the door panel and a small blood smear on the driver's seat. When I checked the trunk, I found a blanket with more blood, and the blanket also had more than 250 white and brown hairs on it that looked exactly like Nero's. That's when I knew, but I called the rental places just to make sure. You got the car at the airport."

I was impressed with my son.

"Overall you've been pretty incredible through all of this. Great detective skills! You ever think about becoming a writer?"

He sighed aloud, still displeased with himself.

"I didn't *solve* it, though."

"What do you mean?"

"I didn't solve the whole thing. Maybe I proved that you hit him, but I never thought you ran him over anyway. For one, that's not like you, and two, you were already home for good when the lady down the street saw the white car screeching its tires. So right now on the last night I can ever talk about it, I'm no closer to figuring it all out than I was on the first day. The killer's still out there, probably laughing at me. I'm no good at this. I didn't solve anything."

While he sat there feeling sorry for himself, I felt liberated, free of the secret at last. Confession had a cleansing and rejuvenating effect on me so that, while he was troubled, I was deeply content.

And so that was the way it ended that night, or so I thought. My wife concluded with afterthoughts about how much trouble would have been avoided if I had just been honest from the beginning. I agreed and thanked my family for being so understanding.

Anyway, just as my wife was ready to close the matter forever, my daughter cleared her throat loudly, indicating she wanted to be heard.

"There's, there's something *I* haven't told you guys about that night..."

The room became so quiet that I thought I could hear my heart beating.

"Something I couldn't tell you."

Stammering, she set forth in an unsteady voice.

"I, I was awake when Daddy came home that night. I was doing my homework. That's when I realized I had forgot to put my assignment sheet in my backpack that day at lunch. Without the instructions, I couldn't finish or turn in my assignment, which would have meant a reduction of one whole letter grade."

Okay, it was good that she was responsible, but what did any of it have to do with Nero?

"I called my friend Natalie and asked if she had the assignment sheet, which she did. So I waited for Mommy and Daddy to go to bed, then I got up and found Daddy's keys."

Finally, it was all beginning to come together for me.

"Natalie only lives about a mile away, so I went out and got in the car. If there was a dent, I didn't see it when I got in. Well anyway, I had to drive real slow because it was a really creepy, eerie kind of night. The fog was like thick smoke that seemed to breathe as it flowed back and forth like the waves in a tide pool. I couldn't see more than a foot in front of the car."

My son, my wife and myself—we were all there, with her in that evanescently animated fog.

"After I'd gone a half block, I wanted to turn around and forget the assignment, but I was nervous. I thought I had doubled back, but I couldn't tell what side of the street I was on or anything. I was going to pull over on the right and just walk home when I heard a crunch and hit a bump that jolted the car so hard my head hit the ceiling. I thought I had run up on a hedge or a brick barrier or something because I could feel the car had only three tires on the ground."

Both hands and voice shivered as she paused and resumed the story.

"I didn't want to get out of the car, but eventually I did. That's when I saw what had happened: the car was sitting right on top of this big ugly hairy dog! It was Nero. I started crying because I didn't know what to do. I couldn't just leave it on him, so I got back in the car and tried to back up, but when the car got about halfway up the body, it stalled and rolled back down. When I tried to a second time turning the tires to left a little, I heard a terrible crunching sound, so I had to let the car roll back on him again."

She cried in agony.

"When I, when I got out of the car to see how badly he was hurt, there was blood all over the street. I thought he was dead, but then he started to moan and wail like he was really suffering. It was horrible. He almost sounded human. That's when I lost it. It was everything, like a horror movie: the dampness, the darkness, the spooky fog, and the way

Nero was howling in pain. I was terrified, so I jumped back in the car, threw it into drive and floored it and I finally found my way home. That's when I saw the huge dent in the front of the car."

Wiping her face with the napkin in her lap, she recomposed herself and steadied her voice.

"I swear I wanted to wake you guys up and tell you about it when I got home, but I was completely neurotic at the time. I just wanted to forget the horror of it all. I figured you'd be asking me about it anyway when you saw the dent in your car, but then when Daddy came home with a car that had no damage to it, I figured he somehow knew what was happening and that he was just *covering* for me. That's why I was arguing his side. I couldn't let him take the blame for something *I* did. I had no idea he had hit the dog earlier."

Then the table fell into silence. We all just sat there trying to digest all the new facts we had heard. Finally, each of us could piece together the truth of what had happened that night. As usual, my wife was the first person to offer a smug commentary.

"Well, I suppose it's safe to say that between the boy's stabbing the dog in the face, your ramming the dog with the car and the girl's crunching him under the tires, this family really did a number on Nero."

No one laughed. No one was even amused. We just sat there in silent thought. After about five minutes, my son asked the inevitable question.

"So, what do we do now?"

I answered.

"Nothing. We're going to let it all blow over. I had a talk with Dan the newsman today, and he promised me the story was dead, that it wouldn't be mentioned on air again."

That's when we heard a forceful knock on the front door. Looking over at the clock beside the family portrait, I couldn't imagine anyone visiting at nine-thirty without a courtesy call.

"I'll get it."

I was blinded by intensely bright, flickering paparazzi the moment I opened the door. As my eyes focused, I made out the images of a mob of people, some with cameras on their shoulders and others angling lights into my eyes. Further out, I was just about sure I saw a pitchfork. Then right in front of me... appeared Dan the newsman, with a microphone in his hand.

"It's over, *Piso'd.* We found you. Do you have anything to say for yourself?"

He shouldn't have asked. I had never committed a violent act in all my life until then, but I reacted in reflex, punching the microphone, sending it in a path directly toward Dan's mouth. When I looked again, his mouth was bleeding and he was complaining about me breaking two of his porcelain dental caps.

Certain my life would never be the same after that moment, I ducked back in and slammed the door. Mute because of the shock of it all, my wife and kids just stared at me as I walked over to and plopped down on the couch. My son followed, taking a seat across from me.

"Dad? Do you realize what's going to happen to you now? I mean, you just made newsman Dan eat his microphone."

"I don't care what happens. I just hope they got it all on tape."

I knew my life would change, but I had no idea how much. The newspaper must have hired a student of Picasso to alter the picture of me they ran on the front page the next morning. I don't know where they got the original photo, but after they had retouched it, my face was darker and the lines in it seemed absolutely sinister, my eyes were squinted and bloodshot and my mouth twisted up in a depraved manner.

Below the picture was the caption, "*Piso'd Off Slug's Dear Dan*." And that was just the beginning. All three local news channels ran negative stories on me that were full of inaccuracies. My former teachers and childhood friends were interviewed, and not one of them doubted that I was the nutcase who had killed hundreds of the city's pets over the past five years.

"I always knew there was something mighty peculiar about that boy," one teacher said before he was joined by my best friend in the fifth grade who added with a serious expression, "We went fishin once, and he *killed* up all the fish he caught."

Caught up in the *newsy* quality of it all, various people in the city drove over to my house everyday and placed pet tombstones on my lawn. My kids, well grounded though they were, were nevertheless harassed at their schools while my wife felt inclined to take a leave of absence from her job.

Finally, I opened the front door one day only to be served papers which indicated pending legal action brought on by pet owners, the Humane Society and the local S.P.C.A. After that came a suit filed by Dan for dental damages, pain, suffering and public embarrassment. Lost about how to respond, I found my lawyer friend in the restaurant again, and after having told him the entire story of what had happened to Nero that night, he sipped his chardonnay and responded.

"Technically there are things you could do legally, but you'd lose. Besides, do you *really* want to put your family through all that?"

Then came the solemn advice.

"You're best off getting on the bandwagon and using the media for your *own* purposes. Dan might be big, but there's always someone bigger. Get out there and tell *your* story."

And that's what brought me to the place where I am today, sitting here in this studio's Green Room. The best lesson I learned, the best lesson my wife and kids learned from all this was in the way we viewed the news as it came to us in its various forms.

We learned to examine it critically and learned that there was a profound distinction between news and the truth. So finally, it had come to this, fifteen minutes of fame on the *Oprah Winfrey Show*. I had written to the show and explained much of my story, while in a pre-screening interview I revealed more, but I was still nervous about what story I would tell when I went on air.

Was I going to mention my son's involvement? Would I tell the public that it was actually my daughter who ran Nero over? Was it better for me to take the blame for everything or fabricate a story with a killer still at large? Finally, as I there just to expose Dan? Would I be any better at telling the truth than he was? Was I there because Oprah or her staff considered my story newsworthy? Or was I there to tell the truth?

I looked at my watch. Only four minutes before it was time to go on! Then I looked at the two other troubled guests Oprah had invited. I couldn't help but wonder what they'd say. Anyway, I was still sitting there in quiet contemplation when Oprah's pretty assistant came in to escort us out.

"Mr. Jackson, Mr. Ramsey—we're ready for you."

She looked toward me, a little perplexed.

"And you—"

I swallowed, nervously.

"Yes?"

"It's time for you, too."

Flipping through the pages on a clipboard, she stopped and scanned the page.

"Um, *what* did you say your name was?"

THE ATTIC

Because I have always loved good stories, I have spent a great deal of my life pursuing them, actively reading and listening to them. The various yarns I've enjoyed have ranged from the lyric verses written by ancient Homer of Ionia to colorful African-influenced tales steeped in oral tradition as told by my ancient grandfather Homer of Mississippi. Born to American parents in a place between Berrechid and Fédala in Morocco during August 1960, I have been blessed to share in the experiences of many wonderful people inside and outside the United States.

While the family moved to California when I was nine, I remember writing my first complete story at age ten. It was a silly story about a sardonic and ill-tempered T-bone steak that suddenly came to life on my plate and engaged me in argument. Notwithstanding, my fifth grade teacher, Mr. Winans, loved the story and suggested that I should pursue a career as a writer.

The rest of the meaningful people in my world however, steered me toward more reasonable and secure ends, and I was encouraged to endeavor in the legal and engineering fields, which I did. I never wrote another story again until my second year of college.

I certainly could have become a lawyer, and I could have no doubt finished the rigorous engineering curriculum, although I don't know how content or competent I would have been in either career. I never found out because I forsook all that "celebrated" security to pursue the quixotic dream of one day becoming a successful writer.

I remember the moment of epiphany in which I accepted writing as my destiny. It was during a Calculus mid-term in my sophomore year. As I sat there, writing proposed character dialogue in between test problems, the professor approached and asked me to stay after class.

Anyway, during the course of our conversation I found out that he was a frustrated writer who had chosen the security of a teaching career over "just getting out there and giving it my best shot." He told me that if I wanted to write, I should find a major that was more compatible with writing and that I should *stay on course right to the end.*

Taking heed, I promptly moved over to the Communication Studies department, intent on law school after graduation. At that point I took up writing in earnest. I started with prose, and then I moved to poetry. Eventually, the poems got longer and evolved into dialogue.

Eager to delve into a new genre, I took a playwriting class and wrote a play in verse about two star-crossed lovers called *Solomon and Constance* (1980-1981), yet I found the Elizabethan style and language unsuitable to contemporary preferences. My second play, called *Michael Angelo* (1982), took up the debate on Black English, or Ebonics, within the setting of a modern-day art academy. The next play was called *Stevie: the Eighth Wonder of the World* (1982), a musical based on the works of Stevie Wonder. I directed and produced it at a small theater in Sacramento during July, 1983.

Shortly thereafter, I wrote three short stories called *Mr. Peacock* (1983), *Till Death Do Us Part* (1983) and *Anthropophagi* (1983). Then came the plays *Caesar* (1983) and *Table 21* (1983), two plays I never got around to producing. Still, they were great studies for writing dialogue, which was useful for the writing of *No More Cheesecake!* (1984), a musical comedy I wrote in twelve days, and one I later produced, directed and starred in at the Sacramento Community Center Theater in 1990.

Enjoying the plays, I wrote one of my favorites called *Kidstuff* next (1985). During 1985 and 1986, I wrote a 500+ page mainstream suspense novel called *Deus Ex Machina*, a quasi-political work about an aspiring presidential candidate with an alarming past. That novel was followed by another play called *Dream* (1986), based on the writings and philosophy of Dr. Martin Luther King, Jr. I spent seven months of 1987 converting *Dream* into screenplay form and trying to manage funding for production.

Failing to acquire necessary financing, I decided to explore a new genre, so I wrote a series of stories that I called *The Love Tragedies* (1987- 1993), an ongoing set of original stories written in *blank iambic meter*. Seeking to take up still another genre, during 1989 I began an ambitious project on a major figure in California politics: a biography on erstwhile Speaker of the State Assembly, the Honorable Willie L. Brown, Jr.

The work was ponderous, painstakingly detail-oriented and took over six years, more than 300 interviews and involved 2,000+ research hours, let alone the time involved for the actual writing. I titled it *Willie: The Man, The Myth & The Era* (1990-1996). It was my first and last biography, as I did not enjoy the genre.

Because the project was so onerous and "un-creative" in comparison to other works, I took a number of breaks to write stories. *Synchronicity* (1991) was first, followed by *Remember* (1993).

I decided to write the Willie Brown book in the "passive first person," but because I had never written in the narrative form, I needed an exercise to find a comfortable voice. My narrative experiment resulted in the first story of the *Four Stories* series: *The Felinicide* (1992). The subsequent stories, *Dick* (1996), *The Doctress* (1997) and *Nero* (1997) involve the same first-person narrator, a person I like to think I know very well.

My most recent works include *Legal Thriller* (1998), a 430 page suspense thriller, *Estéban*, a cynical story about a talking pig, and the beginnings of a screenplay (1999), called *The Last Year*.

Because I was loath to include a "Preface" in this collection, I feel a degree of obligation to say a few words about the background of the book. All *Four Stories* are loosely based on my own experiences and the experiences of various people around me.

Notwithstanding, *The Felinicide* was written after April 1992, in the wake of the publicity surrounding Robert Alton Harris. In fact, a character from the story utters a disturbing line attributed to him. The media-concern from *Nero* was partially inspired by a Ted Koppel speech I heard and analyzed years ago in college classes, while the nature of the debate over dinner was influenced by elements of the O.J. Simpson murder trial.

At present I am working on the screenplay, a few literary projects, 11 new stories and a proposed collection of stories from the South. Enough of all that.

Anyway, I hope you've enjoyed our little chat up here in the attic as much as I have, but more than that, I hope my *Four Stories* have made you curious about other works and future stories. If they have, then perhaps someday much more of my work will be available for public perusal.

Until then, I thought I'd end this book with a little extra: a poem I wrote as a tribute to one of my favorite storytellers, Edgar Allan Poe, in the rhyme and meter of *The Raven*. It is titled *Black Bertha*. I hope you enjoy it. Until later, I'll see you between the covers!

Good Reading,

Marcus McGee

BLACK BERTHA

On a farm in Petaluma, lived a hen whose
name was Bertha,
Whose dark feathers were a source of discontentment,
gloom and more.
As she walked about the farmyard, looking out she
spied a barnyard
Full of hens with plumage lighter, whiter than the
Ibis wore.
Thus said Bertha, "Black no more!"

It was more than her flecked brownness. She despised her
beak's cruel wideness,
And her breast was slight and formless as it drooped right
to the floor.
Her physique was meant for laying, in the hay for
who was paying,
Daily eggs with no delaying, staying till her
rump was sore—
Till groaned Bertha, "Lay no more!"

To an older hen she muttered, cursing fate as
foul she uttered.
Clucked and crew, harangued and fluttered, stuttered on
the farmyard floor,
"Why have I such swarthy feathers? teeny breast? a
butt that tethers
High above two thighs so shabby, flabby as the
farmer's boar!
Why! oh why me? I implore!"

"On *that* farm as I was saying, live white hens who
do no laying.
Since I've seen them I've been praying for the chance to

join their score.
Theirs are days of always eating, up-scale pens and
better-treating,
While my nights are full of moaning, groaning like the
farmer's whore?"
Swore bold Bertha, "Pimped no more!"

"In the dark I'll cross the highway, walking or by
secret flyway.
Then I'll have a life that's my way—free of our fowl
loathsome chore.
With the whitest cocks I'll cuckol, flit about and
cack or cluckle,
I'll be there while you, my neighbor, labor at what
I deplore.
There I'll stay forevermore."

But the older hen thus pleaded, "There you'll surely
be mistreated,
You'll no doubt be rudely greeted from the time you
reach the door.
They will ridicule the inference that you seem to make
in difference,
Criticize your beak and breast and test your patience
to the core—
Make life *worse* than e'er before."

"While we sometimes wish for better, thinking grass is
always wetter
On the other side of fetter, road or fence or
chain or door—
True contentment lies inside us, happiness and bliss
abide us.
Thus we're better seeking solace, solace from our
inner store—
Only then our spirits soar."

But young Bertha, feathers ruffled, swore aloud, then

huffed and puffled.
Yet the worst she said was muffled as they scuffled
on that floor.
Beak to claw the hens grew bloody, staining darkened
feathers ruddy,
Till at last her mother, muddy, muddy for the
blood and gore,
Sighed at last, "I'll fight no more!"

Then flew Bertha to that haven, fast as swift and
grave as raven,
To the perch that she'd been cravin, boldly bravin
fates in store.
In the barn house she got nested, and when
finally she rested,
All the hopes that she'd invested, rested on the
farmyard floor.
She walked slowly out the door.

In the bright of day her blackness did such contrast
with their whiteness
That the other hens in excess *sans politesse*
swarmed the floor.
Clucking, squawking, crowing wildly, they went
mad to put it mildly,
Snatching till young Bertha's feathered, weathered wings
could take no more.
Yet one hen quelled that uproar.

"Let her answer plain my query, on a point that
makes me leery,
'Why would such a hen so dreary, over-weary,
haunt *our* corps?'
Sure her story is a sad one, full of
tragic tone, compunction,

Woe and pain to such extreme the theme of which
we can't ignore—

Let her that sad tale outpour!"

Then stood Bertha, preening sprightly, clearing throat to
speak politely,
And with feathers ruffled slightly, sobbing lightly
she forswore,
"Here I now renounce my darkness, feathers
ugly for their starkness,
Teeny breast, a beak so wide I'm teary-eyed
a troubadour.
I'll be black and foul no more!"

From a bottle she acquired, she poured bleach till
she was tired,
Till she had what she desired—white blow-dryered
plumes she wore.
"Now I'm just as white as any hen in all
you birds so many!
Now I've joy beyond compare—the *laissez-faire*
esprit de corps!
Geeked!— (to trash the metaphor)."

"But!" said others, "there's the matter being that your
breast is flatter!
Ours are bigger, juicy, fatter!" did they chatter
in uproar.
Yet cool Bertha, still unflap-ped, answered those vain hens,
so vapid,
"Moneys I invested make me breasted more than
all your score.
Heads will turn in true rapport!"

From her purse came a prosthetic meant to flatter
the aesthetic—
Where her breast was once pathetic this *cosmetic*
now she wore.
Now her breast was wholesale bigger, doing wonders for
her figure,

All her flaws were quick forgotten as upshotten
Bertha swore,
"Breasted well! Forevermore!"

"Wait!" cried others, beaks still gaping for the sudden
breast reshaping,
"There is surely no escaping that you're aping
breasts and more.
But your beak is wide, unsightly, setting you apart
outrightly,
Thus you don't conform completely, so discreetly
leave the floor.
You're rejected on that score!"

Yet bold Bertha stood there daring to ignore their
grudging glaring,
Speaking out she was not sparing the comparing
anaphor,
"Have I made my feathers whiter? Is my breast not
fuller, tighter?
Now you dingy, smaller-breasted, bested birds have
lost threescore.
Rhinoplasty!—to the fore!"

She had gone through measures drastic to procure a
nose in plastic,
Made from some refined elastic, a fantastic
beak restore.
When she put it on she muted jealous hens who were
out-cuted.
Bertha had with great aplomb become the envy
of the floor.
Loud she crowed through the uproar.
On the farm there is a saying: *Crowing hens
forebode great slaying.*
Thus with Bertha crudely braying all were praying
en rapport.

Till one hen who seemed the warder, who was top of
pecking order
Did for all of chicken-kind remind her of that
farmyard lore.
"*Oops, my bad! I'll crow no more!*"

"Why?" said warder, "are you staking so much in
this undertaking?
The decision you are making should mistaking
underscore.
On this farm we do no laying, but the life that we're
portraying
Is in truth a counterfeit, a shallow, fallow
dreadful bore.
You are *worser* than before!"

"Here they lust our bodies only, caring not that we
are lonely,
Not at all that we hormone-ly are not *chickens*
anymore.
Daily breasts are fondled lightly while our rumps are
handled nightly,
Legs and thighs caressed and pressed and patted by
false paramour.
Laying eggs is less a chore!"

"Whence you came the hens are wanted for their
qualities unflaunted,
And have confidence undaunted in their vaunted
inner store.
Ours is superficial beauty while they have a
sacred duty
And by laying are displaying strength from
inner reservoir,
Thus their lives mean so much more."

List'ning, Bertha slow admitted she had common
sense forfeited

When she thoughtless had committed to half-witted
foolish splore.
"When I can undo my action, I'll go back and join
that faction,
But for now I'll recreate and celebrate as
ne'er before—
Might as well your side explore!"

"It's too late!" said warder, plainly, though young Bertha,
feather-brainly,
Did not understand how vainly, what immanely
was in store.
Not what every other bird did, as the hens were
rudely herded,
Right inside the chamber room that sealed the certain
doom in store—
Till was *slammed* that chamber door!

Then poor Bertha, loudly squawking, stopped at once,
demurring, balking,
Then at last she ceased her talking and stood gawking
on that floor.
Floor and ceiling both were bloody, once-white plumes were
stained and ruddy,
Heads fell from a cruel machine—a guillotine all
Smeared with gore!
Bodies lined the corridor.

Senseless, headless hens were prancing, in a sort of
gruesome dancing,
While poor Bertha, shocked, advancing, barely glancing,
cursed and swore.
"Why such wanton, pointless killing of the splendid
and unwilling?
I must know before I die the reason *why*
if nothing more!
Someone answer on that score!"

Then the warder, axes nearing, answered Bertha
nervous, fearing,
"On this farm it was appearing we were
cavaliering corps,
But it seems your eyes were liars as this is a
farm for *fryers*,
You have come on harvest day, the slaying day
we all abhor.
We are slain, forevermore!"

"Stupid me!" vexed Bertha, crying, "It's my fault that
I'll be frying!
I was vain, inane, for sighing and denying
my own corps!"
Then came razors, whirling, whacking, sending Bertha
off to packing.
You might buy her as a fryer at your local
poultry store.
Feathers gone, she's poor once more.

Thus was Bertha's tragic ending, meant for candid
reprehending,
And for careful comprehending when commending,
furthermore,
For the girls who flutter vainly, for the boys who lust
Inanely—
Meant for all the discontenting through
inventing metaphor:
Tap your *inner* reservoir!

OTHER TITLES
AVAILABLE BY MARCUS MCGEE

LEGAL THRILLER
(Suspense thriller, 439 pages paperback,)
Murder mystery set in San Francisco

SYNCHRONICITY
(Short Stories, 298 pages paperback)
"The Club," "Anthropophagi" and other stories

SHADOW IN THE SKY
(Suspense thriller, 263 pages paperback)
Asteroid threatens Earth, Last year of life

THE SILK NOOSE
(Short Stories, essays, 217 pages paperback)
"Denouément," "On Niggers and Squirrels," and others

MURDER FROM THE GRAVE
(Suspense thriller, 425 pages paperback)
Berkeley professor-turned-SF police detective matches wits with a killer who wants to commit seven murders after he is already dead

Coming Soon:

SANITY SLIPPING
(Short Stories, @ 275 pages)
VIRAL VECTOR
(Suspense @ 375 pages)
Sequel to Legal Thriller

order at www.pegasusbooks.net

www.ingramcontent.com/pod-product-compliance
Lightning Source LLC
LaVergne TN
LVHW091044080826
845145LV00002B/613

* 9 7 8 0 9 6 7 3 1 2 3 0 9 *